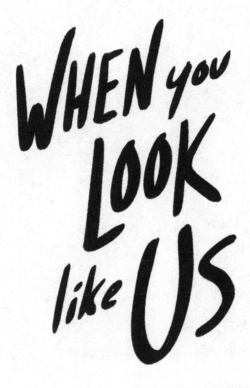

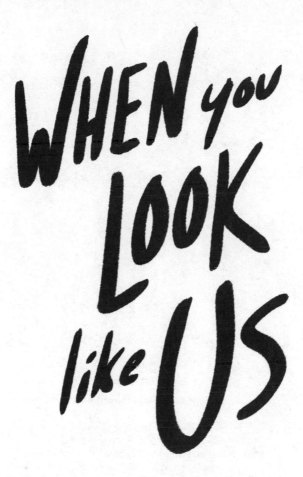

PAMELA N. HARRIS

QUILL TREE BOOKS

An Imprint of HarperCollins*Publishers*

Quill Tree Books is an imprint of HarperCollins Publishers.

When You Look Like Us

Library of Congress Control Number: 2020946925
ISBN 978-0-06-294589-1

Typography by Carla Weise
21 22 23 24 25   PC/LSCH   10 9 8 7 6 5 4 3 2 1
❖
First Edition

FOR MY PARENTS, WHO NEVER HAD TO REMIND
ME TO MAKE IT HOME BEFORE THE STREETLIGHTS
CAME ON—I WAS ALREADY INSIDE DREAMING
WITH A NOTEBOOK AND PEN.

ONE

IT BEGINS WITH A *THUMP, THUMP, THUMP.*

A steady bass line, throbbing against the normal rhythms of Canal Street. The *rat-a-tat-tat* of car backfire, the staccato grumblings from the neighborhood pit bulls. The chirping of Mrs. Jackson's laughter drives the tempo for the evening's lullaby. But it's the *thump, thump, thump* at my window that unnerves me. It's not like the usual gunshots that punctuate the night, but a gentle knock. An invitation for me to crack open the window and let the night swallow me whole.

"You're not listening, Jay."

I pull my eyes away from my bedroom window. I'm tripping. Who the hell would be knocking at my window this time of the night? The guys in my neighborhood joke that I don't need a pit bull when I have a MiMi. Her smirk alone could leave the most thuggish of thugs shook. I lean on my headboard, press my cell real cozy against my ear so Camila feels me feeling her.

"Actually," I say to the phone. To Camila. "I'm listening too much." My eyes shift back to the window, expecting another thump. Stillness greets me. My nerves are on autopilot tonight, doing their own thing. Must be from all the Red Bull I downed to finish up Meek's paper.

Camila lets out a heavy sigh. I try to imagine her. Maybe she's sitting on her bedroom floor, waving an issue of *Cosmo* over her toenails so the polish dries. She probably spots a smudge. Probably wants to redo them all but won't. Redoing them requires using both hands, but one of those hands belongs to me right now. Or maybe that's just wishful thinking. Camila and I've been shooting the shiz every night since she kissed me two weeks ago at some party Bowie and I stumbled into. Yeah, it was a dare—and yeah, I could taste the wine cooler on her lips that made the kiss sloppier than it needed to be. But she liked how I didn't try to do more with her that night. And I liked that she liked me after years of insisting my name was Ray. So yeah, the idea of Camila Vargas creating a crime scene with her nail polish just to speak to me was pretty dope.

"It's like you're here but you're not," Camila keeps on. "Tell me—where's Jay?"

"I'm still here." I close my eyes and wish I were some-where else. Somewhere outside of the Ducts, where I don't have to check my locks three times before running out to grab MiMi's blood pressure meds every month. Somewhere with Camila. Sitting on soft carpet, watching her paint her nails. Eyes trailing up her lotiony legs but stopping at the hem of her shorts. I try to respect her even in my daydreams.

"When Bowie told me what you were up to—"

I jolt away from my headboard. "Bowie's a clown. A corn nut. About as trite as a dad joke."

"Lo que sea," Camila says under her breath but heavy enough for me to hear it. "Jay, you could get suspended. Hell, you could even get expelled."

I laugh. Can't help it. Camila goes from zero to one hun-dred at lightning speed. That's one of the things I dig about her. One minute she's rolling her eyes at me in class because I'm staring at her too much, and the next she's scribbling her name on the back of my hand to mark her territory. "I tutor, Mila," I explain. "Can't get in trouble for helping out classmates. Isn't Youngs Mill teaching us to be helpful and productive citizens?"

"Tutoring doesn't mean you write the whole damn paper, Jay, and then charge people for it." Even with Camila not in my bedroom I feel her eyes on me. Sandy brown, poking tiny holes through anything that'll come out of my mouth next. But I don't get a chance to bullshit her. The *thump, thump,*

3

thump returns. This time, I spot a hand at my window.

"Shit." I jump out of my bed. I really wasn't tripping—someone's out there.

"What? What's wrong?"

My feet are glued to my carpet as the hand raps against my window again. I always wondered what I would do if something went down. If it was *my* bedroom that was the scene of one of the random break-ins our neighbor was always warning us about. I finally have my answer. I would freeze.

"Jay? You okay?"

Camila's voice snaps me out of it. I can't be a bitch right now. She'd break up with me before we even put a label on whatever the hell it is we're doing. She has to hear me man up. "Someone's at my window," I croak, in my least manly voice ever.

Camila sucks in a breath. "Why is someone at your window?"

Excellent question. My brain races for an answer. Something logical that'll put Camila at ease. That would put *me* at ease. "Maybe they're lost?" The hell, Jay?

"What the hell, Jay?" Camila asks. "Why would someone be knocking on your window in the middle of the night because they're lost? That's what Google Maps is for."

Great point. Someone's more likely to pull up to a gas station than a random-ass window in the hood to ask where to find Main Street or Whatever the Fick Boulevard. Even better point? If someone were trying to pop me, I'd doubt they'd politely rap on my windowpane first. Psychos don't really give a damn about manners. So, there was one somewhat logical answer.

"Probably a blisshead," I say. Javon Hockaday lives in my neighborhood. The guy's notorious for selling bliss or crinkle or anything else you might want to get high on a Saturday night. He's also notorious for being my sister's boyfriend and, thus, a pain in my family's ass, but I'll save that for another time. Anyways, sometimes lowlifes make their way to my building, looking to score, too high to realize that Javon lives a block away from me.

"Really? A blisshead, Jay?" Camila utters something in Spanish that I can't quite catch. She said she'd teach me more. Said bilingual dudes were sexy as hell, but we can never quite find the time between school and my odd jobs and general high school bullshit—plus all the time I spend thinking about her during school and my odd jobs and high school bullshit. "You got some thot over there, don't you?"

I frown at her even though she can't see me through the phone. "Mila, ain't no thot creeping into my bedroom. And I'm pretty sure they wouldn't like you calling them outside their name."

"Why you care what I call that ho if there ain't no ho crawling through your window?"

I push air out through my nose. I learned pretty quickly

that there's no talking to Camila when she's like this. The girl gets salty if I use too many words to answer a female teacher's question. *Like you give that much of a damn about the Constitution*, she told me after we had a sub with too much estrogen in history class two days ago. I mean, damn, shouldn't I, though?

I grab the baseball bat under my bed. The most bliss does is give you the munchies or a serious case of the chuckles, or so I've heard (and seen). But every now and then, some of these blissheads need an extra push to back off. "Look, I gotta go, Mila, before they wake up MiMi."

"Jay, you best not let whoever's at your window in," Camila says as I cross my bedroom floor. I pull back my curtain some more and raise my bat high, ready to wreck shop. Or make someone think I'm ready to wreck shop in case they try anything funny.

Pooch peers back at me from the other side of my window.

I smirk and drop the bat to the floor. "Gotta fade," I say to Camila, and end our call before she can tell me otherwise. I'll pay for that later. The bad news is that I'm right—there's a blisshead at my window. The good news is that it's just Pooch, the friendly, neighborhood degenerate. As narrow as a string bean, goofy as all hell, and the absolute antithesis of dangerous. About two weeks ago, he showed up at my window asking for ten bucks to grab a meal at Wendy's. He and

I both knew that he could buy a meal for less than five bucks at Wendy's, just like we both knew my ten dollars wouldn't actually go toward a burger, fries, and a Frosty. Like always, it'll probably take me five minutes to get rid of him. Though I'd much rather keep spitting game to Camila, I know she doesn't have much patience to hang out on the other line while Pooch tells me for the hundred-and-third time about the night he thought Mary J. Blige hit on him in the club. Spoiler alert: Ms. Blige was just some black chick with a honey-blonde wig and a fierce two step.

Pooch motions for me to open my window. I shake my head and then hitch it to the side, tell him to beat it. He clasps both hands together in a prayer and, I don't know, maybe it's his ashy knuckles. Or the Dallas Cowboys jersey he wears so much you can barely still see Tony Romo's number. Or the rings around his eyes that tell me he hasn't had a good night's sleep since Romo was actually the Cowboys' quarterback. Either way, he looks just sad enough for me to humor him for a few minutes. I pry my window and rest my elbows against the sill.

"I don't have any change tonight, Pooch."

One of Pooch's eyebrows quirks up. "Huh?"

"Change. I don't have any change tonight, Pooch," I repeat, even as a pair of twenties burns a hole in the pocket of my jogging pants. I guess the correct thing to say would be that I didn't have any change for *him* tonight, but it's late and

I'm not trying to wake up MiMi so . . . "Later."

I reach for the window and Pooch throws up his hands. "Hold up, youngblood. I ain't ask you for no change."

"Yet," I say.

"I came for information, not coin."

It's my turn to raise an eyebrow. Pooch has a way of keeping me on my toes since I never knew what the hell was going to come out of his mouth—when he wasn't talking about his almost hookup with the queen of R & B music.

"You know where I could find Javon?" Pooch asks me.

I give him a look that I'm pretty sure he gets every day in his life but never from me: one of complete and utter confusion. "Don't come at me with that, Pooch. Why the hell would I know what Javon's up to?" Lies. Nic took off with him earlier tonight. Right after MiMi told her she didn't need to be going to any parties on a school night. Nic yelled a few words, MiMi yelled a few words back. Both glared at me, waiting for me to pick a side. But I'm Switzerland. I retreated to my room and Nic retreated to Javon's car. The whole scene was too much of a headache to give Pooch the play-by-play.

"Him or his boys ain't on the stoop." Pooch looks over his shoulder and toward Javon's building, completely ignoring my question. "Kenny's not at his spot, either. I just needed to, you know, ask them something."

Yeah, like could they spot him an ounce of whatever. I

raise both my hands into a shrug. "Don't know what to tell you, man."

"Well . . . maybe your sister could tell me something. Where's she?"

His question hits me like a hammer. "I'm not my sister's keeper, Pooch." More lies. I mean, kind of. I've tried to keep Nic a few too many times, but she doesn't like to be kept. She slips through my fingers every time I think I get a good grip on her. Kind of like tonight. It's almost midnight, we got school in the morning . . . and Nic still hasn't slinked home from the party she wasn't supposed to go to in the first damn place. Good thing MiMi fell asleep right after *Grey's Anatomy*. I have too much going on than to referee another shouting match between those two.

"Hit her up then. She gotta be with Javon . . . or Kenny." He lowers his lids, all *you know what I mean?* But I don't know what he means. Kenny's Javon's boy—the main guy Javon trusts to push whatever he's pushing. Kenny looks out for Nic from time to time, but only when Javon needs him to. And to think anything else is to think that my sister is some kind of skank.

"Fick off, Pooch. Don't come around my window anymore. Don't even glance at it on a leisurely Sunday stroll, you hear me?"

Pooch stumbles as if I actually used my bat on him.

"Come on, Jay. I didn't mean anything by it."

"Sure you didn't. Now beat it."

"Jay. Jay? We cool, youngblood. We cool. Here." He rummages through one of the pockets of his jeans. "Want a Jolly Rancher?"

I frown at him. "Pooch, I don't know how long you've had them Jolly Ranchers." I pause and think about all the Red Bull I guzzled earlier. I could use something else sweet to keep me awake instead of drinking more caffeine. "What kind?"

He looks down at the candy in his hand. "I'll give you my watermelon if you got five bucks to spare."

I scoff at him. "Man, ain't nobody tryna give you no five dollars for some watermelon Jolly Ranchers." If he had green apple, we could've negotiated.

"We cool still, right?" He pleads at me with his eyes. He and I both knew that my family were the main people in this neighborhood that looked out for him. I sigh and give him a slight nod. He claps his hands together. "My man! Did I tell you about the time I rolled up in The Alley a few years back?"

"Night, Pooch," I say.

"It was ladies' night," he continues, smiling at the sky as if he was back in the nightclub. "Drinks were flowing, Frankie Beverly was bumping through the speakers, and out of the corner of my eye, who did I see tearing up the dance floor? None other than Ms. Mary J.—"

I close my window and draw my curtains closed. I had to finish Meek's paper and try to squeeze in at least three hours of sleep before waking up for school. Enough with his shenanigans. I plop back down on my bed and rest my iPad on my lap. Crack my neck from side to side and get ready to dive into an analysis of *Othello*. As soon as the words start flowing, my phone buzzes and knocks against my windowsill . . . almost making me drop my iPad—and a deuce in my pants.

I sigh. "Come on, Mila," I say under my breath when I realize I left my phone across the room. I almost ignore it but ignoring a call from Camila is far worse than hanging up on Camila. I'd have to promise shoulder rubs for a week to get out of that one. I trudge over to my phone, prepping a string of apologies in my head. But when I grab it, Mila's name isn't on the screen. It's Nicole's. Speak of the Devil.

"MiMi's sleep," I say as soon as I answer. "The coast is clear. For now. But you might want to book it before she gets her two a.m. sweet tooth." Without fail, MiMi wakes up early in the morning with the taste for something that'll spike her blood sugar. Then yells at me and Nic the next day for eating up all the cookies or graham crackers or whatever.

"Jay?" Nic says, or I think she says. Her voice is muffled, hushed. And there's a steady bass line in the background like she's taking a break from bumping and grinding in somebody's cramped living room. "You . . . gotta . . ." More thumping music. Someone yelps in the background, followed by laughter.

I roll my eyes. Glad she's off having fun while I'm here researching *Othello* and fending off blissheads. "What is it this time, Nic? Crinkle? Bliss? Or were you adventurous and partied with both?"

"No . . . *no*. Just . . ." More bass. More laughter. Nicole says something else and lets out a heavy breath that turns our connection into static. Almost like she's stifling a laugh. I grip onto my phone. I've seen or heard her like this too many times in the past couple of years. When she's so cranked up on bliss that MiMi can't even get through saying grace over dinner without Nic breaking into a fit of giggles. She'd been doing okay lately. Gone to school at least four days during the week. Even pulled up her grades in two classes. Not necessarily the honor roll student she was back in middle school, but at least she was thinking about her graduation in a few months. But here she is, dirtying things up on the other side of my phone, expecting me to clean it all up again.

"Kind of hard to talk straight with all that bliss bopping through your veins, right?" I have to push the words out of my throat. If I hold them in, she'll keep clowning around. Maybe move on to something more twisted than what Javon's pushing. We had already lost so much, so I wasn't trying to lose her, either. "Call me back when your head's clear."

"Wait! Jay—"

I hang up. Don't let her get out what she needs to get out because it's all bullshit. At least when she's like this. My phone buzzes and her name pops up again. She's not letting up. Javon's probably putting her up to this. I could see them now—laughing as she redials my number. Trying to pull a fast one on her dope of a little brother. That's what Javon called me the first time we met. Like *met* met, not just me avoiding his side of the street as I walked to the store or waited for the school bus. He rode up to our building in his Charger, rims blinging brighter than the custom-made platinum grills hugging the bottom row of his teeth. Righthand man, Kenny, sat in his passenger seat, warning the neighborhood kids to not toss their balls too close to the car. Nicole bent over to kiss Javon through his window, pointed at me over on the curb as I clicked through the latest from Colson Whitehead on Bowie's hand-me-down iPad.

Javon scoped me out, the only thing shining on me was the silver cross around my neck that matched Nic's. "Yo, that's one dopey-looking nigga." He made sure the whole neighborhood could hear it over the booming bass of his sound system. And my sister laughed. She fickin' laughed at me. I pulled the iPad closer to my face but the words on the screen lost their form.

Before I can hit ignore on my phone, Nic hangs up. A couple seconds later, she shoots me a text:

Never mind. All good.

All good? Of course she is. She's always good when she's buzzing. Hell, she's good even after the buzzing goes away because I'm always here to help quiet the storm, like the dope I am. I shove my phone under my pillow and get back to work on Meek's paper. Nicole won't remember any of this in the morning. Why should I?

✳ ✳ ✳

I go to sleep that night and dream of snakes. It's Nicole, not Pooch, outside my window, and the braids in her hair have been replaced by snakes. They curl around her neck, squeeze at her throat until she can't even choke out my name. Every time I reach for her, one of the snakes strikes at me—so close I can feel its venom spritzing my skin.

TWO

THE ALARM ON MY PHONE GOES OFF AT 5:57 A.M., PER usual. The sanitation truck beeps down the street, collecting the week's trash, per usual. I hear my neighbor through the walls, trying to wake up her three boys for school. Per usual. Canal Street lives on.

No lie, sleep was thin last night. Every creak, every tap, every whistle my apartment made during the night, I assumed was Nic. Tiptoeing into her bedroom, sleeping off her latest head trip. She's probably in bed now, snoring the bliss away. We have things to iron out, but I'll let her catch some extra z's before I begin my Q&A session.

"Jay!" MiMi taps, taps, taps on my door. "Jay! I know you heard that alarm go off. Get up." I mouth along to her

15

follow-up threat: "If you miss the bus, I'm not driving you!"

I peel away from my mattress and let my feet graze the carpet. Scratch the side of my face. "Easy, MiMi," I call out. "Can't a brother take a moment to collect himself?"

"A brother can collect the crust out his eyes and come eat this breakfast. Get a move on. That bus driver of yours is crazy. Showing up all early, making y'all miss the bus so folks gotta waste gas to get y'all to school. Ain't got time for her shenanigans today." She knocks against my door one last time—as if I could still be sleeping through all her killjoy-ing.

I grab my phone, expecting to see my usual morning text from Camila. Nothing. Great. She's pissed about how I ended the call last night. I send her a winking emoji before pulling up my calendar, glancing through all my alerts for the day: meeting with Meek before first bell, Taco Bell interview right after school, then hitting up the CVS around the corner for MiMi's meds. Now I have to find time to check in on Nic, make sure all that bliss she smoked up with Javon last night is not seeping through her pores before she heads to school. Last thing we need is for her to get suspended. Just another Friday for me.

Before I hit the bathroom, I poke my finger through the slit I cut in my box spring. Let my fingers run across the bills I've collected so far. Can't start my day without touching them, seeing if they're still there. $4,210 so far. I have a long way to go until I reach $112,000. Not even sure if MiMi has seen that amount of money in her lifetime. But she's had to. After a Google search, CNN told me that it costs about fourteen grand a year to raise a child. Multiply that by the eight years I've been here, and MiMi has spent over a hundred grand making sure I'm fed and still breathing. Money that could've gone toward her retirement. That's not even including Nic's expenses. I don't care how long I have to hustle. If I have to stuff burritos or write Meek's English papers until his dumb ass graduates—MiMi is going to retire in Florida, or wherever the hell else she wants to.

Florida was always my dad's endgame. "Soon as I hit sixty-five," he'd always say. "Mornings with Mickey, and sunsets by the sea." I found out that Mickey Mouse and the sea aren't near the same city in Florida, but it didn't matter. Dad never made it to sixty-five. The cancer barely allowed him to make it to thirty-five. It ate away at his smile, his laugh, his everything, until Dad was nothing but an outline with a pout. Did the same to my mom even though she never had cancer. She was a different kind of sick. Mornings with her were the toughest after Dad passed. Nic making me pause at Mom's bedroom door so she could be the first to peek in, see if Mom was sleeping in her own vomit or worse. I can still hear the loud sigh that tumbled out of Nic's mouth when Mom got caught behind the wheel with too much booze in her system for the last time. Nic wasn't disappointed—hell, she wasn't even sad. That breath was relief.

Once again, I pause outside a bedroom door, but this time it's Nic's. MiMi's distracted, clattering away in the kitchen, humming to a hymn that Reverend Palmer insists the choir sings every Sunday. I've lost count of how many times I had to be reminded that Jesus's blood saved me. My hand lingers on Nic's doorknob before I take a deep breath and twist it, peek inside her room. I deflate just a little when I notice that her bed is fresh to death, not a crinkled sheet or rumpled pillow in sight. She probably crashed at Javon's last night. He's an ass, but at least he won't let her roam the streets when she's off the chains like that. I slink into her room, pull her comforter and sheets down. Plop down on it and make it look real lived-in for MiMi. The last time MiMi found out that Nic had crashed at Javon's, the second civil war almost got started here in the Ducts. I'm talking tears, threats, and lamps busting against the walls. Our plaster couldn't take another argument. Nic's favorite rapper, Travis Scott, glares back at me from the poster next to Nic's dresser. I glare right back. Why the hell is he so pissed? I'm the one that's losing shower time to cover Nic's ass. Yet again.

"Jay!" MiMi booms from the kitchen. "I don't hear any water running!"

I close Nic's bedroom door behind me and make my way to the bathroom. Take a five-minute shower, knowing MiMi would twist if I take any longer. Once I dry off, I put on my threads, top them with my favorite gray hoodie, then head to the kitchen. MiMi has two plates of eggs and a fried bologna sandwich sitting at the table, waiting for me. Waiting for Nic. If my sister gave me a dollar for every time I had to lie to MiMi for her, I wouldn't have to consider this Taco Bell gig.

"Milk or orange juice?" MiMi asks, her head buried in the fridge.

I curl my lip. "Can't I just munch on some Cap'n Crunch? My stomach gets all jazzy this early in the morning."

MiMi pokes her head out of the fridge, two rollers eating up half of her forehead. "Your stomach gets jazzy because you like eating junk for breakfast. Now sit down. You got five minutes." She decides for me and pours a glass of orange juice, sets it down in front of my plate. "Check on your sister?"

"Yeah." I take a huge chomp of my bologna sandwich, way more than needed. But a full mouth is a muffled mouth, and a muffled mouth can sell lies to MiMi. "She got picked up early. Grabbing breakfast on the way." I take a swig of orange juice to swallow down my fable with the fried meat.

MiMi shakes her head and sits across from me, smoothing out any wrinkles from her khaki pants, pressed and ready to go for the packing plant. "I better not get another call from that school telling me she's a no-show." She slides the plate meant for Nic in front of her. "Can't win for losing with that child." She pokes at her eggs with her fork, eyes on her plate but mind somewhere swaying with Nic's. What little bit Nic has left.

Pretty sure Nic lost most of her mind three years ago. I know the exact moment. It was the summer before I started high school. Nic had a full year on me, so she felt it was her duty to make sure I didn't walk into school looking like a sucker. We took the city bus to Ross to buy name-brand threads on the cheap. Nic spent most of her allowance on me but made sure to buy a pair of red mini shorts to beat the summer heat. She insisted on wearing them on the way back home.

"I'll take them off before MiMi gets home," Nic told me.

"What if she wants to see what we bought?" I asked.

"I'll just hold them up real swift-like for her. She won't even notice how short they are."

I raised an eyebrow as I scanned her shorts. *She'll notice all right*, I remember thinking. Javon Hockaday noticed, too.

No sooner than we stepped out of Ross to head to the bus stop, he happened to be leaving the Verizon store, picking up the latest phone that took pictures when you blinked your eyes. Or something nifty like that.

"Ms. Murphy's people," he said to us, but not really. He spoke to Nic's legs. His eyes traced every muscle and curve that my big sister wasn't supposed to have.

Nic giggled, made some kind of noise to affirm him. I stared down at my shoes. We weren't supposed to bump gums with the likes of Javon Hockaday. MiMi made that very clear when she rolled up her car windows every time we drove past his building.

"If y'all heading home, I can give you a ride." Again, this was directed at Nic. Hell, not even sure if he knew I was there.

Nic looked at me, bit on the cross dangling from her necklace. I knew she always thought Javon was cute. Most of the girls in the neighborhood do. He has the look of one of those rappers who knows how to bang out both party anthems and baby makers—high yellow skin, good hair, and enough tattoos to make him look dangerous. Only thing, I heard enough stories to know that Javon really was dangerous. I shook my head at Nicole. She chewed her cross even more and I shook my head three more times. Finally, she dug in her pocket—handed me some change for the bus. "Don't talk to anybody," she said. "Go straight home and lock the door behind you. I'll be there in a few."

Before I could even protest, she was trailing behind Javon toward the parking lot. She glanced at me one last time before entering his car. *Straight home*, she mouthed. She went her way and I went mine. We haven't been on the same path ever since.

"*Can't Win for Losing*," I say to MiMi at the kitchen table. "Isn't that the name of one of those plays on the chitlin' circuit?"

MiMi looks up and tries to hide her smile with a smirk.

"Not to be outdone by my personal favorite, *Mama, I Want to Twerk*. Coming to a concert hall near you."

MiMi laughs and reaches over to smack one of my hands. "Boy, you are too much."

I take one last swig of orange juice and leap from my chair. "Gotta fade. Can't miss the bus, right?" I peck MiMi on the cheek, then snatch my backpack from the floor by the front door.

"Jay, when you see your sister, tell her to—"

I close the door behind me. I have lots of things to tell Nic once I see her. Like this is the last time I cover for her. Like it's either the bliss and Javon, or me. Like I'm too scared to know who she'd choose.

✳ ✳ ✳

The thing about Youngs Mill High is that there is no thing about Youngs Mill High. You got students that come from the shitty parts of Newport News like me, and you got students who live in the bougie neighborhoods. Three-car garages, white picket fences, fireplaces in master bedrooms. All the jazz that would run cats close to a million dollars, but costs half that in Newport News because who wants to live in Newport News? Even the Youngs Mill football team isn't special, but fools will still sell their first-born child to get and keep a spot. Feels good to have a purpose in this hellhole. Plus, it's the golden ticket out of here for some of us. Exhibit A: Meek Foreman.

"How it do, Jay?" He presses his broad frame against the

locker next to mine, eclipsing my view of the rest of the hall.

I give him a nod. "Meek." I pull out the books I need for the first two periods, real crushed ice–style. Thing is, you can't let clowns like Meek see you sweat, no matter how much they resemble a bouncer in a ratchet hip-hop club—all biceps, no brain. Meek and his kind run the school, and guys like me just try to stay in the race. My hustle at Youngs Mill keeps me in the game, but only if I feign power. So if this deal is going to go down, I need to keep my cool and keep it brief.

Meek pounds fists with a couple of fans. Spottiest record for a running back in Youngs Mill history, but still has fans. That takes real talent—or lack thereof. "Thought I'd wish you a good morning before running off to English."

I slide my red folder from my backpack. The most obvious color, hence why I chose it. People never dwell on the obvious. "Right on. Hope you did your homework."

Meek digs into his pocket, coughs into the baseball mitt he calls a hand, and then reaches inside my locker—leaving a crumpled twenty-dollar bill on top of my binder.

I cock my head, stare down Andrew Jackson's wrinkled face. He stares right back. I chew on the inside of my cheek to keep it from twitching. To keep myself from blurting out: *"Twenty dollars? Do you know how long it took me to type this up and pretend you actually know the difference between allegory and metaphors?"* I don't because: A.) Smart businessmen don't crack under pressure, and B.) Meek is anything but meek, and having my ass whooped in front of my peers is definitely not on my To-Do List for the day.

"He's missing a friend," I say to Meek, slowly and measured. As if his girth doesn't make me want to crawl into my locker and hide until the coast is clear.

"Bowie told me I'd get a discount. Being a first-time customer and all."

Fickin' Bowie. First spilling my wax to Camila, and now making deals behind my back? He and I need to have a conversation that doesn't include many words. "Is Bowie the one doing the actual work?"

Meek shrugs his mammoth shoulders and the world shrugs right along with him. "Seems like you and Bowie don't understand the art of communication, but that's not my problem. The bell's about to ring, so . . ." He takes a step closer to me because that's what big guys do when they want to make a point.

I nod. Point taken. I slide Meek's English essay out of my red folder and rip away the final three pages. I shake out my hand to keep it from shaking on its own. Try to pass the rest of the essay to Meek with my you-can't-rip-out-my-spleen-in-public smile.

"The *fuck*, Jay?" Spit flies from Meek's mouth and lands dangerously close to my upper lip.

It's my turn to shrug. "Third of the price, third of the work. Better than nothing, right?"

Meek's nostrils flare in and out, in and out—keeping time with my heartbeat. I think about the desert, sandpaper, Nic's meatloaf. Anything dry enough to stop me from melting right at Meek's feet.

Alarms go off in my head, telling me to flee. Run for cover. Except Meek seems to hear them, too, and takes a step back. Thankfully, it's the warning bell, letting everyone in the hall know to carry their asses to class now. I've never been so appreciative of Youngs Mill High's tardy system. "We'll chitchat later, Jay."

"Any moment with you, Meek, is always a pleasure."

Meek swings his bulky body away from me and sideswipes some kid minding his business, trying to get to class. The kid tumbles against a locker, but still feels compelled to apologize to Meek. Meek's too pissed to even respond with a grunt, which means I won't be taking the bus home today. He'll be waiting for me near the bus ramps, and then everyone will have a video of him stomping my face in. I'll have to keep it low-key until Meek blows off steam on some other unassuming punk. No offense.

I head toward first period, make sure to take a swift sip of water at the fountain right across from the girl's restroom. Nic's usually in there every morning when she decides to show up to school. She sheds MiMi's approved attire and squeezes into something that barely covers her ass. "Javon likes when I show off my legs," Nic always throws out as an excuse. Apparently, Javon also likes when his girlfriend is late to school because I've had too many gulps of water and Nicole and her legs are nowhere to be seen. I wipe my mouth with the back of my hand and take one last look at the bathroom door. *The New Jay wouldn't be worried*, I think over and over until I believe it. So New Jay moves his feet toward first period.

"Clock's ticking, Jay," my Math Analysis teacher, Mr. Branch, says to me outside his classroom door, sipping from his Black Power coffee mug.

"Wouldn't be a problem if y'all would let us sprint to class," I call out to him.

"Coach Vines told me your mile-run time last year. You'd get to class quicker with a powerwalk, homey."

I pretend to duck from the shots he just fired. Mr. Branch is one of the only teachers I'd let bust my chops like that. He always finds a way to quote Jay-Z, even when preaching about distance formula. Who knew math class could be so turnt?

The final bell rings just as I slide into US History class. Mr. Booker's at his desk, nodding along to whatever Missy Johnston's complaining about this morning. I can tell from his hooded eyes that he hit the town too hard last night and hasn't yet had his first sip of coffee. Camila's at her usual seat by the window, already jotting down Mr. Booker's icebreaker question like a good little student. I linger a beat at her desk, gauge her temperature toward me.

"Hey," I say.

Camila peeks up at me through her bangs, then shifts her whole body to the window.

"We're doing this today?" I ask.

She continues scribbling a response in her notebook, pretends I'm not there.

"Come on, Mila. I said bye before I hung up." At least, I think I did. I had so much Red Bull running through my veins that my fingers were still twitching this morning.

Camila smirks and looks up at me again. "I'm trying to get my work done. Don't you have *other* people's work to do?" At that, she raises her hand and flutters her fingers at me, sending me away. Okay, she's salty about my side hustle—which means instead of answering Booker's time filler of the day, I'll be drafting my epic apology note to her. Camila's old school, likes to watch old Boyz II Men and Jodeci music videos on YouTube. She'll want to see my sorrow in handwriting. I'll lay it on extra thick.

"Yooo," Bowie says as I take my seat in the back next to him. "Cold front this a.m., am I right?"

"I wonder why." I slam my binder onto my desk, hope he feels it.

Bowie strokes his cheek on cue. "She still mad you skipped out on helping her babysit her sisters last weekend?"

"Among other things." I pause as the principal's voice crackles through our shoddy PA system. Know I have about a minute to speak my mind before Booker does his job and makes us keep quiet for the Pledge. "You have a big mouth."

"The ladies aren't complaining."

"The ones in your dreams who never talk to you in person?"

Bowie rubs his fist across his chest. "I am wounded, friend."

I lean in real close so he catches every syllable. "I pulled you in to help me franchise. Get the word out. Not to snitch to Camila, and definitely not to negotiate prices." Over the speaker, Principal Gilbert reminds us that the AC's busted in the cafeteria.

"You pulled me in because I'm business savvy. Giving discounts to first-time customers is business savvy." Bowie jabs his finger on his notebook, as if his shitty business practices are written down. "As for Camila . . . thought she was a potential customer."

"You mean the girl who's been on honor roll since the first grade?"

Bowie scratches the top of his trusty Steelers skullcap. That cap is stapled to his head—teachers don't even bother to ask him to remove it anymore. His curly hairs poke out from the front, and they look like they've been dipped in grape Kool-Aid.

I shake my head at him. "Your hair's purple. How am I supposed to school you when your hair's fickin' purple?"

Bowie adjusts his skull cap and tucks his hair back inside. "Got bored last night."

"Pick up a book next time. Not a bottle of Dimetapp."

Bowie lets out a silent laugh to tell me to fick off. He's weird. Hella weird, as he'd put it. One of the only white kids to not be on Youngs Mill's swim or golf team, he latched onto me in ninth grade after I didn't pick him last in gym for dodgeball. Almost three years later and I still can't shake him off, no matter how hard I try. Not that I try that hard or anything. Bowie's the zig to my zag, the Chewbacca to my Han Solo—without him, I'd be pretty one-note. We even created our own cuss words to feel badass around adults. MiMi still thinks *fick* is some kind of texting acronym.

Gilbert announces it's time for the Pledge, and Booker motions for us to stand.

"To be continued," I say to Bowie as I climb to my feet. I mouth the words to the Pledge of Allegiance but don't say them aloud. I stopped doing that about a year ago. Don't have the balls to take a knee like three of the football players in class but figured my silent protest would do for now.

As we reach the climax of the Pledge, Mrs. Pratt, the school counselor, slinks into the room with her designer heels and chunky earrings she got from her trip to Panama or Trinidad or some other place more exotic than Bad News, Virginia. She keeps a map on her office wall with pushpins outlining her summer travels.

"This could be your map one day," she likes to tell me before our mandatory class-scheduling sessions. *Yeah right, lady*, I want to say. *Guys that look like me and come from my neighborhood don't go no farther than Williamsburg for a vacation.* I lost count of how many times I had to see the Jamestown Settlement.

I'm about to take my seat when I notice both Booker's and Pratt's eyes on me. I can't help but glance at Bowie. This is the moment I've been dreading since I started charging clowns for papers last fall. Of course the moment I pull in Bowie, it all goes to hell. *The hell you do?* I mouth to Bowie. Bowie throws up his hands to show me they're clean. It's Camila's turn to feel my scrutiny, but she stares back at me. Wide-eyed.

"Can I borrow you for a minute, Jay?" Mrs. Pratt asks, inevitably.

"Do I have a choice?" I ask, add a smile for good measure.

"Boy, go with Mrs. Pratt. Bowie will catch you up," Mr. Booker orders.

My sneakers squeak louder than necessary as I follow Mrs. Pratt out of the classroom. Before we reach the school counseling office, I glance at the main entrance. Count how many steps it'll take me to reach it. If I double-timed it, I could be out the door before Pratt even looked back at me. Make up some excuse about MiMi. She's old, she fell. She needed me. It'll give me some time to clear past assignments off the computer we all share in the kitchen. Maybe even dump my iPad somewhere.

"You want to take a seat, Jay?" Mrs. Pratt asks me.

I blink and I'm staring at Mrs. Pratt's infamous dotted map. My feet failed me and led me right into her office. I fold into the chair across from her desk. Link my hands over my lap so they won't shake.

"You probably already know why I brought you in here," Mrs. Pratt says.

If not Bowie or Camila, did Meek sell me out? I'd rather have taken the ass whooping.

"Jay?"

I shove the thought out of my mind and give my full attention to Mrs. Pratt, who's in full-on counseling mode. Leaning forward, giving me direct eye contact. The whole nine.

"Mrs. Chung told me she asked you to be co-editor of *Run of the Mill*," she says.

A gush of air seeps out of my mouth and I float in Mrs. Pratt's office. The lit magazine. Mrs. Pratt's trying to bully me into joining that damn lit magazine. That's all.

"She also told me that you said you'd get back to her," she continues.

"Yeah, I did." I settle more in my seat. Check out the blinds for dust, scope out any new thumbtacks in her map. Wonder what the hell is a Bhutan and why Pratt would want to visit it.

"Jay, that was two weeks ago. I have to ask—what's the hold up?"

"I mean, it's a lit mag," I say, then shrug.

"Don't do that." Mrs. Pratt folds her arms across her chest. "Don't play the cool guy routine with me. Not when I know how often you check books out of the media center each week. And not when I know you could list all Colson Whitehead's books in order of publication."

"First of all, *run-of-the-mill* basically means, well, basic. Not a strong selling point. Second of all, nobody reads print anymore," I say. "Everyone's too busy clicking and swiping." Plus, time spent working on a lit mag means less time working, period. MiMi always said: "If it don't make dollars, it don't make sense." I get what she means now. Pratt wouldn't understand, though. She's too busy traveling the world to see what's going on in her own hood.

"See? Mrs. Chung needs your fresh ideas. You could propose a digital magazine instead. Maybe a new name." Her hands dance in the air now, getting more and more jazzed up about something I didn't sign on the dotted line for. "Besides, it's not like you're doing anything else, Jay. You're not playing sports. Not doing any extracurriculars outside of Sunday school. You're not even signed up for many AP classes even though you could probably do most of the work with your eyes closed. Colleges look at everything, and you're nearing the end of your first semester of junior year."

It's like she's been conspiring with MiMi. Everyone's trying to box me up and ship me away for four years. It's not that college hasn't crossed my mind. It crosses everyone's mind, even if it's just a fleeting thought while taking a stroll or deuce. But I've done the research. Lots of people make good grades, so why would someone offer me a full ride instead of some other dopey black dude in my school? It's not like I can handle a ball. Basically, if I wanted to go to college—a *good* college—I'd be relying on loans and MiMi. She's done too much for me already. I have to pay her back, and a degree in African American lit isn't going to cut it.

But man, studying African American lit would be pretty, well, lit. I could be sitting in a student union, arguing the merits of Alex Haley with a dreadlocked kid named Zahir who wears skirts over jeans as some kind of political statement. Maybe I'd have my own map in my dorm room, pushpins on the places I planned on visiting. Hell, maybe I'd even give Bhutan a chance. But that dream danced away the day Mom decided to crash our Chevy into the back of a squad car. If I went away for four years, who would take care of MiMi? Can't necessarily rely on Nic anymore.

"Jay?" Pratt frowns. "I thought you wanted to go to

college. Of course, there are other routes you could take, but I thought with your grades and—"

"I'm figuring it all out," I say. I lie. "And I'll get back to Mrs. Chung soon." I can't stop lying. "We good? I really need to fade—get my history on."

Pratt exhales loudly, her hopes for me drifting through her nostrils. "I'll be in touch. Tell Mr. Booker thank you for letting me borrow you."

My ass is out of the seat like it has a fever. Hard to think about my future when I could hardly keep my sister present. I grab my phone, open the texting window to shoot a message to Nic, but then catch myself. That's Old Jay rearing his worried head. New Jay shoves his phone back into his pocket and heads to Booker's class to learn about the past. *Nic can wait.*

New Jay repeats that until it sticks.

THREE

"YOU'RE BREATHING A BIT TOO HARD ON MY NECK, BRUH,"
I say to Bowie.

Bowie huffs and puffs behind me, pressing down on his
bike pedals as we make our way up Warwick Boulevard. I'm
perched on his handlebars, hanging on for dear life as he
maneuvers past cars and pedestrians.

"My apologies, Your Highness," Bowie says in between
breaths. "It usually doesn't take this much exertion to ride
my bike, but I'm carrying deadweight at the moment."

"I'm typically described as lean."

"Can you *lean* your ass more to the right as I whip this
turn?" Bowie asks.

I shift to the right as Bowie grunts under his breath and

turns on Colony. Poor guy. We wouldn't be in this predicament if Meek hadn't been waiting for me at the bus ramp, as expected. I hid behind a shrub and watched his nostrils flare as he paced back and forth in front of my exact bus. Homeboy did his research. I had two options: endure the beatdown and show up to my Taco Bell interview half-dead, or ask Bowie for a ride that would get me to Taco Bell in one piece, albeit with a sore ass.

I chose the handlebars and sore ass.

"You can drop me off here," I say to Bowie as we reach Canal Street.

"I got you this far, might as well give you door-to-door service."

Panic crawls up my throat as I spot the opening to the Ducts. "It's all good. I have to regain the feeling in my ass anyway. Walking could do me some good."

"It's not a big deal. I could use some water and—"

"Stop the fickin' bike!" I jump off the handlebars before Bowie can get to a complete stop. The pavement skids so much under my sneakers that I expect to see a trail of smoke behind me. Instead, Bowie stares back at me with question marks in his eyes.

I should've known this would happen. Bowie tried to invite himself to my place for years, but every time I made up some bullshit excuse, like the air conditioner was busted, or MiMi was having the carpet cleaned. Eventually Bowie figured out I was dishing lies, so stopped asking like the good friend that he is. And I liked that about him. How he knew when to drop things. When to cut the tension with some whack-ass joke. Like when the other white kids at school find out about where I live, he puts the cap on that real quick.

Random White Kid: The *Ducts*. Holy shit. Have you ever been shot?

Bowie: My nana gets shot every day. I mean, she's diabetic, but still . . .

Hearing about the Ducts is one thing, but actually seeing it is a whole other beast. The beat-up furniture spilling out of the dumpster. The neighbors inspecting said beat-up furniture to add to their collection . . . and that's not even mentioning all the foul shiz that goes down when the moon's at its highest. But that's what all the assholes talk about. The ones that consider the Ducts to be the worst kind of stereotype. The ones that have never been to a neighborhood fish fry, or tasted Mrs. Jackson's sweet potato pie on Thanksgiving. If Bowie starts looking at me like those assholes do, I don't know how I'll get through the next year at Youngs Mill. I couldn't.

"Man," I say, pushing out a smile. I rub my backside to dim the awkward, but rubbing your ass is always awkward. "If we're going to make this a thing, you should invest in a pillow or something."

"I don't live in a palace, Jay," Bowie says, ignoring me. He looks me dead in the eye, speaks in a low voice. Last time I saw him like this, I had spent the night at his house for the first time and just told him about my parents. "That sucks, bro," he said after the longest five seconds of my life. Then he let me have the last slice of pizza. Bowie would eat his own underwear with the right amount of tomato sauce, so that last slice solidified our friendship.

"Yeah, pretty sure they wouldn't let you into Buckingham with that hair." I slip my backpack off his shoulders and give him a salute. He studies me and I don't move. He and I both know that I'm not taking another step until he pedals in the opposite direction.

Bowie finally gives in and returns the salute. "Text me later. Let me know how it goes at *El Taco Bell*." He lays on the accent extra thick, but every time he tries any accent, he always ends up sounding like some sweaty guy that works in a pizzeria in the Bronx.

"Yeah, and send my regards to your uncle Vito," I say.

"Why I oughta . . ." Bowie shakes his fist at me like a true stereotype as he gives himself a push on his bike. I wait until he rounds the bend before I trek the rest of the way to my apartment building.

It's weird to call the Ducts home. My tongue still gets in my way when I try, as if it's embarrassed for me. Dad's eyelid twitched more times than his doctor would have liked when he found out that MiMi was moving here. It isn't that the Ducts are the projects—it's the neighborhood that everyone migrates to when they move on up from the projects. The buildings might be newer, but the chaos inside those buildings remains the same. Behind these walls, there are still families living paycheck to paycheck, and the occasional idiot creeping into windows to steal those paychecks.

I walk past the security booth stationed at the entrance but, of course, the guard is nowhere to be seen. The booth is just something to make government officials sleep better at night. To show that even though the Ducts is part of the public housing system, they still care about our well-being. So they hire security guards as twisted as some of the folks who live here.

The most twisted of them all, though, is Javon. Remember when I said I'd get back to him later? Here goes: Javon Hockaday is the Ducts' resident Don Corleone or Walter White or any other badass who makes money off fear. And he has the whole fear factor thing on lock. I've never actually seen him lay a hand on anyone, but I *have* seen grown-ass men—big dudes who like to show off their biceps in wife beaters even when the sun isn't shining—cross the street to avoid eye contact with Javon. There are rumors Javon and his boy, Kenny, once seared a guy's eye with a lit blunt for staring at Javon too long after asking for directions. Kind of surprising to hear that about Kenny. Though he rolls with Javon, he still takes the time to help MiMi carry her groceries upstairs when I'm not around. Sometimes, when he isn't making runs for Javon, we'll catch him playing freeze tag with the younger kids in the hood. But Javon is a different story. Only time I've seen him smile is when something sinister lurks behind his eyes. Like he's plotting all the ways to dismember you and where to hide every limb.

Javon's apartment building is in the parking lot to the left of the security booth. He does his business right under the guards' noses, slinging out bliss, crinkle, and other drugs du jour. A part of me figures that's why he got into the business. A big ol' middle finger to the system that gives the side-eye to guys who look like us.

As expected, two of Javon's goons, Slim and Quan, are perched outside of Javon's building, ratchet hip-hop music spilling out of one of their Bluetooth speakers. They both crack up as they check out something on one of their phones. Slim even pounds one of his chubby feet against the pavement, punctuating the hilariousness of whatever he's watching. Usually Nic's on the stoop laughing right along with them. Other times she's holed up somewhere with Javon. I prefer her out in the daylight though, that way I can check to see if her eyes and head are clear. When she's off with Javon, no telling how cloudy she might be when she makes it home.

No lie, Old Jay shows up when I don't spot Nicole with Slim and Quan. Maybe I should try calling her before my interview. But she did text that she was all good . . .

"Ay yo, come here!" a voice booms.

The air around me freezes. I turn around and Javon stands at his stoop. His platinum chain rivals the sun for light. Even Slim and Quan know that staring directly at him will scorch their eyes. Half of Javon's hair is zigzagged into crisp corn rows, while the other half is full on 'fro. He chews on a Black & Mild cigar, face warped with irritation.

I point to myself like an idiot, and Javon frowns at me to validate I'm an idiot.

"Nah, the dopey nigga behind you," Javon says.

Do not look behind you, I think—knowing if I do his crew will start clowning me for at least two minutes. I walk back over to Javon's stoop, but make sure not to walk up the steps. No one walks up there unless they live in the building, and even residents take pause.

"Ay," Javon continues, "where's your sister?"

His question hits me in the gut. I peek at the window that, based off my own floor plan, leads to Javon's living room. Expect to see Nic peering back at me. "What do you mean? She's not with you?"

"Wouldn't be asking if she was." Javon flicks away his cigar and I jump to my right to dodge it. "Haven't seen her since last night."

Last night. Last night, Nic was tripping hard, talking so much nonsense over the phone that she must've smoked up whatever Javon didn't sell yesterday. Figured she was coming down from her trip with him this morning, like usual. But if Javon's lost in the sauce, where the hell could she be?

"I don't know where she is," I admit. Saying it aloud makes it even truer, and the fried bologna sandwich I had for breakfast crawls up my chest.

"You wouldn't have a reason to lie to me, would you?" His question isn't just any question—it's a warning. And I hear it loud and clear.

"Why would I lie?" I ask.

Slim and Quan both suck in a breath and I wince. My attempt at sincerity was seen as a dig. Dig too deep with Javon and someone will have to dig you up. Or so they say.

My biggest fear comes true as Javon steps off his stoop, approaches me. "Fuck you just say to me?" I can still smell the smoke from his cigar on his breath. See the smoke seeping from his nose and ears. I swallow so hard that I taste the burnt vanilla remnants.

"Huh?" I ask, knowing damn well I heard every syllable. But "huh" was the only thing my throat would let me squeeze out.

"Bruh," Quan calls out from the stoop, scratching the angry scar across his eyebrow. "I think he's clowning you."

My throat gets even tighter. "What?" I practically squeak. I clear my throat as much as I can and take a stab at articulation. "I wasn't clowning anyone. Just trying to get home." I take two tiny steps back from Javon in case he doesn't believe me.

With one large step, Javon eats up the space between us. "You playing me?"

"Huh? No. *No*. That was the exact opposite of what I just said."

"Now he's saying you can't hear, Von!" Slim says. He buries his hand in a bag of pork rinds and then passes the bag to Quan. My impending death is much more amusing than whatever they were cracking up at on their phone.

"Nigga, if you're covering for Nic, I'm going to find out." Spit flies from Javon's mouth and lands inside mine. I'm too frozen with fear to gag.

"Javon . . ." I speak to him slowly, calmly. Just like I do with Nic when she's floating. "I promise you, I'm not covering anything. I haven't spoken to Nic since—"

Javon's palm eclipses my face and I'm knocked off my feet. My mouth and nose are against the sidewalk and I'm munching on concrete. My arms flail. I try to push myself up for air, but Javon's hand is glued to the back of my head. Pushing me down so hard against the pavement that I wait for my nose to crunch.

Slim and Quan whoop and holler in the background, egging Javon on. "Kill that nigga!" one of them says with a laugh. *Kill?* For asking a question? The fick are these guys on? I slap my hands against the sidewalk to show Javon that he wins the game I didn't know we were playing. I feel more pressure on the back of my head, and then Javon's mouth is right next to my ear.

"When you see Nic . . ." he begins in between breaths, like punking me is his cardio for the day. "Tell her to hit me up. Immediately."

At that, he loosens his grip. My head snaps up and I gulp so much air that I almost choke from it. Tiny drops of blood fall from somewhere on my face and kiss the sidewalk underneath me. My self-respect spills with each drip. I scramble to my feet, don't look back as Slim and Quan cackle at me like black folks at a Kevin Hart movie. Javon hisses more words in my direction. Something sharp and dangerous. But the words never stick because something else runs through my head: Where the hell is Nicole?

✳ ✳ ✳

As soon as Joshua Kim slides into the booth across from me, his managerial facade goes to shit. He pauses, cocks his head, and furrows his eyebrows so hard that they basically shout: *Dafuq?*

I get it, though. My face looks like it just made out with a cheese grater. My dance with Javon's palm left me with a busted lip and enough scratches to form their own constellation. I thought about rummaging through Nic's drawers, finding makeup to cover the nicks—but I know as much about makeup as I do about self-defense. So, I made sure to wear the crispest button-down in my closet. Tucked it into my pants like a productive citizen. My dad was all about appearances and passed that eager-to-please gene down to me. I even push my bottom lip into my mouth to hide the cut as much as possible, play it off like I'm serving severe thinking face.

Joshua finally remembers the reason we're sitting together and flashes a quick smile before shuffling through papers. Can't imagine what else he has in his hand aside from my application, which was nothing but two sheets with my contact information and my answers to a few math problems. It's hard to imagine anything else, actually, aside from where the hell Nic could be—and why the hell Javon seemed so pissed when he mentioned her. I only remember her getting into it with Javon one time. It was just this past Halloween. Nic came home early in short shorts, a white tank top, and heels. Beyoncé from her "Crazy in Love" music video. I'm assuming Javon pulled out his best Yankees fitted cap to be her Jay-Z. I was lounging on the couch, committing to my yearly Halloween tradition of being a loser at home watching some Michael Jackson movie about ghosts.

"You're home early," I said to Nic.

Nicole frowned at the old white guy on the TV screen. "Why does that old white dude look like Michael Jackson?"

"Because it is Michael Jackson."

Nic's frown shifted toward me.

I shrugged. "I guess the makeup artist wasn't that good. Why are you home? Thought Kenny was having some huge blowout."

She bites down on the cross hanging from her necklace. "He was. But Javon decided to be a jealous dick, so now I'm here."

"Sucks to be you," I said. Then offered her my bowl of popcorn.

Nic knocked my feet off the couch then curled up on the cushion, eating the majority of my popcorn. She ignored Javon's calls the rest of that night. I still remember her laugh as I tried my best to mimic Michael's dance moves from the movie. The sound was light and airy, like nothing weighed on her shoulders. Just like we were kids.

The next day, she grew up and answered Javon's calls again.

"I asked if your name was Jayson Murphy."

The smell of queso infiltrates my nose and Joshua Kim is across from me again. He's wearing eyeglasses and, by how shiny they look, I can tell he doesn't really need them. Probably something he throws on to make himself look like an official supervisor and not some college kid picking up a gig at Taco Bell to pay for textbooks.

"Yeah." I clear my throat. Fold my hands on top of the table between us. "Yes, sir," I say again. More formal. I put on my polite white boy voice to show Joshua that despite my face looking like the last scene of a horror movie, I could be trusted.

"Hi, Jayson. Welcome to Taco Bell." He smiles as if he built the restaurant with his own two hands. "It says here you're a junior at Youngs Mill. Tell me a little more about that." He leans forward, as if he expects me to say more than: "I'm an eleventh grader at Youngs Mill."

I make up some shit about how much I enjoy school, how English is my favorite subject. How Youngs Mill has such an inviting atmosphere, which helped me build my team player skills. I think I add in something about math, since the application wanted me to demonstrate my math skills. The words just tumble out of my mouth so I can fill up enough space to push Nic out of my mind. The past year or so has been me covering for her, or worrying about her, or doing *something* for her. It was time I did something for me. Who cares if she pissed off Javon? They should break up anyways.

"And I decided to lighten my load. Take it easy on extracurricular activities this year to gain some work experience," I conclude. I punctuate it with a nod since that's what I've seen people in the movies do when they nail a job interview.

Joshua nods back, pleased. "Aside from school, what do you like doing in your free time?"

The fick does that have to do with working at Taco Bell? I rub my hands together, buy myself some time as I try to conjure up a bullshit response. But all I can see is Javon's hand smacking me in the head. All I can hear is the rage in his voice as he asked about Nic. If he could knock around his girlfriend's own brother, what did that mean for Nic? I shake my head and shake out the image.

"I like to help out my classmates with homework," I say. "I'm usually their go-to guy for essays. I also tend to walk my neighbors' dogs from time to time. I don't have one of my own, so it's a good way to sneak in a couple of pats. Oh, and I have a sister." I wince as soon as the words leave my mouth. Dammit, Nic. All I needed was five—ten minutes tops without her interrupting my life. But now Joshua Kim thinks that my sister is my hobby, whatever the hell that means.

"Um. Okay." Joshua blinks at me. "I have a sister, too. They're kind of pains in the you-know-what, am I right?"

I smile and nod at him again. He has no idea.

Joshua exhales and leans back in his seat. "I'm going to give it to you straight, Jayson. Since I've begun managing this shift, this Taco Bell has been receiving top marks with our health inspections and customer service surveys. We run a clean, friendly place here. No time for riffraff, follow me?"

"Yes," I answer, though it comes out more as a question.

"Don't get me wrong, you look like a good guy, but . . ." He points to his face. Probably because it would be too rude to point at mine.

"Oh. This?" I rub a hand across my mouth and my lip

cusses at me. "This isn't what you think. I fell off a bike."

Joshua blinks at me again. "How many times did you fall?"

This interview was over as soon as Joshua slapped on his fake eyeglasses and got a clearer look at me, but I play along as he tells me about the next steps in the process. Phone call at the end of the week, and then I get to meet with another shift manager. I hadn't realized Taco Bell had as many clearances as the FBI. But that's what usually happens when you come from my neighborhood, live down the street from a guy like Javon, plus walk in with a face like a Picasso painting. Still . . . the run-around feels kinda shitty.

As I wait outside for the city bus, I glance at my phone, but there's nothing new from Nic. I had called her, but she never picked up. I even left a voicemail, but she didn't bother to send another text to check in. Her last text stares back at me: *Never mind. All good.* If she's all good, why the hell is Javon tripping? I keep the phone in my hand, as if Nic could sense me waiting to hear from her. I hold on to it for the entire bus ride home.

She never calls.

FOUR

WHEN I GET HOME, I HEAD TO NIC'S ROOM AND DON'T EVEN bother knocking. If she can't respect me enough to return my call, I can't respect her privacy.

Nic's bed is just like I left it this morning. Hell, everything's exactly like it was this morning. She still hasn't made it home. I snatch my phone out my pocket and stab at her name. After the fifth ring—voicemail. Again. I grit my teeth as Nicole's recorded voice commands me to drop her a line.

"Okay, so check this," I begin after the beep, "I don't know where you are or what you're up to, but since you just cost me a job, I'm going to start charging you ten bucks an hour for all the time I spend covering for you. May not sound like much, but I want backpay. So yeah, you're going to need your boo to spot you more than a couple of bucks. And speaking of Javon, he's a fickin' psycho!"

I push Nic's door closed behind me, just in case MiMi comes home from work and hears me spazzing out. "I'm done, Nic," I say in a hushed voice. "Capital D as in dead. Which is what you're going to be once MiMi finds out you haven't been home in almost twenty-four hours." I hang up the phone and wince as soon as I do. I didn't even say goodbye.

No. *No.* Old Jay worried about polite farewells. New Jay was so cold that Nicole was probably going to catch a chill just listening to that message. I reach for the doorknob, but my hand feels heavy. *Dammit, Nic.* I tighten up the sheets on her bed, nice and tidy as if she's been home. But this is the last time. I promise.

When I enter my room, I open Snapchat on my phone. Search through my friends until I come across Sterling Simmons's profile. Her page is flooded with selfies of her glossy lips and platinum-blonde hair and random shots of her baring her abs in her bathroom mirror. A basketball wife in training.

Nicole and Sterling have been Frick and Frack since they both joined the track team during their freshman year. Of course, Nic got kicked off once her grades started slipping like her mind, and everyone knew that Sterling only latched onto Nic to give the middle finger to her ultra conservative, ultra–Confederate flag supporting parents. Otherwise,

Sterling would just kick it with the other bougie white girls at school. The ones who eat their ramen in fancy broths and not from a twenty-cent packet.

She's currently active on Snapchat, so I send her a private message: **You with Nic??**

She takes her sweet time to respond to me. I drop the phone on my bed, yank off my interview clothes while I wait. I don't think I ever shook Joshua Kim's hand. *The right kind of handshake seals the deal*, Dad always told me. He used to take my hand, squeeze it the right amount, and have me copy him. Sometimes he'd show me the street way—a gliding of the palms punctuated by a half hug. Both handshakes showed respect, but linger too long or squeeze too limply, and folks'll look at you funny. I was so eager to check my phone for any missed messages from Nic that I never got the chance to extend my hand to Joshua. Maybe, just maybe, that would've salvaged the interview. Now I have to go back to walking neighborhood dogs and other side hustles to give MiMi her due.

My phone dings and lets me know I have a new Snapchat message.

Sterling: Who this??

I smirk so loudly that I hope she can hear it. Forget the fact that my handle is literally *JayMurph*. Sterling has to prove that she is in a higher social stratosphere than me.

I stab a response: **Nic's brother.**

Bubbles appear then disappear on my screen. Appear and disappear. Over and over as if Sterling is trying to perfect her response for little old me.

Sterling: Nope

I groan in frustration. All that waiting for a one-word response. A possibly deceitful one-word response at that. A simple no would've taken a second to type. Sterling was too deliberate with her message, like the breath a sax player takes before leaking out the final, seductive note.

Me: You sure?

More bubbles. Finally:

Sterling: Think I would know. Come find me Monday morning at school, tho.

I frown at her last message. If she hasn't seen Nic like she's claiming, why would she need to see me? Sterling has always spoken to me in clipped sentences, as if she's saving her adverbs and adjectives for somebody that counts. Now she's scheduling meetings with me? The only explanation is that there's something she wants to tell me that she doesn't want in writing.

Me: You good?

The blue dot in our chat window disappears. Sterling's no longer active. What the hell? I open the contacts on my phone until I remember that I don't have Sterling's number. Nic has always been our link, and without her, the assemblage is rusty.

"Jay! Nicole!" MiMi's voice booms from somewhere in the front of the apartment. I didn't even hear her get in. "Wash your hands and come eat dinner!"

I shove my phone in the pocket of my jogging pants, wipe the creases out of my old T-shirt as if I'm having dinner with the president instead of my grandma. Finally, I strut toward the front, try to keep the same cadence in my steps as usual. If I double-time it or take my time, MiMi may notice the absence of Nic's footsteps sooner. When I get to the dining area, MiMi's humming a hymn in the kitchen while she pours sweet tea into empty jelly jars. She sucks on her bottom lip, an indication that she is reaching the good part of the song. I grab two plates out of the cabinet, place them in front of my and MiMi's chairs. My subtle way of letting MiMi know that Nic won't be joining us for dinner tonight.

"Hey, baby," MiMi says when she notices me. "You would not believe the sale going on at Picadilly's. Ten-piece chicken meal, two sides, biscuits—all for twenty bucks."

"Mmm," I respond. Hard to focus on fried chicken wings when Nic is out there doing God knows what. Has to be something trippy if Sterling doesn't even want it in writing. How the hell is the New Jay supposed to get the Old Nic out of this one?

"Work was rough today. All I want to do is stuff my face, find something on Netflix, and fall asleep. Where'd you leave my blood pressure meds, baby?"

I grip onto the back of the chair that I was pulling out. Dammit. I was so caught up in my feelings after that interview that I forgot to swing by the pharmacy. Plus, I wanted to rush home, see if Nic made it back. Between her drama and getting my ass handed to me by Javon—

"I ficked up." I wince as soon as the words leave my mouth, even though MiMi probably thinks that what I said was as harmless as LOL. "I forgot," I try again. "I can run out now and grab them."

"Don't be silly. Eat your dinner. I have enough pills to get me through tonight. It's okay." MiMi exhales and I know from her sigh that it's not okay. She's tired and I'm doing the tiring. She walks over to the dining table with the jars of tea and pauses when she sees only two plates. She looks up at me and doesn't even have to ask the question. It's written on the faint lines trailing across her forehead.

I rest my elbow on the table, tuck my chin into my hand to cover my busted lip. I wish I had something to tell her, but I don't even know what to tell myself at this point. And with me dropping the ball on her meds like that, she can't afford to get all worked up. I have to protect her as best as I can.

"Nic stopped by real quick," I say from behind my fingers, each word scratching at my throat. "Said she's eating at Sterling's tonight."

At that, MiMi clicks her tongue. "Shouldn't I have a say? I'm the one paying the bills around here." She shakes her head after setting the jars down with a thud. Tea sloshes out of them, bronze tears dripping onto the table. MiMi mutters a few other things as she snatches the food out of the paper bags. I watch her hands. Knuckles a little large, permanently swollen. Slightly chapped in that space between her thumb and index finger, no matter how many times she soothes it with Vaseline. Her hands are badges of honor, proof of hard work. Still, I look forward to the day when she can rest them.

"Sit down, MiMi. I got it." I rush to her side, take the plastic platter of chicken from her hands. Our pinky fingers graze against each other, but MiMi's in no hurry to move hers. Instead, she rests her head on my shoulder. I let her, taking in the soothing smell of cocoa butter in her hair. Two, three years ago, it was my head on her shoulder. Now she barely reaches my chin.

"You're a good boy," she says. "Always been a good boy."

"Well, I was raised by the best."

Something gets caught in MiMi's throat and she pulls away. "Ya damn skippy," she says, bumping her hip against mine before taking a seat at the table. I laugh. MiMi cusses once every blue moon, but when she does, it's always worth it.

"You going to sit here and play dumb," MiMi begins as I take my seat across from her, "or you going to tell me what happened to your lip?"

Fick. I forgot to keep covering up the lip. I touch it, and then raise my eyebrows as if I forgot it was there. "Oh, yeah.

Chewing on it, then *BAM*. Bumped right into someone during class change. Tooth almost went clear through." I take a bite of my chicken, crunch unnecessarily loud for distraction.

MiMi eyeballs me with her lips twisted to one side. "And what about the rest of your face?"

Right. The rest of my face. "The guy was pretty big. Muscles on top of muscles, know what I mean? Can you pass the salt?"

She slides the saltshaker over to me. "Wham, bam, thank you, ma'am, in the halls, huh?"

I scrunch my nose. "That doesn't mean what you think it means."

"And what about your job interview? How did that go?"

She's on top of her game today. As Joshua Kim knows, I'm clearly not. I think about the money stashed in my box spring. How much longer it'll take me to reach my goal without that job. "Pretty solid. Keeping my options open, though."

"Okay, Jayson." She's pulling out my government name. Not a good sign. "First your sister's avoiding me all day, now you're coming home with your face all chopped and screwed. One of you is gonna end up in a ditch somewhere, and I'll be looking dumb, sitting here at this table. Watching your plates get cold."

The image of Nicole's cold body lying facedown in a ditch is enough for me to push my plate away.

"And now you're not hungry?" MiMi asks.

I'm not sure what I am. I know I should be pissed at Nic for playing some kind of vanishing act. Asking me to look out for her without asking, as if that's part of some brother handbook I only read the synopsis of. But usually, Nic would shoot me a line—a text, a DM, a smoke signal to tell me she's living her best life while I wait at home, letting her do it. Her silence is almost too loud at the table.

"Just remembered I have to finish my English project," I finally say.

MiMi frowns at me. "It's Friday."

"You're the one that's always on me about procrastinating." I stand, peck MiMi on the cheek before she can say more. As soon as I close my bedroom door behind me, I try calling Nic again. Straight to voicemail this time. I don't leave another message. I call again and again, hoping that her real voice will pick up instead of the recording.

It never does.

I dream about Nic again that night. I find her somewhere in the woods, crunching on leaves as she weaves through trees, holding hands with Mom. Real Mom—all bronzed skin and bright eyes. Not Prison Mom—all faded and monochromatic. They look back at me, motion for me to join them. I take a few steps into the woods but Nic and Mom get farther and farther away. I try to call their names but choke on some vines creeping toward me, away from the trees. The more the vines bury me, the smaller Nic and Mom get. Smaller and smaller until they're just specks. And then nothing at all.

I wake up around three in the morning to gunshots.

FIVE

THERE WERE FOUR OF THEM. *CRACK, CRACK, CRACK, CRACK* cutting through the night, like a drummer having a jam session with the raccoons and cicadas. The screeching tires that followed let the neighborhood know that it wasn't just a couple of assholes setting off firecrackers. Only bullets could cause that frenzy.

"Just got off the phone with Roberta," MiMi says to me as our shoulders graze each other in the hallway. "She said they're having a good deal on strawberries at the farmer's market." She stares down at the phone in her hand, strawberries the last thing on her mind. MiMi always gets jittery the day after shots are fired—especially when they're so close that the smell of gunpowder does the hustle with her morning cup of coffee. And especially when Nic's still drifting.

"For real?" This could be my out. My way to pound the pavement, scope out some of Nic's stomping grounds to catch wind on where she might've blown. "I could ride my bike there and pick some up. Need to get some air anyway."

MiMi's eyes snap up at me. "Boy, the only air you're getting today is a draft from the window. Now park it." She points to the couch and I do what I'm told.

MiMi makes another call but heads to her room and closes the door behind her so I can't hear. I also can't just be idle. Those bullets had a destination and I need to be sure that Nic wasn't a pit stop. I open up Snapchat, see if Sterling's signed on again. No luck. I scroll through her followers. Maybe one of them is online and knows if Sterling's really kicking it with Nic. I need to find someone that Sterling follows back. Someone not quite in the same circle as Sterling, but at least on the outskirts. They might give me the answers I need.

Before I narrow down my options, there are three sturdy knocks on the front door. Urgent ones. The kinds that if not answered within a few seconds, hinges will be broken. Those knocks could only mean one thing: the bullies with the badges are on the other side.

MiMi comes scurrying out of her room, gives me a

warning point to stay put. Stay quiet. *Don't give them a reason*, Dad would say. Cops around here are always looking for reasons. Reasons to lay hands on you, reasons to put cuffs on you—but for the most trifling things. Pooch once got his face smashed against the hood of a squad car for complimenting a cop's shades. Took most of the neighborhood to convince the cop that Pooch was just being Pooch—that he wasn't pulling a fast one. After about an hour of being cuffed in the backseat of a squad car, Pooch was released. But when it comes to Javon and his crew, the cops are a little less handsy. Almost like Javon has them in his back pocket.

Two of them are at my threshold now, one smacking on gum every other word to punctuate his smugness.

"So, you didn't see or hear anything last night?" the one without the gum asks, scribbling away in his notepad despite MiMi not giving him anything yet.

"I see and hear something every night. You have to be more specific, honey," MiMi says, leaning against her door. She can cut someone down with one look, but it's much better when she uses her words.

"A kid from Warwick High got killed early this morning. Right outside the security booth."

A sigh seeps out of my pores. I almost immediately regret it. Yeah, if it's a kid from Warwick High, that means Nic's in the clear. Still . . . someone's not coming home for dinner tonight. Their family will have to look at their empty dining room chair forever. The good thing about moving in with MiMi is that the table is different. I don't have to look at the head of it and not see Dad sipping on his morning coffee. I don't have to see the tiny dent in the wood where Mom dropped her hot plate. I see Mom and Dad everywhere else. In the permission slips they're supposed to sign. In the birthday parties where they're no longer swaying to Stevie Wonder's "Happy Birthday." In the mirror when my mom's eyes and thick nose and full bottom lip stare right back at me. At least I could eat a bowl of cereal in peace.

"Why aren't you speaking to the security guard, then?" MiMi asks.

"He was patrolling the neighborhood by foot when the incident occurred," the cop with the gum adds.

"Shame." MiMi's voice, though, is anything but shameful.

The cop takes two more smacks of his Big Red and then leans around MiMi, eyeballs me sitting on the couch. "And where were you early this morning, young man?"

MiMi shifts her hips to the other side of the doorway to block me. "He hasn't left the house since dinner last night."

"Can he answer for himself?"

"He's sixteen. I speak for him until I say otherwise." MiMi places a hand on her hip. In the streets, this move is just as ruthless as taking off your shoes and earrings before a brawl. "Now, neither of us can help you. You may want to move along, stop wasting your time. I'm sure that baby's mama wants answers."

The cops mumble a few words back and forth between each other. MiMi places her other hand on her hip, eating up more space in the doorway. She's getting all biblical like Edom, not letting any jackass pass through. It works. One of the cops hands her a card.

"In case you remember anything else," the one with the notepad says.

"*Mmm hmm,*" MiMi mumbles before closing the door in their faces. She looks down at the card and rips it in half.

She trudges to the kitchen. "They always do this. Put on a big show like they care enough to do their jobs, but then forget about these babies a minute later." She tosses the card into the trash in the kitchen, and then plops down on the other end of the couch. "I'm sick of it. Sick of it, I tell you."

MiMi sinks back into the couch as if her whole body exhales and begins channel surfing like her thumb's on a mission. She stops on some black-and-white TV show and peeks at me. "I don't like Nicole out on them streets when madness is going on," she finally admits. "You would think that she would call, let me know she's at least breathing."

I wish I could bury myself under the couch pillows. It's been almost thirty hours of calling her phone only to get her voicemail. Thirty hours of what-ifs and now-whats. But I couldn't show MiMi I was worried, too. Not when all the pieces haven't been put together. I need to wait and get more answers from Sterling. Until then, I need to slip into Old Jay's skin.

"It's all good," I say. "Nic texted me. She's still with Sterling. Shopping, getting their nails done, the whole nine. You know how Sterling likes to spoil Nic to flash her money."

MiMi gives me a look, and I turn to the TV. Nod along to whatever hijinks the fat white guy and his tall lanky friend are getting into. No clue what's going on, but I'll put up a front to stop MiMi from asking more questions. Seconds of her staring at me stretches into minutes, and soon I'm trying to find something to do with my hands.

"You need to put something on that lip," she says. "Don't want you heading into church tomorrow looking like whodunit."

"Yes, ma'am." I'm on my feet before I get the second word out. I head to the freezer, grab a bag of frozen chopped broccoli and press it to my mouth. Then I go ahead and stick my whole head inside the freezer. Wait until my brain becomes numb, hope it reaches my heart.

✳ ✳ ✳

As soon as I wake up on Sunday, I open my texting window for Nicole. Press the shrugging emoji three times, but then delete them. If I want to get a response from Nic, I have to keep it real.

Me: I'm not mad. Just worried. Come home.

I don't even wait for her response. I try calling again but . . . straight to voicemail. Her phone's still not on, and I can't help but wonder if she cut it off, or someone cut it off for her. On cue, the scab on my lip itches—reminding me of Javon forcing me to eat concrete. I can only imagine what could happen to Nic if he got his hands on her.

But I can't shake MiMi to figure it out, especially not on a Sunday. The Lord's day. Me and MiMi always arrive at Providence Baptist about an hour before service begins. She fiddles away in one of the offices with a calculator and spreadsheet—and does what she does with Deacon Irving when the office door is closed. MiMi and Deacon Irving are the talk of Providence, but only in whispers since the deacon still has a wife who he may or may not be separated from. All I know is that she lives somewhere in South Carolina, and the only time I've seen her is in a picture that the church keeps framed in the banquet hall. Ironically, she sits right next to MiMi in the picture, along with a few other notable ladies of the church. The deacon's wife's smile is wide and oblivious, whereas you could trace MiMi's straight smile with the end of a mechanical pencil.

As for me? About a year ago, MiMi roped me into spending the hour before service co-teaching Sunday school for five- and six-year-olds with Riley Palmer. The church figured the best way to reach the youth was to have the youth teaching them. MiMi said it was something good to put on college applications, but we both know that it was a way for her to keep tabs on me. To make me continue coming to services after Nic started playing hooky. And having Riley as an extra pair of eyes for her was even better.

Riley's the preacher's daughter, which basically means she's obligated to dress like it's winter even if it's ninety degrees outside. She also has Converse sneakers in every color. The only thing dopier than seeing a girl wear a turtleneck with overalls in the summer is seeing her wear them with a pair of white Converses. She goes to Warwick High, which is down the street from Youngs Mill, but Warwick has the IB program. Even though we have a few nerds at my school, the sentiment is well known: we don't fick with the uppity mofos at Warwick—even though some of them try to slink into my hood from time to time to get cool points. Yet here I am, rubbing elbows with one every Sunday morning.

You don't get any more uppity than Riley. We met when we were eight, and her first words to me were: "What's that?" as she pointed to my jacked-up flattop, which leaned a little more to the left than I would have liked. It was right after I moved in with MiMi. I no longer had access to the barber Dad and I went to all the time. MiMi got a discount from this old dude named Man Boo who had a shop around the corner from the Ducts. I soon found out that old dudes named Man Boo weren't really keen on the latest styles, so I kept my fade low ever since. Still, every moment with Riley has been a perpetual string of What's thats as she calls me out on everything, from the generic soda brand I sip on to the masking tape I use to hold my headphones together until I get a new pair.

I enter the conference room where our Sunday school class takes place. Riley's at the whiteboard, tracing the kids' hands with a dry erase marker. Today she graces me with a pair of lime-green Converses to go along with her flannel shirt and jean skirt that reaches her ankles. Didn't even know they sold skirts that long.

Malik, one of the smallest kids in the class, spots me and jogs over. "What it do, Jay? We're all giving high fives to Jesus." He holds up his tiny hand, and I slap him one. Malik pauses after really taking in my face. "Dang, what happened to your lip?"

I swat my hand, indicating it's nothing. "I just fell off my bi—"

"Y'all, Jay got into a fight and broke his lip!" Malik announces to the rest of the class. At that, seven little heads swivel around to get a look. A chorus of *oohs* erupts in the room. Riley looks at me and folds her arms across her chest. If she cussed, I'm sure she would've mouthed something unholy to me.

I bob my hands up and down, up and down. Encouraging them to quiet down. "Jay didn't get in a fight," I say over their inquisitive voices. "Jay fell off his bike, just like most of you still do. It's nothing."

"Did you fall off your bike because you was fighting?" Keosha asks me, questions spilling out of her eyes like the plaits and barrettes spilling out of her head.

"There was no fighting," I repeat. I say it loud enough so that the words could stick to Riley's ribs. Riley chews at the end of her dry-erase marker, studying me. I raise my eyebrows at her, pleading for her to do whatever magical thing she does to get the kids back on task.

Finally, Riley claps her hands three times, and the kids repeat after her as they all take their seats at the round table. "Okay, I think we've heard enough about Jay and his clumsiness, right?" she asks.

Some of the kids snicker. I let out one loud *ha ha*. Phony enough. Hope that sticks to her ribs, too.

"Who remembers what we were supposed to read about today?" Riley questions the kids in the same high-pitched voice as a Disney princess. Several hands fly up, but Riley turns to me. "Jay, do you remember? Or did your tumble from your bike cause amnesia?" She laughs and a snort follows, because Riley's full of swag.

"What's amnesia?" Malik asks.

"It's when people don't believe what you're saying, so they attempt to be cute in front of a group of kids," I say. The kids look at one another, blink, and shrug. I force a smile at

Riley. "I think I'd much rather scope what the kids remember. Since it's their class and all."

Riley's face falls, probably realizing she's not as funny as she suspected. "Of course," she says. She points to Daysia, whose arm is going to snap off if she isn't called on in two seconds.

Daysia folds her hands perfectly together on top of the table. "We were going to talk about David and Gollum."

I choke out a laugh. Just a quick one. But long enough to make Riley step in front of me to block me from Daysia.

"Very close, Daysia. But we're learning about David and *Goliath*. I think someone still may be in the running to get a sticker at the end of the day," Riley says, and Daysia nods—eyes lighting up at the possibility of a new smiley face sticker to paste on the back of her hand. "Okay, let's all go to the reading nook. Remember, crisscross applesauce."

The kids march over to the blue gym mat that serves as Riley's reading nook.

"You up for this today?" Riley asks me, under her breath.

"I'm here, ain't I?" I say.

Riley opens her mouth like she wants to say something else corny, but I turn away from her. Chitchat over. We get through David and Goliath's story from the *Children's Bible Stories* book that was used in my Sunday school class back in the day. The pages smell like stale bread and cough drops, but it always takes me back to a time when I cared more about missing recess than missing sisters. The story only lasts about five minutes, but the seconds drip away like molasses as I mime the actions of the characters.

"Okay, back to the table so you can all draw me *your* Goliath," Riley instructs. "What's something scary that you were able to beat, or are still trying to beat?"

The kids get to it and I retreat to a chair in my corner. Snatch my phone out of my pocket like Hot Pockets fresh out the microwave. Check it for updates. I reached out to, like, three of Sterling's followers on Snapchat last night, but . . . nothing. I do get a text from Camila, though. Kind of. More like a string of question marks for being all MIA this weekend. My thumb hovers over the texting window, conjuring up some energy to give her a satisfying response.

"Okay, spill it." Riley leans against the wall next to me and I shove my phone back into my pocket. Pretty hard to sweet-text Mila when there's a Riley next to you. "What really happened to you?"

I roll my eyes. "Told you. Fell off my bike."

"You're sixteen, Jay. There's no way you're still falling off your bike." Riley gives a smile to one of the kids who holds up his paper to show off the blob he's calling a dog.

"Maybe I'm clumsy. Just like you told the kids."

"Come on, Jay. Do I really look that stupid?" Her perennial ponytail is tucked up into a bun, making her eyes bigger and more prying.

"Don't make me answer that."

"Got into a tiff with your crew?"

I give her the side eye. "I have a crew now?" I don't know what offends me more—her assumption, or that she's tossing words like *tiff* at me without cowering in embarrassment.

"For real. Was it a scuffle over money? Someone step on your sneakers?" Riley snaps her fingers, points at me. "A girl, wasn't it? You threw down over a girl because one of your friends got her pregnant."

And this is exactly why I couldn't tell Riley about Javon. Even though Javon did the slinging, she'd put me in the same category as him. To Riley, both me and Javon strut around with our pants hanging a little too low and the music from our cars a little too loud. Not that I had a car, but if I did have one, rest assured that Riley would ask me why I still used the CD player instead of XM radio.

"Okay, who's ready for our sing-along?" I ask the kids before I say something to Riley that would blow the bun off her head.

"We're not done with our pictures yet," Malik tells me as he holds up his half-empty drawing for proof.

"We'll finish them next week. Do we have any requests?" Never any point asking. We always end with "I've Got the Joy." The kids love pretending to be the Devil sitting on a tack. Three requests for it later, and we're all singing, bouncing up and down, covering our butts like we sat on something pointy.

After two rounds, Riley and I stand on opposite sides of the door, slapping fives to the kids as they file out of the classroom. When the last one leaves, I follow suit. Double-time it to get away from Riley and pull out my phone to check Snapchat again.

"Something really exciting must be happening on your phone," Riley says, catching up to me.

I jump from her presence. Those Converses are irritatingly squeak-free.

"Is it the pregnant chick? Don't tell me she needs you to take a paternity test." She snickers under her breath. Interrupts it with her snort.

I stop walking and Riley crashes against my arm. "You ever notice that you're the only one who laughs at your jokes?"

Riley's laughter dies down. "Lots of people think I'm funny."

"Yeah? The five-year-olds in our class don't count."

"Ugh. Who peed in your Mountain Lion today?"

I groan. Of course she assumes that I drink Mountain Lion instead of its name-brand cousin, Mountain Dew. I do, but still. "You do know that Lion and Dew taste the same, right?"

She snickers again. "Ninety-nine point nine percent of

consumers agree that Dew is better than Mountain Lion."

"Only you would have time to research that." I glance down at my phone. No new alerts.

"You would have time too if you weren't—"

I frown back at Riley. "Let me guess. Out on the street with my *crew*? Busting heads and taking names?"

Riley raises her eyebrows as if that thought hasn't run laps around her brain before. "I was going to say if you weren't always on your phone. Seriously. Who died?" She gasps and clutches her chest. "Wait—did someone die?"

I give up. Riley's like that fly you can't just swat away at a cookout. The one that makes you cover your soda with a napkin in case it wanted to take a dive. "If I tell you what's up, will you stop being so extra?"

She holds up three fingers, scout's honor style, in all her extra glory.

I pause. Riley's the last person I'd spill my wax to, but the pressure's been building so much that I have to let some of it seep before I explode. I step closer to her in case anyone overhears. "My sister's been missing since Thursday night. I have no idea where she is."

Riley covers her mouth with both hands. "Jay," she says in between her fingers. "Jay, I didn't know. Why are you and Ms. Murphy even here today?"

"MiMi doesn't know anything." I ram my fists into my hoodie's pockets. "Don't want to scare her for no reason." My hands tremble at the thought of having a reason to scare her.

"No reason?" Riley's hands drop to her sides. "Jay, your sister could be *missing* missing. She has a right to know."

"I don't know if she's *missing* missing."

"You just said she was."

"Look, you don't know Nic. She does this . . . thing. She tries to break free, but then shows back up at our doorstep like a stray, remorseful kitten. I can't freak out MiMi over one of her dizzy adventures."

"This time is different, though. I can see it on your face."

I step back. Riley's been studying my face enough to see a difference?

"If you're not going to tell your grandma, you at least have to go to the cops."

I'd laugh in Riley's face if my throat wasn't so tight. "Cops don't listen to guys like me—and they damn sure don't care about girls like Nic."

"Not all cops are like that, Jay." Riley blinks at me with all the sincerity in the world. Her eyes are open to possibilities, not muddied from seeing cops laughing at blissheads like Pooch instead of lending a helping hand.

I've said too much. I move away from Riley before I say any more. She calls after me one more time. I pause, glance at her over my shoulder.

Riley squeezes and pulls at her fingers. "I'm . . . I'm sorry."

This time, I do let out a laugh. A small one just under my

breath. "You and me both." But not as sorry as Nic will be after we exchange a few words when she gets home.

If she gets home.

That tiny word haunts me all throughout Reverend Palmer's sermon. *If, if, if.* Over and over like the chorus of a hymn. I need to reach Sterling, get some answers, to make this somber song end.

SIX

I PLAYED A GAME OF HIDE AND SEEK DURING SUNDAY DIN-
ner: hiding the truth about Nic's whereabouts from MiMi
and seeking answers about the truth on my phone. Nic still
wasn't returning my calls, and Sterling's so-called followers
were nothing more than that. Just a few wannabes who comment on Sterling's posts for clout, with no tea to spill. So I hit
up the queen bee herself on Monday morning before heading to my locker. Sterling quickstepped off Snapchat and
remained MIA the whole weekend. She had to know something about Nic. Hell, Nic was probably sitting right next to
Sterling while we chatted, feeding her lines. Hopefully.

I know just where to find Sterling. In the girls' bathroom
across from the gym, touching up her face to take on the role

as the baddest chick at Youngs Mill High. I text Bowie while I wait—mostly so I won't look like some creeper waiting by the girls' bathroom. My phone vibrates in my hand and a number I don't recognize pops up on my screen. I suck in a breath and the phone almost slips through my fingers as I fumble to answer it.

"Nic?" I ask. I plead.

There's a brief pause on the other line. "Uhh . . . this is Joshua Kim from Taco Bell. Looking for Jayson Murphy."

All hope seeps out of my nostrils. Taco Bell? I thought I bombed that interview so bad that they sent a crime scene cleanup crew to mop up after me. "Yeah, this is me. Jay. I mean, Jayson. Me being Jayson." The hell, Jay? You want this guy to think you're even more of a dope?

"Alrighty then. Well, I reviewed your application with the other shift manager. And he and I both agree—you got what it takes to join our crew."

I stifle a laugh. What it takes probably means that I was the only applicant who didn't come to the interview smelling of booze or bliss. Guess they'll take someone on the losing end of a street fight over a blisshead. "That's amazing. Thank you so much, Mr. Kim," I say in my Whiteboy Jay voice.

"We'd love to see if you could come in to meet Maurice, the other manager. And then we could talk about . . ." Joshua goes on and on about background checks and uniforms and W-2 forms, oh my. But his words pour in one ear and leak out the other because Sterling finally slinks out of the bath-room door, heels almost as long as her legs, and reminds me I'm on a mission.

"Excellent. I'll get back with you," I say to Joshua right before hanging up. He's probably regretting the decision to hire me even more, but I'll have to kiss his ass later. Right now, I have bigger fish to fry.

I nod at Sterling and she doesn't even flinch when she sees me. Just nods back as if she was used to having dudes wait for her. "Hey." She runs her fingers through her blonde locks, all wavy and tousled like she just strutted off the beach, then walks past me.

What the fick?

"Wait," I say, catching up to her. "Didn't you want to talk to me today?" I spread my arms and present her the floor. Inside my heart is doing cartwheels. I'm doing the whole duck thing—cool and calm on the surface, but everything flailing where nobody can see.

"Oh, right. Chung asked me to edit the *Run of the Mill* and convince you to do it with me. I mean, nobody really reads print anymore but I figured . . ."

Sterling's words get eaten up by static. The lit mag? The fickin' lit mag? No. *No.* There has to be more. Sterling's my window to Nic. My last gasp of hope before I let the fear of what could be strangle me.

"And don't look at me like that," Sterling continues. "I

know how to read, Jay. I can run a lit mag."

"I don't give a damn about the lit mag!" The words explode out of me. Sterling jumps from the blow. "I thought we were connecting about Nic."

"Nic?" Sterling frowns at me. "Why?"

"I asked if you've seen her. You told me you'd talk to me on Monday then got all sketchy and disappeared all weekend."

"I didn't get sketchy. My parents took away my phone because I got a stupid D on my calculus test."

The window to Nic gets smaller and smaller. I still try to squeeze through. "Be real with me. She hasn't reached out to you at all?"

"Jay, the last time I heard from her was on Thursday."

Thursday? The last time I heard from Nic was Thursday night, too. "What she say to you?"

Sterling's face shifts from day to night. Like someone came and turned off the lights behind her eyes. "I don't remember."

Her response sends my eyebrows flying. "Sterling, was she upset? What she say?"

Sterling rummages through her purse, searching for something. Probably a way out of this conversation. "I said I don't remember."

The hell. "You don't remember anything? Did you see her in person, or was it just a text?"

"Jay." If she could stab me with a look, I'd need at least ten stiches by now. "She hit me up by text. Shooting the shit, like always. No biggie. Find me later if you want to talk about the lit mag." She stops her avid search through her purse and begins to walk down the hall.

"Wait . . . Sterling." I follow her. Can't let her out of my sight. Without her, Nic might disappear for good. "Nic's missing!"

Sterling pauses and looks back at me. "What?"

"I haven't heard from her since Thursday. If you haven't either, then something's off." My knees buckle. Saying the words aloud almost sends me to the floor. "You know this is weird. Even for Nic."

Sterling chews on her bottom lip, forgetting about the gloss she just slathered across it. "Look, I wish I could help, but I don't—" Meek Foreman's arm interrupts our regularly scheduled programming as he wraps it around Sterling's shoulder. Somehow, she doesn't lose her balance from the extra weight. Her shoulders must be used to all that heft after two years of on-ing and off-ing with him.

"Is there a problem here?" Meek asks, glaring at me. By the way his hand clings onto Sterling's upper arm, this must be an on period for their love saga.

"Jay and I were talking about the lit mag," Sterling answers for me. "And now we're rushing to class. Right, Jay?" She raises her eyebrows at me.

Meek flexes his bicep as he continues to hook it around Sterling's neck.

"Right," I say.

"Let me walk you then," Meek says to Sterling. "And Jay, don't forget about that paper you promised to help me with. Mrs. Nelson gave me an extension." Before turning around, he points to his eyes, then points right at me. A weekend hasn't iced him out—he's still seeing red over his decapitated paper. Just like his deadline was extended, so was my pending ass whooping if I didn't come through for him. Like I didn't have enough to worry about.

"Let me know if you hear anything else," Sterling says to me over her shoulder. "About the lit mag." She and I both know the lit mag was code for something else.

I scrub at my hair as I watch Sterling and Meek disappear into the crowd. My window to Nic is completely closed now. Sterling is a dead end, so the only way to reopen that window is to listen to Riley and do the unthinkable. Roll with the cops.

✳ ✳ ✳

There's a dance going on at the precinct on Warwick. Phones ringing off the hook, badges scurrying back and forth, rustling through paperwork. Two drunken idiots sit handcuffed, shouting insults to each other across the room, as another badge types up a report. The chaos makes me wobbly, but my purpose keeps me anchored. Never thought I'd have to turn to the cops for help. I could've hopped on the 107—the bus route would have taken me straight from the Ducts to the station in no time. But I took the long route. Hitched a ride on the 108 toward Patrick Henry Mall, then ordered an Uber near the food court exit just to cover my bases. If Javon and his crew spotted me here, I'd be doing more than just eating pavement. They'd rough me up real good, prop me on the hood of one of their cars and parade me around like an ornament just to make an example out of me. Everyone in the Ducts knows that the only thing worse than a cop is the snitch who squealed to them. But with Sterling being just as clueless as me about Nic, what other choices do I have?

"Can I help you?" one of the white badges in the center of the storm asks me. She has wide shoulders like a linebacker and a general don't-give-a-fick disposition. Her eyes do not leave her computer screen, even as I approach her desk.

I place both hands on top of her desk, keep them visible. "Always let them see your hands," Dad would warn me about the police. He never lived long enough to teach me how to drive, but we practiced drills on what I should do if he ever got pulled over.

I take a deep breath. Look at the exit over my shoulder. I could leave. Pretend I never came here and no one would be the wiser. Including me. I'd still have no answers about Nic's whereabouts. "I need help," I finally manage.

"Came to the right place, kid." She coughs in the crook of her arm, gets back to her computer.

"I'd like to file a missing person report," I try again.

That gets her attention. She raises an eyebrow at me. Leans back in her seat like she's sizing me up. "Where's your mom?"

"In prison." The words come out angrier than I expect. You'd think after all this time of her being locked away, I'd be numb to it all. Telling someone new, though, always hits a nerve I forget is there. Besides, what does my mom have to do with anything? Of course, I keep that to myself. Need to keep my cool for Nic's sake.

"Well, who's supposed to be watching you? Do they know you're here?"

I frown. "I need a guardian to report someone missing?"

"Look, kid." She leans forward now. The nicotine from her pores tickles my nose. "We get a lot of kids like you coming in here clowning around. Filing false reports is illegal, you catch me?"

"You think I'd be here if I didn't have to be?" My patience is razor thin now. Every second I spend farting around with her is another second for Nicole to fade. "If you can't help me, can you find another cop that will?"

The Lady Badge's upper lip twitches as she points a finger at me, ready to give me the reading of a lifetime.

"I'll take it from here, Colleen," a voice says from behind

me. I glance over my shoulder and a black cop peers down at me, with a beard and a frame that could rival Rick Ross's.

"You sure? He's a feisty one," Colleen says, as if she hadn't picked a fight as soon as she spotted me.

Rick Ross chuckles. "Nothing I can't handle." Then to me: "What's up?"

I look over at Colleen, whose wrinkles above her brows form an angry V. Then I look at the two drunken dudes in custody, eyeballing me. "Is there somewhere else we can talk?"

He hitches his head and I follow him to a tiny room near the back with card tables and vending machines. He sneaks glances at me as he helps himself to a Styrofoam cup of coffee. "Take a seat," he orders, pointing to one of the machines. "Hungry? Chips are usually stale, but the muffins are on point."

"I'm good." I sit at one of the card tables. My knee bounces up and down, bumps into the table.

"Your grandmother's Ms. Marie Murphy, right?" Rick Ross asks me as he sits across from me.

My leg freezes. How in the hell does he know MiMi? "Yes, sir."

He nods, and his fingers disappear into his beard as he scratches it. "We go to Providence Baptist together. Your grandma's good people. Helps with the bookkeeping there, right?"

"Yes, sir," I repeat. Try to picture his face in one of the pews, but the clock on my phone usually keeps me busy during service.

"Let me formally introduce myself." He extends his hand. "Miles."

I scope out his badge. Hunter. Miles Hunter. Name like that, he had no choice but to be a cop. "Jay." I shake his hand.

"All right, Jay." He takes a long sip of his coffee. "How can I help you?"

I had to find the one cop in the precinct that knows MiMi. But maybe it's better this way. Nic's been gone longer than normal. MiMi's bound to have questions, and maybe Officer Hunter can help give her answers.

"I want to file a missing person report."

Hunter blinks a few times, stunned. "Who's missing?"

The knee starts again. "My sister, Nic. Nicole Marie Murphy."

Hunter taps a finger on top of the table, creating his own spastic beat. I try to follow his melody, but he's all over the place. "How long has she been missing?"

"Since Friday."

"Friday? Your grandma didn't mention any of this when I saw her at church yesterday."

I take in a deep breath. "She don't know yet. Nic does this thing where she fades, just to get some space from MiMi. Figured I'd give her the weekend to breathe. But this is the longest she's gone without chopping it up with me." I pause as Hunter rubs his thumb across the lip of his cup. "Where's your notepad? Aren't you supposed to be writing all of this down?"

Hunter pushes away his cup and folds his hands together. "Your grandmother's good people, so I need to give it to you straight, Jay. I . . ." He breathes deeply through his nose. His face scrunches up like he's solving a complicated math problem in his head. "The streets talk. I know that Nicole is Javon Hockaday's main girl, and Javon doesn't necessarily keep the cleanest nose."

I wait for more, but Hunter continues to stare at me, as if the silence says everything. "And?" I ask.

"Unfortunately, when you roll with trouble, trouble rolls with you."

"But Nic's not trouble," I bark.

"I didn't mean it like that. What I'm trying to say is . . ." Hunter pauses and takes a breath, like he's about to speak to a kid who just lost his puppy. "I just really wish she hadn't gotten mixed up with Javon. I know the guys here. They take their merry time to help out people they assume intentionally got caught in the fray. Especially when there's already so much going on. Jay, we got over twenty missing black girls in our county alone. Three homicides over the weekend that this precinct is currently investigating—one right in your neighborhood. The Ducts, right? I can add your sister's name to a list, but it might take me a while to get a strong team going. Hopefully, she's lying low. Has she done that before? When anything in the neighborhood got a little dicey?"

Dicey? Hunter's acting like Nic's hiding out from a playground bully when she could be somewhere hurt, trying to get home. Or maybe too scared to come home. I leap from my seat, almost knock the card table on Hunter's lap. "If she was blonde with blue eyes, it'd be another story, right?"

Hunter sighs. "Are you even listening to me? I want to help, and I *will*. But I may not have the manpower right now to snap my fingers and make her appear."

"Yeah, or maybe you just don't even feel like trying." I always assumed that there were some dirty cops doing Javon's bidding, and Slick Ross here's proving me right. I shake my head. "Thought you'd be different, bruh," I say. If I had the balls, I'd spit at his feet. But I'm pissed, not stupid—he's the one with the gun.

Hunter flinches. "If I didn't care, I'd be spitting lies at you—*brother*."

I swat my hand at Hunter, make my way to the door to escape his stale snacks and even staler concern.

"Let me do what I can, Jay—but talk to your grandma. She needs to know," Hunter says to my back.

I snatch open the door without another word. I've done enough talking.

SEVEN

NOTE TO SELF: NEVER LISTEN TO A GIRL WHO WEARS UGLY Christmas sweaters unironically. Riley's suggestion to speak to the cops did nothing but send me crashing into another wall. That Rick Ross wannabe dismissed me like I stood in his way of watching Monday Night Football. Yeah, he went to my church—he even had the same extra dose of melanin as me. But it didn't matter. Homeboy still bled blue. He proved his allegiance when he tried to pin Nic's disappearance on Nic herself.

I hitched my way back home from the precinct, ready to crack skulls and get answers the way that someone from Javon's crew would. But thug fits me as well as a Halloween costume from five years ago. No matter how much I want to storm up to Slim and Quan and give them the business until they spill everything they know about Nic and Javon, I still scurry past their stoop and retreat to my bedroom. I need to prove Hunter wrong. Not everyone from the Ducts is on a fast track to a rap sheet. If I want to find Nic, I have to use my wits and not my emotions. I plop on my bed. Stare at the ceiling like a game plan can be found up there. The more I try to think of something, the more Hunter's words seem to dance around my light fixture: *Talk to your grandma.*

Damn. Maybe he's right. There's only so many stories I can spin about Nic's whereabouts. Besides, MiMi might think of something that I didn't. Or couldn't. Even after years of leading Nic's damage control committee, there's still a part of me that's hoping for the Pre-Javon Nic. The one who tried to shield me from Mom's downward spiral so I wouldn't love her any less. But MiMi saw through Mom's shiz, just like she sees through Nic's. MiMi would be able to take her mind to the darkest corners to find where Nic might be hiding.

I don't get a chance to rehearse my talk. On cue, the front door opens, signaling MiMi's return home. She doesn't crack a smile when I walk to the living room, wave hi. Not even a fake one. She takes a seat on the couch, begins unlacing her heavy work shoes.

Okay then. "You look tired. Want something to drink?" I offer.

"I want you to have a seat with me."

My stomach climbs to the back of my throat. The last two times MiMi asked me to sit with her like that, she was telling me Dad died and that Mom was locked up. "I'm good," I say. "I have homework, so—"

"I'm not asking, Jay."

I sit in the loveseat across from her. Maybe if I'm far enough, whatever she needs to tell me won't stick.

MiMi places her elbows on her knees and leans forward, just like Mrs. Pratt when she's ready to get all up in your bidness. "Where's your sister?"

It doesn't matter how far away I am—MiMi's question knocks me right in the ribs. I open my mouth to spit another story about Nic and Sterling, but the lie sits heavy in my chest. So much so, I brush a hand across it to make sure my heart's still beating. *Talk to your grandma.*

"Before you spin whatever you're about to spin," MiMi begins, "know that the school called to inform me that Nicole hasn't taken a step inside that building since last Wednesday."

I look down at my shoes. The top of my sneakers got scuffed sometime during the storm of this weekend. The storm I had to weather alone. Old Jay would make some smart-ass comment about Nic being blissed out of her mind. But New Jay's realizing that whatever's happening with Nic might be out of her control. That maybe Nic isn't coming home any time soon. That maybe he needs to lean on MiMi to let that sink in.

"I don't know," I mumble.

"What?" MiMi asks. "Open your mouth and look up when you speak to me." She claps her hands together and my head snaps up. I stare her in the eyes even though my eyes sting.

"I don't know," I repeat.

"What do you mean you don't know?"

I try to shrug but my shoulders are too heavy. "I've been calling her. Texting her. She won't pick up. Her phone's not even on anymore. I spoke with Sterling and she ain't seen her, either." The words tumble out of my mouth. I wait for my chest to feel weightless, but the heftiness of dread still hasn't left it yet. "I went to the cops and everything. Spoke with Officer Hunter from church. He ain't trying to help, though."

"Wait a minute." MiMi gets to her feet. No groaning like usual—she's on them in half a second. "You went to the *cops*? Jayson, how long has she been gone?"

My eyes are back on my shoes. "Last time I heard from her was Thursday night."

"Lord have mercy, Thursday night?" MiMi cups her hands over her mouth and says a prayer in between her fingers. When she looks back at me, she has enough tears to turn her golden eyes murky. Just like that, I'm ruined. "I have to find her." She starts patting her pants, the pocket in front of her shirt. "Keys. What I do with my keys?"

"I've tried to find her, MiMi," I say—and then instantly

want to punch myself in the face. I didn't try hard enough. Hell, I hung up on her. Then ignored her call like she was some bill collector. I'm her brother. Doesn't matter how irritated I get with her, I'm always supposed to have her back.

MiMi rummages through her purse now. "I just had them . . ." she says more to herself than to me. Beads of sweat crawl down her face like sideburns.

Now I'm on my feet. "Don't worry. I'm going to get answers. I owe her that much. Just sit down for a minute. You don't look too—"

"No, Jay. No. I'm supposed to take care of both of you. I promised your father I would. It's my job to get that baby back home before she gets hurt." She clutches her forehead. "What if she's already hurt? Lord, what if my baby's out there crying for me right now—wondering why I haven't gotten her yet? What . . . what about her bottle?"

I frown. "Her bottle? What?"

"Don't make it hoo tot. Too hot. Just run some hot water over it and . . ." MiMi takes a wobbly step toward me. Before I can catch her, she tumbles to the floor. My heart right next to her.

✳ ✳ ✳

I get back home right around dinnertime and the apartment is so still, so quiet, that I almost choke on the silence. The doctors said MiMi had a hemorrhagic stroke because of her high blood pressure. They said the ambulance got to her just in time. That I did good and moved quickly and other shiz to pat me on the back.

But all I hear is: MiMi wouldn't be here if you got her meds. If you didn't lose Nic. If you weren't such a shitty grandson.

MiMi's face just before she hit the floor is tatted on my brain. The urgency to get to Nic. The fear that it might be too late to get to her. Parallel feelings sketching parallel paths across her forehead. Not the usual worry lines—MiMi was devastated. And I caused that devastation by pushing Nic away.

I keep beating myself up as I pull out my phone. Stare long and hard at it. I don't know the prison number by heart, but it's somewhere in my contacts. Mom would want to know what's going on with her mother-in-law. With Nic. With me. But having that conversation, after so many years of no conversations, is enough to give me heartburn. I had enough on my plate right now. Instead, I grab a suitcase out of MiMi's closet. Start shoving in some of her belongings. She has to be under close observation in ICU for a few days, and I want to make sure she has everything she needs when she finally comes to. Bedroom slippers, nightgown, her favorite hairbrush. I pause when I reach her lotions and perfumes. She changes up her scent each season, but I can never remember if she prefers Japanese Cherry Blossom in the spring or in the fall. Nic always knows. But she's not here to help because of me. She doesn't even know MiMi's in the hospital.

Because of me.

I'm almost grateful for the knock at the door. The more time I spend in MiMi's bedroom, the emptier it feels. I grab the packed bag and make my way to the front door, peek out the peephole. Frown hard when I spot who's out there.

I open the door and nod at Riley Palmer. Not too enthusiastically. After all, it's just Riley Palmer. "Yeah?" I ask.

"Aren't you full of pleasantries?" She nods back at me. "Are you going to let me in?"

Let her in? Riley is the kind of Black chick who thinks Black guys like me eat fried chicken and watermelon with every meal—and have a crew that eats chicken and watermelon in between impregnating random girls. I'm not giving her any opportunity to scope out where I lay my head to come up with any more tall tales about me. "What are you doing here?"

Mr. and Mrs. Armstrong from upstairs giggle over something just as they crank up the R&B musings of Usher. Mr. Armstrong just got a promotion at the shipyard. Sure I'll be hearing them celebrating all night long.

Riley glances over my shoulder. "Where's Ms. Murphy? I want to say hi."

"She's not here." I grip onto the doorknob, brace myself for what's about to come out my mouth. "She's in the hospital."

Riley's eyes grow wide, circular. I'm sure the color would leave her cheeks if that was possible. "Jay . . ." Her mouth freezes, partially open. Like she's searching for the right thing to say.

"She's fine," I spit out before she finds it. The nurses offered enough *sorry*s that I could take a shower in them. But sorry doesn't help MiMi. "She's just there for observation. She's fine." I try not to repeat it again. "What do you want?"

Riley pauses in case I want to say more, but I chew on the inside of my cheek. "If you or Ms. Murphy need anything . . ."

I keep chewing.

Riley sighs and continues. "I need to tell you something. But I was hoping I could come inside." She leans close to me. So close that I smell the hair gel that keeps her ponytail intact. Almost like candy, but Riley sure as hell isn't sweet.

"What's wrong? Scared that you're going to be grazed by a stray bullet?" I ask. "Think a car with huge rims is going to run you over? If you want to feel cozy, book it back home."

Riley shakes her head. "Jay, you have no clue where I'm from."

"Not sure if I care, Riley," I say. "Either start bumping your gums or leave."

Riley looks over her shoulder, keeps an eye on the door that leads out of my apartment complex. "I have some information for you," she says in a hushed voice.

Information? What kind of intel could she possibly have that I need to know? I shrug at her even though she's not looking at me. The silence makes her look at me again.

"About what we talked about yesterday," she says, even quieter. "About your sister."

Her words, though soft, come with gale force winds, so strong that I fall back against my door.

"That's not funny."

"Does it look like I'm laughing?"

"Everything about me is a joke with you, Riley. But Nic is a topic me and you aren't going to chuckle about."

"First of all"—Riley holds up a finger—"I don't think you're a joke, Jay. That's your own insecurity. And second of all"—another finger gives me the peace sign—"do you want the info or not?"

I picture MiMi in her hospital room. Think about sitting next to her, Nic-less. If Riley gets me closer to changing that image, then I need to hear her out. "Let's walk," I say. I need to get back to MiMi.

Riley follows me out of my building as I lead her to the mailboxes on the corner. This spot is usually a ghost town. Probably because the only piece of mail most of us get around here are bills. "Okay. What you got?" I ask.

Riley fluffs out her ponytail, which she lets roam crinkly and free today. Then she moves closer to me, wraps her arms around my waist. I'm so off guard that I freeze right in her arms, limbs stuck between awkwardness and action. I hear snickering in the distance. My neighbor Lil Chuck and two of his ashy fifth-grade friends pause their game of catch to laugh and point at me and Riley. Lil Chuck antes up, makes kissy faces at us.

"Whoa, whoa, whoa." I snap out of it, step out of Riley's grasp. "It's not even like that." I jump at Lil Chuck and his crew and they scurry away like they hear the ice cream truck nearby. They should be hightailing it home anyways. The streetlights are almost on, and every kid in this neighborhood knew what that meant: beat the lights home or risk a beating.

"Don't you watch movies? I can't just stand here and give you intel. We have to act like we're up to something else."

She's right. Eyes are everywhere around here. I peek over at Javon's building. Slim and Quan are in their usual spots. Sipping something strong out of paper bags while they play cards on an overturned crate between them. The window leading to Javon's living room is open, the curtain blowing in and out, in and out as if Javon's breathing controlled it. I groan and then step back in front of her. She wraps her arms around my waist again, and I follow suit. Timidly. Making sure there's only clothes-to-clothes contact.

"Just don't be breathing your hot breath right in my face," I say.

"Excuse you? I chew Dentyne Ice all the time. You can't get any more wintry fresh than that. Now . . . how often do you go to the corner store on Menchville?" Riley smiles up at me all dreamy like she's my boo. Eyelashes fluttering, fingers laced behind my back—but keeps her thumbs free so she can trace tiny circles of affection over my shirt. It takes me a second to realize that she's gaming the neighborhood still. She's good. She's *damn* good.

I shift and clear my throat. "Not much. Don't really have to."

"Every day after school I stop by there and buy the same thing: a box of Lemonheads, a small bag of peanuts, and a bottle of Diet Cherry 7UP."

"Hence the Dentyne Ice?" I make myself ask. We both need to remember that this cuddle fest we have going on serves a larger purpose.

Riley gives me a quick eye roll but continues. "Every day after school, I see the same two dudes kicking it in front of the store. Kenny and JT. Ring a bell?"

I blink and nod. Everybody knows Kenny, of course— he's one of the most likable dudes from the Ducts, despite the mixed company he keeps. And JT is also one of Javon's boys. One of the crazier ones, who once knocked out a dude's two front teeth for smiling too much. Both Kenny and JT got promoted to deal in areas with more foot traffic.

"Only today, I didn't see Kenny. Didn't see him Friday, either, but didn't think much of it. Today, JT was there with someone new."

I'm careful to not let any part of my face flinch. Keep up the game, especially with Slim and Quan clowning it up a few feet away from me. "And?" I ask.

"And . . . this new dude didn't earn his promotion, so to speak. They needed someone else there since Kenny's been MIA."

I nod, try to connect the dots. But still, the largest one is missing.

As if reading my face, Riley squeezes me even tighter. "Kenny's been missing since Thursday night, Jay. The last time anyone saw him was driving away from some huge party . . ." She leans forward like she's going to kiss me but grazes her lips against my ear instead. "And your sister was with him."

I blink—two, three times. Try to get it all to make sense. "Kenny always gave Nic rides when Javon couldn't, so—"

"So my classmate at Warwick was also at that party. Said that Javon and Nic got into this fight to end all fights. Right before Nicole ran off with Kenny."

The air's too thin, so I pull away from Riley again. *Ran off with Kenny?* There were too many ways to take that sentence. Past scenes run through my head like a montage in a movie, except I'm seeing them in HD now. Kenny in the passenger seat, eyeballing Nic right after Javon called me dopey. Kenny playing tag with the neighborhood kids, only pausing to crack a smile at Nic that broke his face in half. Pooch outside my window, bumping his gums about Nic and Kenny.

Javon and his rage. Tackling me to the ground, almost like he wished I was someone else.

Nicole *ran off* with Kenny. How could I have been so blind? Kenny's into Nic. Hell, he's probably always been into Nic. But did Nic feel the same way?

"Word is that Kenny was a little too accommodating," Riley continues, reading my mind. "And that Nicole was . . ."

"Nicole was what?" I step closer to Riley. "Some thirsty chick that messes around with her man's best friend?"

"What? No. *No.*" Riley shakes her head a little too eagerly to refute me. "I heard she was just really happy to see Kenny. Like relieved. Jay, I don't think your sister was two-timing Javon. At least, not on purpose. Sometimes . . . you can't help who you fall for." She looks down at her hand, pulls at her fingers.

I glance at Javon's stoop again. See the smoke from his Black & Mild curling out of his window and evaporating before it hits the sky.

If that's true, if Nicole really fell for Kenny and booked it with him, I had to find them before Javon did.

"Are you okay?" Riley asks, reminding me she's here.

"Whatever's going on, Jay, we'll figure it out."

My head snaps back in her direction. "You mean me. *I'll* figure it out. You've done enough."

Riley's face crumples in confusion and I immediately know that my words spilled out all wrong.

"I mean, thank you," I try again. Saying those words to Riley was like speaking Mandarin. Felt so foreign to my tongue. "But I'll take it from here."

"But—"

"I'll wait for you to order an Uber." I glance back at Javon's building and Slim's and Quan's eyes are on me now. On Riley. I was right—she's done enough. No way a preacher's kid could handle the pending shitstorm if word about Nic and Kenny reached Javon. So, I wait with Riley for her ride, stand real close to her to block her from Slim's and Quan's gazes.

EIGHT

THE THING ABOUT RUNNING OFF WITH SOMEONE IS YOU don't think about leaving clues behind. No goodbye notes, no breadcrumbs. Because when you take off with someone, you bring all the good stuff with you and leave all the bullshit behind. And that's what I find in Nic's bedroom. Bullshit. Just random puzzle pieces that don't even make a complete picture when you put it all together—unless that picture is a typical seventeen-year-old girl's bedroom. Nic's place to slumber was all scented lotions and scented hair products and scented ChapStick (which, what the hell?). Those, on top of her clothes—her scantily clad looks hidden underneath her regularly clad looks—were all I could find when I raided Nic's room. Twice. First, right after Riley spilled the wax she got from her classmate—and then again after dropping off MiMi's things at the hospital. At least I got good news there. MiMi's stable now, but they got her under a microscope just in case. I try not to think about the just in case.

Even though both raids were complete busts, I couldn't help but feel like there was something I was missing. Yeah, Kenny was crushing hard—I finally saw what everyone else had already seen. But I'm not sure if that crush was reciprocated. Nic went hard for Javon—so hard that she once told me that they were thinking about getting matching tattoos. After telling Nic that walking around with a tattoo on her ring finger of a rose winding around a knife might send MiMi to an early grave, Nic reconsidered. She did other crazy shiz for Javon instead, like skip school or smoke bliss, or talk back to MiMi about skipping school or smoking bliss. Hard to imagine she'd go through all that drama just to hightail it somewhere with Kenny. But where were they? And why was Javon so pissed? I still can't shake that last phone call from Nic. All ellipses and em dashes with not enough words in between.

Those questions haunt me as I sweep up the dining area in Taco Bell. Bad enough that I had to actually work in the middle of MiMi's stroke and Nic's vanishing act, but can a brother at least make a chalupa? Neither Joshua nor the other clown-in-command, Maurice, felt I was ready to handle the cash yet. Hell, maybe I wasn't ready, either, since I just found out I got the job yesterday. I came in today to meet Maurice and they handed me a broom. Guess when you come to the interview looking banged up, people assume you're thirsty for whatever job they'll offer.

My phone buzzes in my pocket. Just as my hope builds, I see it's a text from Bowie.

You got the rest of Meek's paper??? He's trippin HARD.

I smirk. Meek Foreman and his forearms are the least of my worries right now. I've seen those forensic shows. If someone's missing beyond forty-eight hours, the prognosis gets grim. What did it mean if the police didn't care enough to even consider someone missing?

A shoulder jolting against my back jostles an answer out of my head—and sends me stumbling over my broomstick.

"My bad, bro." A tall, white guy stands behind me with a shit-eating grin scribbled across his face. He wears a hoodie with Greek letters on his chest, some kind of triangle with horns. Spins a key chain with a Cadillac emblem around his index finger. I take it the dark mocha Escalade eating up two parking spaces in front of the dining area belongs to him. Wow. What a dude bro.

"Didn't see you there," Dude Bro continues, leaning toward me. He smells like he went running through a Christmas tree lot. Probably some high-end cologne, but the stuff MiMi mops the floor with smells better. "But check this out . . ." He points somewhere behind me. "You missed a spot."

That's when I notice the two white guys behind him, cackling like he's the star of some Seth Rogen movie. They're pretty nondescript—just Lackey No. 1 and Lackey No. 2. Both wearing the same hoodie as their douchey ringleader. The earthy smell of bliss seeping out of their pores, almost overtaking the Pine-Sol cologne. They probably scored in my neighborhood. Guys like them always perch in front of Javon's building, not willing to step outside of their fancy cars and walk in their fancy shoes to the stoop. Instead, they demand full service like they're ordering burgers at a Sonic Drive-In. Most don't bother to look my way, but the ones that do give me the same you-must-bow-down-to-me head nod like these corn nuts. Great. Now I have to catch an extra dose of that condescension working the night shift at Taco Bell. Fick my life.

I snatch up the broom from the floor and give Dude Bro a look that I hope will haunt him during his sleep later. He cocks an eyebrow, amused, and even takes a step toward me. Daring me—naw, *begging* me—to ram my broomstick right in between his eyes. I grip onto my cleaning utensil. Think about all the wonderful ways I could turn it into a weapon. How I could take out all my sadness, my frustration . . . hell, my *rage* on this Alpha Phi Asshole right in front of his fan club.

Someone clears their throat. I look over my shoulder and Joshua Kim's behind the counter, stacking up trays, his eyes firmly and decidedly on me. I feel like I'm in a Western, but instead of drawing guns, Joshua's drawing a silent warning: *Any funny business and I'm calling the cops.* Doesn't matter that I'm the guy in here trying to work. My popping melanin makes me the aggressor in every situation. I loosen my grip on the broom handle, step around Dude Bro and his boys to clean up the crumbs underneath a table behind them. Their laughter is the salt in my wounds as they make their way to the counter.

This is for MiMi, I tell myself. After going through what she's been through this week, she's earned that retirement in Florida. I sweep up every crumb, every scrap that's ever been in this Taco Bell before I even stepped foot in it. If this is what Joshua and Maurice need to see before they give me a promotion and up my pay, then I'll be an Olympic Broom Pusher. The quicker I can get those duckets, the quicker MiMi and me can leave this neighborhood behind. Hopefully with Nic tagging along with us.

Just as I dump all my handiwork into the trash bin, Bowie hits me up again:

Bowie: You alive???

Really? It's probably only been ten minutes since he sent his last message. He acts like I don't have a life outside of him. Like I'm not dealing with moms in prison and missing sisters and grandmothers in the hospital. Not like he knows all those things, but still . . . I wish I had so little cares in the

107

world that my main concern was making sure Meek Fore-man graduated.

"I said all right!" Dude Bro's voice booms throughout the dining area as he and his two friends squeeze into one of the booths. He pauses, as if the rumble in his vocal cords is a power that he just discovered. On some real Harry Potter shiz. He leans across the table to one of the other white guys. "Not here, man. Not here," he says in his attempt to be hushed.

Lackey No. 1 or Lackey No. 2—not sure which one—nods about five too many times as he stirs his straw around his cup. His basic friend sits next to him, slaps him in between his shoulder blades to console him. Two times, brief. All: even though we're sitting together, we're not *together*. As if anyone truly gives a damn.

"No phones while you're on your shift," Joshua Kim says, walking up behind me. I jump, almost drop said phone. His work Skechers are no joke. It's like he's walking on squeak-free clouds. "You could leave it in the breakroom if it's going to be a problem."

Oh really? He better kill all that noise. "My grandma's in the hospital," I say instead. "I need to keep it close for updates."

Joshua's jaw flinches ever so slightly. He wants to tell me and my phone to shove it, but grandmas are a sensi-tive topic for everyone. "Just try to limit checking it to your breaks, 'kay?" He gives me a pat on the back like a caring and empathetic manager is supposed to, then walks away to annoy someone else.

A crash comes from the frat guys' table. Dude Bro's out of the booth, has one of his lackeys in a headlock. An actual damn headlock. They spin around as the lackey tries to pull away from him, crunching piles of nachos underneath their feet. The third idiot leaps up about five seconds too late to pry them apart.

"Chill out, Liam!" Third Guy pleads, finally detaching his friend from the blissed-out clutches of their leader.

Dude Bro pushes his hair out of his pink and sweaty face. He scopes out his friends, who huff and puff across from him. Fists clenched at their sides like they don't know what he's going to do next. Dude Bro shifts his eyes down to his pulverized food, then smirks up at me. Smugness washes over any anger on his face as if he was just reminded that he's the one with the power—and I'm the one with the broom.

"I'm not hungry anymore. Let's get out of here," he orders. He makes sure to step on another pile of nachos before heading out to his obnoxious ride. Lackey No. 1 and No. 2 glance at each other, asking a hundred silent questions. Still, they follow behind Dude Bro like they're supposed to.

"Glad they left before things got out of hand," Joshua Kim says from behind me.

I stare down at the rubble of their order on the floor. *Before* things got out of hand?

"Make sure to clean that up before more guests come."
He slaps me on the back to motivate me.

I take a deep breath and push my broom over to their booth. Try my best not to push it up his ass.

✳ ✳ ✳

Forty-five dollars. That's how much money I made for my five-hour shift at Taco Bell. That's not including what Uncle Sam was going to take from me by the time payday rolls around. I had to spend five hours of sweeping up taco shells and plunging toilet bowls and dodging smirks from high frat guys with too much time on their hands to not even crack fifty dollars. Now it's creeping toward eleven o'clock and instead of climbing into my bed, I have to cram for a Math Analysis test.

I yank off my polo shirt as soon as I unlock my front door and hurl it onto the couch. I reach for it to clean up my mess before MiMi gets here, but then the memory of her unconscious in her hospital bed hits me like a fist. So, I take my actual fist and ram it into the couch pillow. It barely leaves a dent, which pisses me off even more. I'll show this goddamn couch. I use all the breath in me to grab the couch by one of its ends and attempt to flip it over, but the wall's in my way. A grunt rips out of me as I ram the couch against the wall, over and over again until they both feel my anger. Until I feel anything but anger. Soon, my arms start to buckle, so I release the couch. It slams against the floor and I slam down right next to it. I rest my back against it and scrub at my hair. Wish I had dreads or something I could grip onto just to pull it all out. That's what I need. To just let everything out.

There's a loud knock at my front door. I blink and climb to my feet. It's late as hell. Probably Miss Claudine asking me to quiet it down. Her boys have to sleep for school after all. Never mind that they play Fortnite loud enough for the neighborhood to hear every weekend. I snatch the door open, ready to tell her just that if she comes at me the wrong way. The girl standing outside my door wears a red-and-gold track suit with matching Converse sneakers.

"Riley?" I say, frowning so hard that I give myself a headache.

She gives me a meek smile. "Hey, Jay. Somebody order a pizza?" She laughs and a snort escapes her mouth. "That was a joke. I mean, obviously I don't have a pizza—though that does sound good right about now." She looks me up and down. "Did I . . . did I catch you at a bad time?"

I look down at myself and remember that I'm only in my white tank top. That I had partially stripped down during my temper tantrum. I fold my arms across my chest, suddenly feeling naked. "What are you doing here? Isn't it past your curfew or whatever?" I peek out in the hall and nobody else is there. Riley Palmer showed up to the Ducts, after dark, without any backup. Brave girl.

"I may have . . . embellished my whereabouts. And by embellish, I mean I waited to hear my dad snore before tip-toeing out the back door."

"Wait—you snuck out?" Okay, what's a word more impressive than brave? "Why?"

"Okay, I know you told me to stay out of it, but I couldn't sleep, Jay. You seemed so surprised by Nicole taking off with Kenny, that she had to have left you something, right? Some kind of hint of where she took off." She pushes past and enters my living room.

I blink after her. "Sure. Come in."

Riley scopes out my living room and if I didn't feel naked before, I certainly do now. I close the front door behind me, hug my bare arms again.

"Were you searching for clues out here?"

I glance over at the couch cushions strewn across the floor and scratch my ear. "Yeah. Yeah I was." Shove my hands in my pockets. "Didn't find anything, though."

"What about her room?"

I smirk. "Of course I checked out her room."

"I tend to do better on papers after someone else takes a look at them. Fresh eyes can catch more, you know? Where's her room?"

"Riley, I told you. I looked in there more than once. I'm her brother. I'd know where she'd hide something."

Riley starts making her way toward the bedrooms as if she has an all-access pass.

"Ay! I didn't say you could go back there!"

"What's the worst that could happen, Jay? I find nothing, you prove me right. I find something, you get an answer. You win in both situations, right?" She points to the closed bedroom door with a picture of Lizzo taped on it. "I take it this is her room, right? Unless you like them BBW."

I frown at her again. My chin almost hits the floor.

"Big beautiful women," Riley says to me, all slow like she's explaining the theory of relativity.

"I know what it means. I'm just trying to figure out how you do."

Riley shrugs. "I rarely ever get enough credit." She pushes Nic's bedroom door open, and I reach out to stop her. But my hand never connects. Maybe she's right. There could be something I missed because I keep looking in all the same places. Maybe looking in the same places got my eyes all bleary.

So far, though, Riley covers the same territory. Nic's drawers, Nic's closet. Under Nic's bed. The same areas I've scoped out so much that I could draw a sketch of what's in them.

"See?" I say, after a couple of minutes past. "Nothing."

Riley lifts up Nic's trash can and another snort leaves her

mouth. "Obviously, you weren't thorough enough. Check this out." She bends over and picks up something off the floor. A wrapper. A small one, like it used to cover a sucker or something. But the picture on it's all artsy and custom, some smiling face with a tongue hanging out. Not the standard Blow Pop I could grab from the corner store. I look up at Riley, whose smile looks like she ate one too many Blow Pops.

I shrug. "So? Nic's not the tidiest person in the world." One time, MiMi found a paper plate with a half-eaten PB&J sandwich under Nic's bed. And they say boys are the messy ones.

"Don't you get it? Everything means something." She puts the wrapper into her pocket and pats it. "I'll keep it just in case."

Trash? We're resorting to trash now? I could've spent these minutes studying, not building false hope. "Okay, you got to go," I say. Riley was having way too much fun with this. Like she was Dora and exploring some big mystery. But my life isn't a cartoon. Far from it.

Riley blinks at me. "But . . . but I'm just getting started."

"Why are you breaking curfew for someone you hardly know?" I ask. "Nic barely said two words to you at church."

"That's not true," Riley says under her breath, so low that I almost miss it. "And it seems like someone should care that she's gone."

I frown at her. "Was that shade?" Does she know how many sleepless nights I had to deal with since Nic's last phone call? How the guilt clawed and chewed away at me until I wake up barely hanging on and painting a smile on my face just not to worry MiMi any further. MiMi still hasn't come to yet, but I know that my stress would keep her under. So, I smile and rub her hand and tell her everything's going to be okay even though my gut says the opposite.

"I didn't mean it like that, Jay. I just meant—"

"Bye, Riley."

Riley studies me for a second or two, then gives me a slight nod before walking past me.

My legs follow behind her on autopilot. My dad always said you're never supposed to let a lady walk alone. He was old school like that. Sometimes he'd get stuck holding the door at 7-Eleven for a good ten minutes for every woman that needed to walk through.

Riley glances back at me and holds up her hand. "I'm good, Jay. I'm good." She repeats it like she means it, so I let her find her way out. Probably for the best. She'd try to say something else to get my hopes up. I look around at Nic's lopsided mattress. The partially open dresser drawers. The closet light spilling out onto her bed. The same paths I traveled earlier, but Riley had to do the job again. As if I was some kid helping out their mom in the kitchen but couldn't be trusted to peel the potatoes correctly.

But dammit, Riley had a point. She saw an opening and went for it, consequences be damned. I was tired of sitting around, waiting for phone calls or text messages. Or the cops to actually do their job. If I wanted to find Nic, I had to take more action. And if Javon's crew didn't know anything, maybe Kenny's crew did.

NINE

BEFORE KENNY STARTED PUSHING BLISS AND CRINKLE FOR Javon, he was a pretty good baller. So much so that high school varsity teams were recruiting him when he was still in eighth grade. For some reason, he still came to Youngs Mill. Something went foul at the start of Kenny's junior year. Nobody really knows what. Some people say he blew out his knee running from or after someone. Others say his dad blew out Kenny's knee after hitting the bottle a bit too hard one night. Either way, Kenny's hoop dreams faded and he grew even tighter with Javon.

Still, basketball was an itch he never fully scratched. Every now and then when I walked a neighborhood dog for one of my side hustles, I spotted him on the court at the

Boys and Girls Club on Bland Boulevard. I head there after school, each step filled with purpose. I spot some of the usual suspects. Not part of Javon's squad, but Kenny's boys from the team—more varsity than vandals. It's less intimidating to get answers from them than from the thugs on Javon's stoop.

The guys on the court whoop and holler as one of them dunks the ball during a play. "You see that shit?" he bellows, still dangling from the hoop. "Tell me that wasn't a Lebron move right there."

"Man, Lebron's trash," some guy with beads dancing at the end of his corn rows says. I haven't seen beads on hair since my mom showed me pictures of herself in elementary school.

"Yeah, says the guy who just ate the bottom of my sneaker!" The Lebron wannabe finally hops down from the hoop and plucks one of the other dude's braids. The beads shiver and make music from his scalp.

"Man, whatever." He smirks and swats Fake Lebron's hand away as the other guys laugh. That's my cue. I force out a laugh and clap my hands.

"Nice. I see you got some skills," I say, still applauding. "Mind if I join in?" I point down at my sneaks, as if to prove that I have the right gear to play. Sometimes I wonder how I even have one friend at school.

The guys look at me, then at each other. "Yo, get your cousin, Rico," one of them says to the guy with beads.

"Man, I don't know this fool," Rico insists. Frowns at me to prove we're not related.

"I do." Lebron looks me over, tucks the ball into his armpit. "Kind of. You go to Youngs Mill, right? And don't you walk around here with that mutt with scabies?"

I wince. Not necessarily the way I want to be remembered. "You mean Titus? Yeah, he had mange, but he's good to go now. Or so his owner tells me. I just help out from time to time." I hold out my hand. "I'm Jay."

Fake Lebron peers down at my hand, his face pinched like a nerve.

"I wash my hands every time I'm done walking them. Plus, I haven't handled Titus in weeks," I insist.

Lebron gives in and slaps me a five. "DeMarcus," he says. Points at a guy with bright red Jordans. "That's Xavier." Points at a dude with his stomach hanging over his gym shorts. "Chip." Finally, the guy with beads. "And you already know your cousin Rico." The guys laugh again, except Rico.

"Y'all keep playing with me," he warns, fiddling with one of his braids.

"So, can I ball with you guys or naw?" I ask again. Brothers usually don't spill the wax all willy-nilly. You got to keep them preoccupied. Catch them with their guard down. Usually when they're doing something they love. For instance, spot me when I finish the latest Jason Reynolds novel, and I'll tell you all about my mom, dad, and my drunk uncle

Kevin who's slept on every family member's couch at one point or the other.

"Naw," Rico says. "We already got our teams. You'd make us all uneven."

DeMarcus smirks at him. "Fool, didn't you just say your ankle hurt?"

Rico smirks right back. "And? I could ride it out."

"Yo, that's what your moms said to me last night," Xavier says, and the guys whoop and holler again. Everyone, of course, but Rico. He rolls his eyes, like jokes about his mom happen every Wednesday afternoon. I need to keep these guys on track. If one of them gets too salty, then the whole squad might crumble.

I look around as if I'm looking for someone. "Figured we could play a little three on three. Where's your boy?"

The laughter dies. "Who?" DeMarcus asks.

Okay. Fake Lebron is obviously their spokesperson, so I have to appeal to him. "Dark-skinned brother?" I continue. "Little bit taller than me? I think you guys call him . . ." I snap my fingers, try to conjure up some random-ass name, "Curtis?"

The guys look at each other again. It's so quiet you can hear someone's stomach growling. Despite it being after school and the elementary-aged kids are slowly making their way onto the playground next to us, all wired and ready to go after seven hours of sitting on their asses.

"Why you tryna play us?" DeMarcus asks. "I think you know his name is Kenny. Just like I think you know that your sister kicks it here with him from time to time."

I blink a few times at him. Nic. He knows Nic. Enough with the bullshitting then. Good thing, because my balling skills are on the same level as my self-defense skills. "So, you know Nic?"

"Of course we know Nic," DeMarcus says. He looks at his boys and they nod in agreement. Even Rico. Not before curling his lip at me, though. "And we know you all are from the same hood. So what's up with this 'pick me, pick me' shit. You trying to ball with us for real? Trying to pick up some more game for the ladies?"

"Little dude probably ain't got no game," Chip says, and it's the first time I heard Rico laugh since I've been out here. Didn't even think he knew how.

"Okay, so if you know all of that, you know that Nic and Kenny faded about a week ago," I say. The cordiality drops from my tone. If they wanted me to get to the marrow, I will. "You hear from either of them?"

DeMarcus scratches his chin as he studies me. A few seconds later, he points at me. "Matter of fact, I did. Kenny hit me up about two days ago."

"He did?" I ask. Two days ago? That recently? Holy shit! If Nic's with him, that means they're good. That means when I visit MiMi I'd actually have some good news for her. Some answers. "Where is he? What he say?"

"I'm trying to remember . . ." DeMarcus rubs his forehead, concentrates. "I think . . . I think he wanted to tell me what he had for breakfast that day. Cheerios, I believe."

"Original or Honey Nut?" Xavier asks.

"Nigga, is that even a question?" DeMarcus scoffs at him. "Honey Nut. Then he told me that he needed to get some more gas for his ride. Then, the most important part of the call, he asked if I could come over and wipe his ass later that night." That does his friends in. They hang all over each other, laughing at me—the loser who can't ball and points at his sneakers and walks dogs with skin diseases.

Heat rises to my face and it takes everything in me to not snatch that ball from DeMarcus's armpit and hurl it at the back of his big head. But there's four of them and one of me. I didn't need a hospital bed right next to MiMi's.

"I'm serious," I say through gritted teeth.

"I am, too, bruh," DeMarcus insists, wiping tears from his eyes. "Kenny's cool and all, but I don't keep dibs on him like that. Ever since he got all tangled up with Javon we see him when we see him. We don't ask any questions. Got too much riding on our futures to know the answers, know what I'm saying?"

I know exactly what he's saying. They all got free rides out of here just because they know how to toss a ball into a hoop. Maybe if I didn't spend the past few years stressing about everyone else, I could've picked up a skill, too. Do something with my hands that'd make me stand out in a crowd. But MiMi needed me and Nic as much as we needed her. And as long as Nic keeps playing this vanishing act, I'll be anchored to the Ducts until I'm able to get MiMi out of there.

I glance one more time at the guys on the court. The laughter has died down again and they all stare at me, eager for me to say or do something else to give them their next round of chuckles. I'm not anyone's clown, though. I head back the way I came. These guys didn't know shiz, anyways. Too busy chasing their own dreams over Kenny's nightmares.

"Hey! Sherlock Homeboy!"

Like an idiot, I turn around. I expect more laughter, but DeMarcus stares at me like I'm a little kid wandering the hood after the streetlights come on. One eye filled with worry, the other one telling him to mind his own business. "Your sister's good people," he says. "Smart as all hell. She'll find her way back home."

I let his words sink in and nod. I hope so. But I'll do everything I can to guide her back in the meantime.

✳ ✳ ✳

"Here, MiMi. I got it," I say as I take the applesauce off her tray and pull the chair right next to her hospital bed.

"I can feed myself," she says, the words leaving her mouth

in tiny clots. "I've been feeding myself for almost sixty years. Heck, I even fed you your first solids."

"Well, relax. Let me return the favor." I spoon some of the unsweetened applesauce and place it to her lips. She gives me a tiny smirk and I raise my eyebrows at her. Finally, she gives in and lets me feed her. "See? Not so bad, right?"

"Hmph." She twists in her bed. I hand her the remote and she adjusts the bed setting, gets it right where she wants it. "I bet you're not eating applesauce for dinner."

"Imagine it's a juicy steak," I say as I feed her a bit more. "With a side of mashed potatoes smothered in gravy. Your greens on the side, pieces of ham all swimming in it."

"Turkey," she says after swallowing. "I gave up pork a while ago."

I pause midair with her next serving. "Since when?"

"Since forever ago. You're just so busy inhaling whatever I put in front of you that you don't stop to ask what you're eating." At that, she looks at me, eyes in full-on grandma mode. "You have been eating, right? What you have for dinner tonight?"

"I'm good, MiMi. I'm good," I insist. No point of telling her that my last few meals have consisted of whatever wasn't sold at Taco Bell at the end of my shift. And that's when I remember to actually put something in my mouth.

"Okay then." She settles back against her pillow. "I already have one grandbaby to worry about." She closes her eyes and

I hold my breath. I was hoping we'd get through at least five minutes without talking about Nic. I told MiMi about Nic running off with Kenny. I thought she'd be relieved that it was Kenny and not Javon, but all she knew was that Nic was there (wherever there is) and not here. Here is safe. Here is home. She reopens her eyes and they're dotted with tears. "You have to find a picture for Deacon Irving. A nice one, now. Not one of them silly ones with you and her making faces in your phone."

"I know," I say. The good Deacon called me yesterday. Talking about he's praying for my family. Talking about the members of the congregation wanted to put out flyers and get Nic's face out there. The gesture would be more genuine from a man who didn't ditch his sick wife in another state to do whatever's he's doing with MiMi. And now that MiMi's sick, I'm not sure if he stepped one foot in this hospital to see her.

"Now you got to put something in your stomach. We're almost done," I say as I feed her more applesauce.

"Can't wait 'til this place gives me some real food," she grumbles. The doctors say MiMi's doing better, but not great. The stroke was pretty severe and they want to keep an eye on her to see if it's done anything to her fine motor skills. Even swallowing might be a new challenge. Hence, the applesauce.

I start coming up with another dinner for MiMi to imagine—lasagna with just about every cheese you can think of packed in each layer—when there's a knock on the door. "Expecting someone?" I ask MiMi.

She gives a weak shrug. "Just President Obama."

I shake my head as I stand. "He's not the president anymore, MiMi."

"He'll always be my president."

I laugh and go answer the door. Javon stands on the other side, hand extended. I suck in a breath and automatically ball my fists. But there's not a weapon in his hand—only a bouquet of flowers. Bright pink and yellow ones at that. The fick?

"'Sup." He nods at me all casual-like. Like he isn't the neighborhood drug lord. Like he didn't bump and grind my face against the pavement almost a week ago. "Ms. Murphy awake? Thought she might like these." He holds up his flowers even higher, all bright and sunny against his cloudy disposition.

"Who is it, baby?" MiMi asks behind me.

"Uh, one of the nurses needs to chat with me. Hold on." I step into the hallway and close the door behind me. Javon stares at me and I stare right back.

"There a reason you calling me one of the nurses?" he asks.

"There a reason you bringing flowers to my grandma?"

Javon stumbles back a bit, as if he has a reason to be shocked by this whole encounter. "You bugging, right? The whole hood's worried about Ms. Murphy. She's like the neighborhood grandma. The OG, for real."

I smirk. "MiMi don't even like you." I wince as soon as the words leave my mouth. Something about being surrounded by white folks in a hospital has made me stupidly bolder. But hey, in case Javon doesn't care about all these professional eyes on us, at least I'm in the right place to get immediate medical attention.

The flowers drop to Javon's side like they just died right there in his hand. He stares down at his feet for a second too long then shrugs. "She never acted like it. At least not to my face." He finally looks up at me and shoves the bouquet into my hand. I grunt from the impact. "Could you give those to her? Let her know it's from me? Or not. I don't care. As long as she has something nice to look at."

I frown at Javon as he starts to walk down the hall. Wait for him to reach for his face, pull off the mask and reveal whatever alien is hiding underneath. He pauses in his tracks and looks at me over his shoulder. I hold my breath for the big reveal.

"Say . . . you haven't heard from Nic, have you?" he asks. Almost like it's a test. Almost like he wants to see how much I know.

I chew the inside of my cheek, keep my face as steady as possible, and shake my head. "Nope," I finally answer.

"Huh." He scratches at the stubble on his chin and

disappears down the hall. *Huh.* Not a question, just a noise. Not the noise that would come from a worried boyfriend. Hell, not the nonchalant noise that would come from the dude that played whack-a-mole on my face last week. That *huh* was strategic. A way to see just what I knew.

Javon did pull off his mask. But instead of revealing an alien, he showed me who I thought he was this whole time: the guy who's heard the streets talking about Nic and Kenny. The guy who'd do damage once he got his hands on them.

If he hasn't already . . .

TEN

FUNNY HOW WHEN YOUR LIFE GETS TWISTED INSIDE AND out, you're still expected to do normal shiz. Like remember to eat. Like brush your teeth. Like even going to school and pretending to care about multiplying matrices to solve an equation. No, I'm not sure what the hell that means. Yeah, I'm sure I would, had I had time to study for my test earlier this week. But I had several good reasons to flake on it. Not that Mr. Branch cares. He still asks me to come to his classroom during homeroom so he can't tutor me. The good news is that I get to avoid the curious glances from Bowie and Camila, who I'm pretty sure think I'm a complete and utter spaz right about now. The bad news is that I have to be lectured to about matrices on an empty stomach and a head full of questions. Questions about Javon and what exactly he knows.

"You following me, Jay?" Mr. Branch asks, tapping his pencil on the paper on top of my desk. Bringing me back from wherever my head was floating. No place good, that's for damn sure.

I lean forward, nod a few times as if I caught the last few minutes of whatever the hell he was dishing. "Yeah. Yeah, makes sense," I say.

Mr. Branch tilts his head at me and smirks. He's one of them older brothers who wears bowties even on casual Fridays. Who has memorabilia plastered all over his classroom walls to represent the HBCU he graduated from less than five years ago. Who likes to pause class to share what he's learning in one of his graduate classes to make it known that he's going to be a brother with a graduate degree. Basically, he's too clever not to sniff out any of my bullshit.

"Where's your head at, Jay?" he asks me. "Come on, earlier this school year, you could solve these problems in your sleep. Now it's like you haven't woken up yet. You got to make it to your senior year before you get senioritis, my man."

I scrub my eyes with the heels of my hands. Try to snap out of it. But Nic's been officially missing for almost a week. All the resilience in the world can't make me bounce back from that. "I'm cool. I just picked up a part-time job, so I'm still figuring out my time management. That's all."

"That's all, huh?" Mr. Branch shakes his head at me then rips off a piece of my paper. He starts scribbling something on it. "How 'bout this? When you're ready to get real with me, you shoot me an email, okay? No questions asked. Just if you need me, holler." He passes me the scrap of paper and I look down at the email address. Gmail—not the one tied to his school account. I look back up at him and raise an eyebrow. Mr. Branch laughs. "I'm not trying to skeeve you out. You just remind me of me, that's all. I remember how hard it was to open up. Sometimes it was easier to write it down."

"Thanks," I mumble as I shove the paper into the sleeve of my binder. I don't look back up at him because what the hell else can I say? I'm not used to older dudes being nice to me unless they're family—and even then I had uncles who put a little too much rough in the roughhousing. "So, yeah, the bell's going to ring soon and—"

"I'll catch you later today, Jay," Mr. Branch says. He just gets it. "And I'm not playing those tardy games, my man. So tell that grape-haired friend of yours to stop cutting up in the halls with you so y'all can get your butts here on time."

I laugh and give him a salute before heading out into the hall. I wonder how Mr. Branch would react if I spilled all my wax to him. It might be nice to have someone else shoulder the burden. Someone who looked like me and from a hood like mine that could point to where I needed to go next. But the last OG I put my trust in was that Rick Ross–looking mofo from the station—and that didn't turn out well. For all I know, Mr. Branch could believe all the rumors he heard about Nic in the school hallways and somehow pin her disappearance on her. Like it was her fault for falling for a thug. Mr. Branch was one of my favorite teachers I didn't need a reason to hate him all of a sudden.

"Jay . . . Jay!" I look over my shoulder and Mrs. Pratt is *click-clack, click-clack*ing toward me. Her dangly, exotic earrings shimmy along with each step as she shuffles in my direction. I exhale through my nose. What the hell is this? Save a Jay Day?

"I stopped by Mr. Booker's class looking for you," she says once she reaches me. "He told me you were getting help with math during first period."

"Yep," I say. Glance at the clock over her head. I had better things to do than have Pratt recap my steps. Like call the hospital before the next bell to check in on MiMi. Like try to find Sterling to see if she's heard anything.

"That's good, Jay. Glad you're taking charge of your grades like that. Speaking of which . . ." She gives me a smile and, fick, I know this can't be good. "Have you spoken to Mrs. Chung about the literary magazine yet? First meeting is coming up real soon."

I chew on the inside of my cheek so I won't let out a groan. "Yeah, I've been meaning to reach out to her. I have

this new part-time job that's been keeping me busy, though."
Hell, if I knew that having legit work could be my excuse for
everything, I would've tried to nab one much sooner.

"Work? That's good, Jay. Real good. As long as you balance your time well. And Mrs. Chung understands that
students are busy. She'd work with your availability when it
comes to the magazine."

Dammit, she's really not letting this go. I scratch the back
of my neck. "Mmm," I say. That's all I can say. Anything else
and I'm pretty sure she'd scope out my irritation.

"Besides, it might be good to take your mind off things."
She glances around the empty halls and takes a step toward
me. "I heard about your grandmother . . . and I know that
Nic hasn't been around lately," she says in a lower voice. "You
know my office door is open if you need to talk. I'd hate for
the truancy officer to show up at your door asking questions
about Nicole when your grandma—"

"Yeah. Sure," I say. Last thing I need is for her to pry even
more about Nic and ambush me in the halls with her so-
called concern. Kind of like now. The bell rings and students
start spilling into the hall. I point to wherever the bell sounds
from. "I need to get to my next class, so . . ."

"Say no more. I have a meeting to get to myself." She
backs away and points at me. "Oh, Jay! SAT registration is
right around the corner. Stop by my office to get more info."

I nod and plaster on a smile as I wave bye to her. "Leave

me alone, lady," I say through my clenched teeth, still keeping up my grateful charade. As soon as she turns around, my hand and smile both drop. SAT registration? Really? I can't even pass a math test this week. How in the hell did she expect me to do well on the SATs with all I have going on? Now, if they asked questions about how to be the worst brother and grandson out there, colleges would be knocking down my door. But I've never been that lucky.

I reach my locker. Grab my books for next period and double-time it to my next class. I'm a few steps away when a boulder knocks against my back and sends me propelling down another hall. After regaining my footing, I spin around and Meek huffs and puffs at me. His fists balled. Ready to give me that ass whooping I deserved a week ago.

"Hey, Meek," I say. I check my surroundings for an escape. We're in the corridor that leads to the living skills classrooms. The ones with all the ovens and sewing machines. The ones that are rarely used except for some of the special needs classes that are held at the end of the day. The ones that are absolutely empty now. Something tells me Meek has been planning this for a while.

"Don't 'hey, Meek' me, bruh!" His voice shakes the ground underneath me. Unless my knees are just giving out on me. "I told you I needed the rest of that paper. I can't ask for another extension. And if I don't turn that shit in, that means I can't play this weekend."

Fick. His paper. Bowie tried to warn me. But just like I haven't had time to study or even eat breakfast today, I certainly didn't have time to find what the hell I did with the rest of Meek's paper. I was so worried about everyone else's well-being that I didn't think about mine.

"And if I can't play this weekend . . ." He takes a step toward me. I take a step back. Bump into a wall behind me. "That means you're not playing, either."

I blink. Okay, he's pissed. When you're pissed, you don't pay attention to whether or not the trash you're spewing makes any logical sense. I'll give him that. "I got you, Meek," I say. "Let me talk to your teacher. I can tell her that you used my computer to type it up. That I'll grab it for you tonight and you can hand it in first thing in the morning."

"I told your dumb ass no more extensions!" he hisses in my face. I wonder if he spots the irony in his statement. That if I were the dumbass, why would he want me to write his papers? But if Meek even knew what irony was, we wouldn't be in this situation. "I've about had it with your slick mouth! It's time for someone to shut it."

Meek raises his meaty fist over my head and he doesn't need to say anything else to prove he's the one who's going to shut my mouth. I swallow and squeeze my fists as tight as I can. If I'm going down, I'm going down swinging, dammit. If I fend him off enough, maybe a teacher could spot us before I'm completely black and blue.

Meek takes a swing at me and I duck. His fist collides against the wall as I flee under his arm.

"Fuck!" he shouts. I see the opening to the main hall but he grabs at the back of my shirt, flings me backward. I'm on my ass in point-two seconds. Before I can climb back to my feet, Meek's on top of me. He straddles me, pinning his knees on top of both of my arms. Cutting off the circulation until I feel nothing but static in them. He takes his hand and covers my entire face. Seriously. He presses down so hard that I wait to hear my nose crush under the pressure. I can't let that happen, so I pull the biggest bitch move I can think of. I bite down on one of his fingers.

Meek cries out and yanks his hand away. I can breathe again. I can see again. And unfortunately, I see his fist come barreling down toward me.

Before his fist makes a landing, someone collides against the side of Meek and knocks him off me. I blink a few times to return to my senses and Bowie hovers over me, holding out his hand. "You good?" he asks.

I blink again, make sure it's him. The purple hair pokes out of his Steelers cap. I grab his hand and he pulls me up.

"The fuck, Bowie?" Meek demands, climbing to his feet. Bowie steps in front of me.

"Hold on, Meek. If you got problems with Jay, then you got problems with me," Bowie says. I frown at the back of his head. Does he have some kind of death wish?

Meek looks at me, looks at Bowie, then shrugs. His fist flickers away from him and jabs right at Bowie's face.

"Gah!" Bowie cries out, covering his nose. I flinch for him. Grab his shoulder.

"You cool, man?" I ask.

"No!" Bowie bellows through his hand.

Meek could care less. He takes another step toward us. I pull Bowie behind me and prep my fists again. This time, hoping to at least land one blow.

"Wait . . . wait!" Bowie shouts. He removes his hand and there's a little blood trickling down from his nose. "You didn't even let me finish, Meek. We got you. Jay . . . did you save his paper in the cloud?"

I keep my eyes on Meek. Ready to stick and move in case he tries anything funny. Or at least attempt to. "Yeah."

"Perfect. Meek, your English class is after lunch, right?"

Meek grits his teeth as he glares at both of us, then gives a curt nod.

"Cool. I'll hit up the library during lunch. Print out your paper. Boom, bop, bip, everyone's happy. Right?" Bowie looks at me.

"Right," I say. I study Meek's hands. Wait to see if he's ready to use them as weapons again.

"Right?" Bowie asks again, this time to Meek.

Meek huffs through his nose and loosens his fists. So do I. "Right . . . but I know where to find you clowns if you try any funny shit."

"We'll be as unfunny as possible, Meek. Promise," Bowie says.

Meek sucks his teeth at us then storms down the hall. I feel bad for anyone who accidentally gets in his way.

I wait until the coast is clear then pat Bowie on the back again. "You sure you good? Want me to walk you to the clinic?"

"I'm fine." Bowie shrugs me off him. "Though we wouldn't be in this predicament if you'd just answer my fickin' texts. But . . . I get it." He wipes his nose with the back of his hand then peeks at me. "I heard Nicole took off."

I frown at Bowie, the words stuck in my mouth.

"People talk, Jay," Bowie explains. "My only question is, why haven't you? I thought we were . . . you know. I mean, we're business partners, but we're friends first, right?" He has so much sincerity in that question that it makes my teeth hurt. That's because Bowie's too saccharine—not all bitter like me. Yeah, he'd get my saltiness if I'd let him in enough to know the ins and outs of the Ducts. But if he tastes too much he might spit me out—like those frat guys and Joshua Kim and even Officer Miles Hunter.

"I'm handling it," I tell Bowie. "Just like I would've handled this situation with Meek."

Bowie scoffs at me. "Yeah. I could see that while he was straddling you on the floor."

"That was a misunderstanding. I was going to mention the library as soon as he got everything out of his system." Lies. I wasn't even thinking about the damn cloud. I had forgotten that Bowie showed me how to save stuff up there as a backup. My head was too caught in the clouds to come up with a rational solution like that. Bowie saved my ass, but I couldn't let him know that or he'd try to do it again. I point to his nose. "You should get that cleaned up before teachers ask questions."

Bowie touches his nose again then winces. "Yeah. Sure." He looks at me one last time. Waiting to see if I'll sing a different tune. But not another note escapes my mouth. Bowie sighs and heads to one of the bathrooms.

I scrub my head in frustration just as my phone buzzes in my pocket. I pull it out, see a message from Riley:

I have an idea . . .

ELEVEN

RILEY WASN'T JUST SHOOTING THE BREEZE. SHE DID HAVE an idea and it's a good one. So good that I want to kick myself because I didn't think of it myself. As soon as school ends, I book it to Heritage Trace Apartments. Wait in front of the sign as Riley's Uber pulls up. She and the driver share a quick laugh before she climbs out of the car. The driver waves a hardy goodbye at Riley before driving off.

I raise an eyebrow at Riley as she walks over to me. "Make a new best friend?" I ask.

"Who, Keisha?" Riley points at the car driving down the street. "She's nice. About to graduate from Hampton University at the end of the year. Plans to continue her studies in psychology. I think I'll request her again."

"And you got all of that from a ten-minute car ride?"

Riley shrugs. "It's amazing what people will tell you if you ask the right questions. Speaking of which . . ." She hitches her head toward the apartment complex. "You ready to do this?"

"Either way, I guess we're doing it," I say. We tread our way toward one of the apartment buildings. The one that Kenny's folks live in. They moved out of the Ducts a little less than a year ago. Even though they moved only a few lights away, I'm sure they figured that any distance away from Javon was good. Didn't matter. Kenny stayed as much in the hood as before. We reach their front door and I lift my hand to knock, but then pause.

"What's wrong?" Riley asks.

I drop my hand to my side. "I don't . . . I don't know what to say." Lately, whenever I opened my mouth to try to help Nic at all, my words come out all sideways and I just hit another wall. I'm not sure if I can take another dead end.

"It's okay," Riley says. "Follow my lead."

Before I can even ask her what she means, Riley knocks on the door. I hold in my breath. Part of me hoping someone answers, but the other part hoping that nobody's home. At least with the latter, I can avoid more disappointment.

"I don't think anyone's home," I say to Riley, just as the door cracks open.

"Yeah," a gruff voice says on the other side.

"Hello? We're looking for Mr. and Mrs. Boyce," Riley says, taking a step forward to peer through the door. I grab her arm and nudge her back. Curiosity is a great trait to have, but not necessarily in this neck of the woods. Pry too much and you just might get popped.

"Who's looking for them?" the voice asks. He punctuates it with a cough that chokes up something I don't want to see.

"Jay and Riley," Riley says. "We're friends of Kenny. Kenny borrowed something from Jay and Jay was hoping to get it back."

I look over at Riley. She gives me a sideways glance. Not bad . . . but let's see how far this gets us.

The door pulls open farther and Mr. Boyce stands in front of us, looking like a shorter, more crinkled version of Kenny. Like Kenny got folded into origami and they tried to undo the work but ended up with Mr. Boyce. "Look now. Kenny don't have anything here that you're probably looking for. I made sure of it, you feel me?"

Riley blinks, perplexed, but I dig everything Mr. Boyce is tossing. He thinks Riley and I are here looking for drugs. All this time I've spent shooing away blissheads, I never thought I'd be mistaken for one myself.

"Jay?" Mrs. Boyce peeks out the front door, tightening the waistband of a house robe around her. "That you? Goodness gracious you grew up."

"Um, thank you, ma'am?" I didn't mean for it to come

out as a question, but what does one say when someone mentions you going through puberty? Not the typical conversation piece.

Mrs. Boyce taps her husband on the arm. "That's Ms. Murphy's grandbaby. They're not here for any shenanigans. Let them on in."

Mr. Boyce doesn't hesitate. He steps back and waves a hand, motions for me and Riley to enter. It's obvious who runs the show in this household. Mr. Boyce flashes me a quick grin like he suddenly remembers my face. The smile lasts only a second, but still sticks with me. However Kenny got that knee injury, I can't imagine it being from his dad. Mr. Boyce seems warm. The kind of dad that scolds you in front of your mom, but sneaks you your favorite snack later.

"Have a seat. I'll get you both some sweet tea," Mrs. Boyce continues and disappears into the kitchen, not waiting to see if Riley or I even wanted sweet tea.

Mr. Boyce takes a newspaper off the coffee table and uses it to knock off imaginary crumbs from his couch. He points to it and Riley and I take a seat. Mr. Boyce hobbles to the recliner across from us and grunts as he follows suit.

Me and Riley's knees bump against each other as we sit in silence. I clear my throat and scoot farther to my end of the couch, my foot banging against the leg of the coffee table. A framed picture of a snaggle-toothed Kenny at about nine or ten vibrates from my clumsiness.

"Sorry about that," I mutter.

"No apologies necessary," Mr. Boyce says. "It gets a bit cramped in here."

"I think you have a lovely home," Riley says, and points to a framed picture of footsteps in sand on the beach. "And I love that painting. My mom keeps it and the poem that goes with it in our guest bathroom."

"You guys keep poems in your bathroom?" I ask.

"It's a poem about the Lord," Mrs. Boyce says, returning from the kitchen with two plastic cups filled with sweet tea, I presume. "The Lord is always with you, Jay. Even when you're doing your business."

"Good to know," I say, taking a cup from Mrs. Boyce. "And thank you."

"And he's especially with you now." Mrs. Boyce hands Riley her cup, and then sits on the arm of the recliner, right next to her husband. "I heard about Ms. Murphy. I've been meaning to send flowers. How's she doing anyway?"

"Much better, ma'am. The doctors said she might be able to come home in the next few days as long as she promises to take it easy. I might have to handcuff her to her nightstand, though."

Mrs. Boyce cackles. "I know that's right. Ms. Murphy's been a busybody for as long as I remember. I always told her that when the day of reckoning comes, she'd be right next to God, giving directions to people on which way they're supposed to go." Mr. Boyce and Riley join in with her laughter. I guess that's my cue as well. I force out a laugh, though it's such a foreign feeling that my ribs strain from it.

"You said that Kenny borrowed something from you?" Mr. Boyce asks.

"Yes, that's right." Riley takes a sip from her tea and peeks over at me. Right, that's my cue again. Step up your game, Jay.

"Yeah," I say finally.

Mr. and Mrs. Boyce both look at me, waiting for the next part of the story.

"My shirt," I say, and immediately try not to frown. How many guys borrow shirts from each other? "Dress," I add. "Shirt comma dress. My dress shirt." Riley takes a huge gulp from her tea. I'm alone on this one. "He needed to borrow mine for a job interview, but now I need it back. For a job interview."

"Kenny? Job interview?" Mr. Boyce asks. "Must've been a cold day in hell."

"Now stop that." Mrs. Boyce swats at his arm. "That's good. He's showing he can be responsible. Kenny's not here, but it might be in his room. What color is it?"

"White?" I try.

"I could help you look," Riley says. "I mean, if you need me to."

"I think I can manage. I'll be right back." Mrs. Boyce

shuffles toward the back and Riley glances at me, somewhat defeated. I know she wanted to lay eyes on Kenny's room to find another dot to connect. But maybe we could find one some other way.

"Kenny's not home?" I ask Mr. Boyce. "I haven't seen him around lately. What's he been up to?"

Mr. Boyce huffs. "Your guess is as good as mine. That boy's been dizzy ever since he got kicked off the basketball team."

"Kicked off?" I repeat. "I thought he got injured."

Mr. Boyce shakes his head. "Only thing he probably injured is his mind. That would explain why he took up with that punk Javon."

"Not a fan, huh?" Riley asks.

Mr. Boyce leans forward in his seat. "Ha! Is a cat a fan of baths?" He starts stabbing at the air with his finger. Now we really got him going. "As soon as Javon entered the picture, Kenny's been up under his thumb. Stopped caring about school as much. His grades started slipping—and his coach wasn't having that. So as soon as Kenny lost basketball, guess he figured he didn't need school anymore. Just stopped showing up."

I stare down at my tea. It's like he's singing the opening chords to Nic's song. If I can find her, maybe she can have a different outro.

"But I can't blame Kenny entirely. Doug probably has something to do with it, too."

"Doug, sir?" I ask.

Mr. Boyce rolls his eyes. "My knuckleheaded nephew. Out there pushing things he shouldn't be pushing. He even got busted a few times, but Kenny doesn't care. All he sees is his cousin living in some fancy condo in Richmond. Driving around in a Bentley or whatever's popular these days." He reaches out and adjusts the framed picture of Kenny on the coffee table. His hand lingers on the top before pulling it away.

"If only we could all stay that size, right?" Riley says.

Mr. Boyce gives her a soft smile. "He's a good boy. He really is. I know that he thinks he's doing the family good, especially with me being laid off and all. But I keep trying to tell him there's a better way." There's a thud in the back of the apartment. Like Mrs. Boyce closes a drawer or a closet door. Mr. Boyce leans over to me and Riley. "Could y'all do me a favor?" he asks in a hushed voice. "Can you tell the missus something good about Kenny's job interview? She just worries so much about that boy. I'd like to put her mind at ease some kind of way."

My heart sinks for them. They really had no clue that Kenny's been gone for a week. Apparently, he does the disappearing act even more than Nic. Mr. Boyce still has hope, even when he erased any lingering bits of mine.

Riley smiles and nods at him just as Mrs. Boyce returns to the living room, empty-handed. "I couldn't find it anywhere," Mrs. Boyce says, somewhat sheepishly. "Sorry about that. You need us to reimburse you?"

I shake my head. "That's not a big deal. I could pick up another one. I think Roses has a sale."

"Besides," Riley adds, "Kenny probably needs to keep that shirt anyway." She turns to me. "Didn't you say he nailed that job interview?"

I look over at Mr. Boyce who raises his eyebrows, hopeful. "Yeah," I say. "He did. I'll let him hold on to it until he gets his first paycheck or whatever."

Mrs. Boyce clasps her hands and rests them against her chin. She gives a silent prayer before beaming at me and Riley. "God is good," she says.

Her words follow me as Riley and I thank the Boyces for their hospitality and head out the front door. God is good? Not sure if I can agree after this week. Hell, after the past few years. I'm still waiting for the silver lining after all the challenges He's thrown at me.

But the Boyces still have hope. Faith that Kenny can be that little boy in the frame on their coffee table again. I saw it in the way Mr. Boyce's hand lingered on Kenny's picture. Saw it in the way Mrs. Boyce's eyes lit up when I dished her the possibility of Kenny having a legit gig. If I told them Kenny's been missing, that hope might wither and send them to the hospital just like MiMi. And what would going to the cops do for them? We have nothing to go on that something's even wrong with Kenny, so they'd just hit a roadblock in the form of another Officer Rick Ross. Best I keep them in the dark until something else sheds more light on all of this.

"Good work, Jay," Riley says, smiling and poking me in the arm.

I smirk at her. "Good work?" I ask. Way to patronize me. Yeah, I'm glad that I could make Mrs. Boyce feel good for a few minutes, but what about me? I'm still as lost and clueless as I was a week ago.

"Wait, you don't get it, huh?" Riley pulls a wrapper out of her purse. The same wrapper she found in Nic's bedroom a few days ago.

"Ugh, you actually kept that?" I ask.

"So, I did some digging," she says, completely ignoring my question. "Tried to figure out what stores use this kind of branding. I finally found a bakery that sells cake pops. Kee Kee's Goodies. They only have one location—in Richmond."

I shrug. "Yeah?"

"And Kenny's cousin lives in Richmond."

"Oookay," I say. Riley grabs my arm and makes me stop walking.

"Use that big brain of yours, Jay. Do you know any reason why Nic would go to Richmond?"

I pause, think about it. "No," I answer.

"So, it's mighty convenient that Nic just happens to have something from a bakery in Richmond. Right in the same city as someone Kenny's tight with."

I shrug again. "Yeah, but Richmond's a large city and . . ." And what? Nic doesn't have a car. It's not like she's driving over an hour away just to buy a cake pop. If Kenny had a reason to be there, it could mean one of two things. First, he's bringing back treats for Nic to try. Or two . . . "They ran off to Richmond together," I say aloud, connecting the dots.

Riley smiles at me again. "Just think about it, Jay. You've mentioned that Nic runs off from time to time. The Boyces said Kenny does the same thing. What better way to hide your trysts than to crash at your cousin's condo in a large city like Richmond?"

It sounds so weird hearing Riley actually say the words, but it makes sense. The last time anyone saw either of them was leaving the party together. And it seems like they've been doing a lot of leaving together before I even knew about it. All those times I figured Nic was off somewhere spinning on bliss, she was cozying it up with Kenny at this Doug guy's place. Javon must have pissed her off for the last time for her not to find her way back home yet.

"You're a genius," I tell Riley, then pull her toward me. I wrap my arms around her and give her a tight squeeze. Her ponytail tickles the tip of my nose and smells like baked goods. Something with honey in it. Riley smells like cake and honey. Wait, I'm smelling Riley Parker. And I'm so busy smelling Riley Parker that I don't even realize that her arms are wrapped around me, too.

I clear my throat and pull away. Riley pulls at her sleeves and stares down at her Converses. "Good work, Detective," she says to me.

"Right back at you," I say. "Let's get out of here, okay?"

Riley nods and pulls out her phone to order another Uber. I crack my knuckles and stare at the lettering of the Heritage Hint Apartments sign. Anything to avoid eye contact with her. But still, the lingering scent of honey tickles my nose.

TWELVE

I FINALLY FOUND THAT SILVER LINING. RILEY AND I WERE able to get the address to Kenny's cousin's condo from Mr. Boyce. The Boyces had figured that's where Kenny was lying low—he tended to do that from time to time when he wanted to feel like a man and get from up under his parents' thumbs. I spat Mr. Boyce a few lines about heading to Richmond anyways, and maybe I could reach out to Kenny and tell him to check in on his mom. I guess it wasn't a complete lie. Whatever it was, it was convincing enough for Mr. Boyce to give me the intel. Riley was going to see if she could borrow her parents' car for our road trip.

Can you even drive, I text to Riley the next day.

I spot an empty staircase in one of the school halls. Plop

down on one of the stairs to scarf down my chicken nuggets, my first meal of the day. Figured it would be best to avoid the cafeteria after the whole Bowie-Meek kinda, sorta smackdown. I couldn't stand to see Meek gloat in my face, and Bowie? I figure the more I stay away from him, the more likely I won't mix him up in all this Ducts drama. It's bad enough I have Riley walking around here like Veronica Mars—I can't have someone else I care about potentially getting into this mess.

Wait, does this mean that I care about Riley? Thankfully, my phone buzzes before I can even consider an answer.

Riley: Does it matter? You need a ride, right?

Me: Yeah . . . kinda want to get there in one piece, tho.

Riley: Wait a minute . . . you DON'T want to die? Let's call this whole thing off then.

I laugh. I actually laugh. Who knew Riley could make a comment about death that almost makes me snort aloud like her. And the laugh feels good—not strained like the one I had to force yesterday for the Boyces. I think about a clever rebuttal for her, something to send her snorting in the middle of lunch or class or wherever she might be at the moment. I wonder what her schedule's like, anyways. Not like we ever talked about it during Sunday school. Not like I gave us many opportunities to talk about anything during Sunday school. Maybe when we find Nic and the dust clears, I could ask her that question. I could find out what she wants to do when she graduates Warwick. But that's in the future, and this is now. Now, I need to text something back to make her laugh.

My thumb hovers above my keyboard just as a pair of legs casts a shadow over my phone. I peek up and I see Camila standing over me. Hip cocked to one side along with her mouth. Hands folded tightly across her chest. She stares down at me like she can't decide where she wants to hit me first, but rest assured, she definitely looks ready to strike. I quickly shove my phone inside my pocket.

"Hey . . . 'sup, Mila?" I ask. I push out a smile to show her I missed her, but my cheeks feel heavy. Smiling at her always came as easy as chowing down on MiMi's homemade lasagna, but now it seems like my muscles have to put in extra work. The hell's that about? Then it hits me: Camila and I haven't talked, like *talked* talked, since forever. No late-night phone calls. No morning texts. Yeah, we had first period together, but spent that hour doing this awkward dance of who's breaking the ice first. We both felt a wall but didn't know how to tear it down. Hell, did we even want to? But now that I'm really seeing her for the first time in like a week, I stare at her hair tucked behind her ears and try to remember if she got it cut recently.

"'Sup, Mila? That's it?" I didn't even recognize her friend, Pilar, behind her. Apparently, she's Camila's hype woman. She never quite understood what Camila saw in me in the first place. She's quick to cut me with her eyes and reminds Camila of all the reasons she's better off without me.

"And what's up to you, too, Pilar," I say, giving her a curt smile. I turn back to Camila. "I was going to call you later," I lie.

Camila knows it. She gives me an eye roll that's worthy of applause. "And when were you going to do that, Jay? When you were writing papers for the football team?"

"Mila." I raise my eyebrows at her then shift my eyes to Pilar, reminding her we're in mixed company.

" . . . or when you were hanging out with that nerdy girl," Camila continues, not even catching my hint.

I pause. "What nerdy girl?"

Pilar scoffs and throws her hands up, annoyed.

"Are you kidding me right now?" Camila asks, irritation piquing because of Pilar's actions. "I know you've been kicking it with that girl from your church."

Riley. How did she find out about Riley? On cue, my phone buzzes in my pocket. Riley's probably still being clever. My hand itches to see what she says next but I'm sure that Mila's hand is itching to clock me upside the head if I even dare respond right now.

"Pilar's brother saw you and her at Heritage Hint yesterday," Camila explains, answering the question written all over my face. "What the hell was that about?"

I open my mouth to answer but the words get stuck.

That's probably a good thing since they'd be paired with exclamation marks. Camila was grouping me in with all these other high school dudes that hook up with the whole female population. I never really had a girlfriend but knew that wasn't my style. I saw how happy one woman made my dad and that's what I wanted. One girl to share inside jokes with and to sit next to without having to say anything because our energy said it all. But happiness certainly wasn't being accused of doing something I didn't do.

"And don't even lie, Jay," Pilar adds. "Victor knows it was you. You were wearing that dusty hoodie you wear even when it's a thousand degrees out. And he says you were with some chick wearing some doofy Converses."

"You told me that annoying girl from your church has like a thousand pair of Converses," Camila says.

"Why you talking to Mila about another girl, huh?" Pilar this time. My eyes zigzag, zigzag, trying to keep up with the conversation.

"Well?" Camila shifts her weight to the other side. I almost expect her to tap her foot, but she's not stereotypical like that. Instead, her nostrils flare in and out, in and out, like she's trying to keep herself from crying. I noticed that when we watched *The Lion King* remake together, right after Simba's dad croaked. "I got popcorn butter in my eye," she insisted.

My whole body sighs. Seeing this girl cry would melt me

to the floor right now. I can't handle that on top of everything else. "Can we talk alone?" I ask Camila.

"Why? You weren't alone at Heritage Hint," Pilar snaps.

I plead to Mila with my eyes. Her arms loosen just slightly across her chest.

"I got this, Pilar," she mumbles.

"You sure?"

Camila's silence is all the response she needs. Pilar pokes her lips out at me, then squeezes Camila's shoulder before disappearing down the hall.

"It's not what you think," I say as soon as Pilar's completely out of sight.

"Don't tell me what I think, Jay," Camila says. "You wouldn't know, anyway, since you've been a ghost lately."

Fair enough. I've been a jackass to her. I've been a jackass to a lot of people lately, but I was trying to make up for it. Funny how when you try to right the wrongs you add a couple of more wrongs along the way.

"I know, and I'm sorry. I am. I just have a lot going on right now with MiMi and . . ." I almost let Nic slip. "And . . . work," I try again. "I listened to your concerns about the paper stuff, so I got a legit gig. I come home every night smelling like ground beef and taco seasoning, but at least I won't get expelled for that, right?" I try another smile with Camila. She does not return it.

"And these are all things you could talk to me about,"

Camila says. She pinches the bridge of her nose and folds her arms across her chest again, toughens up. "I tell you when things are going down at my house. Like when my mom skipped out on dinner to do something for work?"

"Yeah, because you hate watching all your sisters alone," I say, and immediately wish I hadn't. It sounds like I'm picking a fight. And, I don't know, maybe I am a little. But now's not the time to question what we are and why she likes me. To ask if she's just using me for free babysitting services and an arm to hold on to until something better comes along. She doesn't deserve the asshole routine. "I didn't mean it like that. You know I like your little sisters." I reach for her hand but Camila steps back. Holds up both her hands so I can't lay a finger on them.

"Don't even bother, Jay. Because I don't care what or who you like. Not anymore." She looks me right in the eye and pauses a second or two before laying it on me: "Because we're done."

I blink. I knew that's where she was heading, but I didn't expect to feel turbulence along the way. "Mila, there's nothing going on with me and Riley," I say. Saying Riley's name so close to hers gives my stomach the ups and downs. Almost like I committed some kind of crime and was afraid of getting caught. "She's just helping me out with something . . . that's all."

"I said I don't care, Jay. She can help you until the cows

come home. You're not my problem anymore." She whips around and her hair smacks me right in the eye.

I rub my eye, my good one watching her walk away. I wait for my heart to sting just like my cornea. Camila's been my dream girl since eighth grade. When she finally gave me the time of day, I was the clown who wondered what colors we were going to wear to prom together. But I never really wanted to go to prom. That was more her thing—like dressing up for spirit week or going to football games. I never looked good in Youngs Mill's random colors of purple and gold, and I could never find a comfortable way to sit on a cold, hard-ass bleacher.

I finally wipe Camila's hair out my eye and take a seat back on the stairs. I try to force the rest of my nuggets down, but they're a little tough to swallow.

✳ ✳ ✳

Camila officially kicking me to the curb is yet another thing on my mind as I pretend that restocking the napkin dispenser at Taco Bell is the most riveting task on the planet. Joshua Kim likes all employees to paste a smile across their face—whether it's the guy pumping cheese on your nachos or the lady showing you where to insert your credit card chip to pay for said nachos. Smiles make people want to spend more money, Joshua says. Funny, I just assumed it was a late-night case of the munchies after a bliss break.

The good news (and yes, I still try to find good news even as a toddler crushes cinnamon twists in her tiny palms and then blows the dust on the floor—cinnamon dust that I'll have to clean up later) is that Joshua Kim is not the tool in charge this shift. I get Maurice instead. Granted, Maurice and Joshua are pretty much cut from the same cloth. Maurice is just a bit thicker around the belly and a bit darker in the pigment, but Maurice is a little older than Joshua. He's not taking this manager job to score brownie points with some professor in his MBA program. Nah, Maurice is a family man. Has a wife and two small kids at home. River and Parker—or some other unisex names that he probably let his crunchy wife choose. But anyways, Maurice is good people overall. Probably willing to help out another brother when needed. I catch him giving me a look sometimes when a customer is getting a little too hype after accidentally getting soft instead of hard tacos. Same look that MiMi gives me when we see a kid cutting up in the grocery store, all: "If that was MY child . . ."

I decide tonight's a good time as any to test out Maurice's brotherhood. I spot him asking the lady with her toddler wreaking havoc on the cinnamon twists if she was enjoying her food. The lady gives a half-hearted nod in his direction. I mean, we are just a fast-food restaurant and not some authentic restaurant in El Paso or whatever.

"All right, you just let us know if you need anything else,

okay," Maurice practically sings, the smile on his face so wide that the whites of his eyes disappear. As soon as he turns around, though, someone hits the off switch and his jaw is as slack as usual. I sweep my way over to him.

"How it do, Maurice?" I ask.

Maurice looks up from his clipboard. Probably inspecting the inventory in the dining area. Probably pretending to inspect the inventory in the dining area but doodling something on his paper instead. Either way, he gets paid. "Keeping my head up as always, Jayson. How about yourself? Been here a couple days now, right? Getting the hang of everything?"

Yeah. I've learned that the broom works better if you sweep from the right to the left and that you can't stuff more than one hundred fifty napkins into the dispenser at once. Important life lessons. "Sure am," I say instead. "Everyone's been mad cool here. And it's been a trip meeting all different kinds of people."

"Yeah. A trip's the right word," Maurice says, staring at the toddler who throws herself on the floor and kicks her legs up and down. All because her mom tried wiping her hands. Maurice gives me the MiMi look for a second before turning back to manager mode. "Been hearing great things about you, too. From what Joshua tells me, we'll get you back there on the drive-thru line in no time."

"Really? That's what's up," I say, nodding like he just told me I won ten thousand dollars.

"Yeah. Just keep on keeping on and we'll try to get you in there in the next month." He looks back down at his clipboard and it's now or never.

"That would be great," I continue. "Listen, while I got you, I was wondering if I could change shifts tomorrow. Between coming here and visiting my grandma in the hospital, I've been a little behind on schoolwork. It'd be great to knock out as much as I can in the morning, and then come here tomorrow night instead." Guess it wasn't a complete lie. I mean, I do have mad homework to catch up on. But the real truth is Riley said her parents might feel more comfortable about her driving in the daytime instead of night. Originally, I told Joshua and Maurice I could do day shifts on Saturdays since it was the weekend and all, but this new lead on Nic is too hot not to follow.

Maurice taps his pencil on his chin. "That probably wouldn't be a problem. Might be someone willing to work doubles," he says.

I smile. That was easier than expected. I knew that Maurice was good people. "For real? Cool, man. I'll be here right at four tomorrow." I shuffle my broom to the other hand and turn around, ready to sweep the rest of this floor with more pep in my step.

"But," Maurice continues—and something about his tone makes me pause. I'm too afraid to even look at him over my shoulder. "If I do you that favor, I'd have to do everyone that favor. Soon, I'd be doing so many favors that I might not have enough folks to cover a shift."

I curse under my breath. Of course, that's the moment the toddler decides to stop throwing a tantrum. She stares at me, wide-eyed and widemouthed. I reluctantly face Maurice again, who stares back at me with both hands on his hips. All broad shouldered and power-hungry. Like he just morphed into some sleazy guy on Wall Street.

"I get that," I say. "But it's just this one time. I promise."

Maurice shakes his head. "It always starts with just one time. One time is all it takes. You can rock a boat just once and the whole thing can tip over. Soon you'd be choking off salmon."

I blink at him. What kind of water is he sailing on around here? I doubt you'd find much salmon in the James River. Hell, we rarely find it in our grocery stores. That's why MiMi's always frying up whiting.

Maurice walks over to me. "You're a good kid, Jay. I told you—we see your potential. But remember . . ." He looks me up and down. "You could also be replaced. Other cats around here would kill to have your job. Recession is no joke." He slaps me on the shoulder. "We'll see you tomorrow at eight a.m., then. Okay?"

I grit my teeth. I want to spit in his face. I want to take his clipboard and shove it up his ass. I want to make him eat all the crumbs and scraps and insect carcasses that I sweep up every night that I'm here. But with little time left for my side hustles, this job is all I have to contribute to MiMi's retirement fund. With how her health has been lately, she needs to get off her feet for good sooner than expected.

"Yeah," I force out. "Cool."

Maurice gives me a wink and then whistles his way over to the counter to torture some new customers that just walked in.

"Welcome to Taco Hell," I want to tell them. But I go sweep up the toddler's cinnamon crumbs instead. Hope it makes the time go by faster.

THIRTEEN

THE SUN STARTS TO KISS THE LAND AS I WAIT FOR RILEY to pick me up to find Nic. Autumns in Virginia meant more hours of night and less time for visibility, which is why I tried switching shifts at Taco Bell. But Maurice used his large, ashy hands to squash my plans. After work, I'd run home and washed the stank of queso off my skin, then hightailed it to outside of Man Boo's barbershop for Riley to scoop me up. Not that I'm putting her in a box like Bowie. Riley's already seen where I lay my head. But there are too many prying eyes at the Ducts. Even tonight, Slim and Quan were perched in their usual positions as I headed to Man Boo. The last thing I need is for Javon to catch wind of where Nic might be and get to her first. I still have hope that he hasn't caught her scent yet.

I hear a tap on the store window behind me. Man Boo raises both hands, as if asking why I'm not coming in. I smile and shake my head: *I'm cool.* Man Boo smirks at me and then shuffles toward the shop's entrance. Should've known he wouldn't take no for an answer.

"Oh, I get it," he says, walking up to me on the sidewalk. "You got a little coin in your wallet now because of that new fancy part-time job of yours. Now you got some swanky guy named Federico cutting your hair." He smiles and he has to have an extra tooth in there or something. Nobody can have that much joy.

"Marco," I correct. "He usually has a waiting list, but I was able to slip right on in. Taco Bell perk."

Man Boo laughs as he rubs his hand over his bald head. He no longer has to subject himself to his own haircuts, lucky dog. "We miss seeing you around here, man. How's your grandma doing? We're all pulling for her."

"She's hanging in there. Should be home soon," I say. MiMi's tough. Probably the toughest person I ever met. Still, even the idea of losing Nic is enough to break her. Hell, it almost did. That's why I'm going to do what it takes to get Nic home and give MiMi the family reunion they show in them Hallmark movies. Even if it means dragging Nic to Riley's car.

Man Boo blows into his hands and nods. He was in so much of a rush to come out and bust my balls that he forgot to throw a jacket over his smock. "And your mom?" He peers at me over his fingers, keeping his hands up like a shield. Like I was going to lash out and strike him at the mere mention of my mom.

I shrug. "She's . . . you know." I shrug again for good measure. Truth is, I don't know how she's doing. Never called to give her the deets about MiMi like I was supposed to, but I'm sure MiMi filled her in by now. Every time I pulled out my iPad to email her or whatever, my fingers locked up. Froze. As if they didn't know what to type. I didn't know which was worse: drafting a letter to let Mom know how twisted our family had become or seeing that I had a response from her. Even if she sent a sentence or two, I'd read so much more in between the lines—none of which would fully scratch that itch I get when I think about her.

Man Boo nods at me again, eating up everything I was feeding him even though it's just crumbs. But he's cool like that. He always knows the fine line between chopping it up and keeping it moving. Too bad his barbering skills aren't just as on point.

A black Lincoln Continental pulls up to the curb in front of us. Man Boo lets out a whistle and I look down at my shoes. Check my laces in case I have to take off booking. Fancy car like that in a neighborhood like this usually spells trouble. The passenger window rolls down and I bend my knees, prepare for takeoff.

"Hey, Jay!" Riley leans over and pokes her head out the window. "Hop on in."

I blink. I don't remember the Palmers rolling in a ride like this to Sunday services.

"Fancy friend to take you to your fancy haircut?" Man Boo asks, raises an eyebrow.

"Something like that." I slap him a five and slide into the passenger seat. "I'll tell MiMi you said hello," I call out through the window.

Man Boo gives me a salute and lets out another whistle as we pull away.

"Seatbelt," Riley says like a mom in training.

"Yes, ma'am." I snap my seatbelt into place. Peek into the sideview mirror to make sure Man Boo got back into his shop without any drama. Most folks around here know better, but there's always some clown from the next town over who thinks they can shake up someone in this neighborhood for some quick cash.

"Who's your friend?" Riley asks.

My smirk comes out as a laugh. "Friend? It'd be kind of creepy for me to be friends with an old dude."

Riley lifts one hand into a shrug, keeps the other on the wheel. "I don't know. You two looked friendly together."

"He just used to cut my hair, that's all." But that doesn't

feel like a hundred percent the truth, especially after saying it aloud. Yeah, he cut my hair until I outgrew his high fades, but he also spotted me a few dollars to sweep up hair or clean his windows. He let me chill out in one of his chairs whenever MiMi's shift ran a little late and Nic was too distracted with her phone to distract me. If he wasn't just a barber, but wasn't a friend, I didn't know what the hell to call him. So instead, I look around the car. Leather seats. Navigation system. Some kind of clip on the vent that makes the whole car smell like lavender. My knee bumps against the dashboard as I continue my snoop fest.

"My mom usually sits there. She's way shorter than you. You can adjust the seat if you need to," Riley explains.

I reach in between my legs and under the seat for some kind of handle. Nothing's there.

"No. It's on the side. Just press it toward the back—it's automatic."

I find the button on the side of the seat, press it, and, like magic, the seat glides backward. The transition is seamless, like a private jet landing on a runway. Don't think I've ever been in a car as fancy as this. The fanciest, probably, was the back of the hearse escorting my dad to his final resting place, but I've always tried to push out that memory.

"We don't drive this one to church," Riley explains, almost sheepishly. "We just use it for trips."

"You have a car specifically for trips?" I ask. "La-di-da.

And Reverend Palmer entrusted you with the vacation vehicle for our trek to Richmond?"

"Weeellll," Riley begins. Okay, that was one too many
l's to not be a little suspicious. "They don't necessarily think
we're going to Richmond."

I look at her. "Where do they think we're going?"

"They might think we're just going to the bookstore to
check out a few more books and stuff for Sunday school. And
by we, they mainly think me." She peeks over at me. "I'm not
allowed to have other people in the car."

I grab my chest. "Riley Palmer. First sneaking out and
breaking curfew, now lying to your parents. What's next?
You gonna get a face tattoo?"

Riley shrugs. "I've always been a fan of unicorns."

I laugh at the image. The day I see Riley Palmer with a
tattoo is the day you'd see me with a full ride to Harvard.
"Unicorns, huh? For some reason, that doesn't surprise me."

"I'll have you know, I'm full of surprises."

She has a point there. If somebody would've asked me
even two weeks ago, I would've never guessed she'd step
foot into my neighborhood after dark—let alone without
a can of mace or guard dog. But these past few days have
been like a Tootsie Pop. Going through layer after layer
without truly getting to the core. Like Riley still has some
things she wants to share with me, but I need to put the
work in first.

"Whereas with you . . ." she continues, "complete open book."

I scoff at her. "Lies. I'd like to think I'm dark and mysterious."

"Just because you think it, Jay, doesn't mean it's true." She holds up a finger and I know she's about to count off a few things. "One, you always have a book with you, which means you love to read."

"Sharp detective skills," I say, rolling my eyes.

"But your books never really have creases in them. Which either means you only carry the books for show, or you treat books like precious things you need to handle with care. I'm going with the latter since it doesn't seem like you care too much about what people think."

That last part's not quite on the nose, but still, I nod, somewhat impressed. "Okay. What else you got?"

"Two." She continues counting with her fingers. "You wear the same hoodie almost all the time."

I shrug. "I live in the Ducts. Money's tight."

Riley shakes her head. "That's an excuse. Ms. Murphy makes sure you look sharp. Even if you're not wearing labels, you have a variety. Which tells me that your hoodie must hold some sentimental value."

I hold my breath. Damn. She's good. I run my thumb along the zipper of my hoodie. It gets caught from time to time. I remember having to help Dad get it up to his neck sometimes, when he got too weak to fight with it. Think it took me five months before I let my mom wash it for the first time after he passed. His scent is long gone, but if I close my eyes tight enough when resting my forehead on the crook of my arm, it's almost like he's still right here.

"And three . . ."

I almost forget that Riley's in the car, even though she's the one driving.

She finally rests her hand back on the steering wheel and gives me another quick glance. "I'm really sorry about you and your girlfriend."

The back of my head hits the seat. "How'd you know about that?"

"I have my ways," she says with a one-shoulder shrug.

"Apparently." I shift in my seat. This big-ass car suddenly seems very cramped. "And she wasn't really my girlfriend. I mean, she was but she wasn't."

Riley gives me a skeptical twist of her mouth and my foot hits her dashboard as I shift again. I take a breath, try to find the right words.

"I think we were together because we both needed something. And sometimes it feels good to be needed." Okay, that sounded so much better in my head. Still, Riley gives me not one but two nods.

"I get it," she says. "Still . . . it must feel pretty weird, huh?"

I glance over at Riley. Her tan Converses perfectly offset her caramel complexion, and her ponytail shows just how high her cheekbones are. How long her neck really is.

I finally shrug. "Could be weirder," I say.

✳ ✳ ✳

Mr. Boyce wasn't lying—Kenny's cousin's condo is fly as hell. It's in downtown Richmond, but artsy downtown Richmond. So instead of bumping into blissheads and crinkle clowns, you might be walking side by side with a theater professor with leather elbow patches on his blazer. Only residents of the condo complex get to park in the garage; everyone else has to find parallel parking out on the street. It's walking distance from a shopping center that has one of those movie theaters with a bar and a bowling alley. Nic wanted to take MiMi to one like that back in Newport News for her birthday, but once we caught wind of how much the food would cost us, we Netflixed and Pizza Hutted instead.

I knock on the door to Kenny's cousin's unit, then crack my knuckles while I wait. Riley glances over at me and rests her hand on top of mine.

"It's okay," she says. "We're bringing her home."

I nod. She's right. This is it. Over a week with roadblocks and, finally, I get a green light. I look down at Riley's hand on top of mine still and can't remember if we've touched like this before. Yeah, our hands grazed each other's when we had to pass out something to the kids at Sunday school, but I always whipped mine away like Riley's had just come out of the oven. Now, though, her hand doesn't feel too hot. Just warm and soft.

"Who the hell is it?" a voice booms through the door.

I swallow. This doesn't sound too inviting. "Jay," I say. "Jay Murphy," I add, like that makes any kind of difference.

The door opens and a young dude stands in the doorway. Lighter complexion than Kenny, but close to the same height. He wears a tank top with khaki shorts and socks pulled up to his knees, like one of them wannabe gangstas in some hood movie made in the nineties. But his thick biceps and the grimace on his face make him a little less wannabe and a lot more dangerous.

He glares at me, then at Riley, then back at me. "I ain't buying shit," he says.

"Are you Doug?" Riley asks, not even flinching at his menacing appearance.

His glare returns to Riley and my feet move, stand slightly in front of her. Just in case. "Who wants to know?" he asks.

"We're friends of Kenny," I say before Riley can get another word out. I really should've made her wait in the car. Right next to that swanky shopping center where I'd know she'd be safe.

"Friends of Kenny?" The guy I'm assuming is Doug raises his eyebrows at us. I hear people chuckle in the background.

Two separate voices. Could one of them be Nic? "Not sure if Kenny has friends that look like you two."

"Could you ask him?" I try. "I mean, he's here, right?"

"I mean, he's here, right?" This Doug dude tries to imitate me but speaks in a high nasal voice. The hell? Is that how I sound? He turns his head toward the people behind him. The people out of sight. "Yo, y'all should hear this clown out here!" More laughter. If Nic were in there, she'd run to the door if she heard my voice. Then again, she's been avoiding me all week. She probably wants Doug to get rid of me so she could continue doing whatever she's been doing these last eight days. I'm not letting her off that easy.

"We're friends of the family—we know Mr. and Mrs. Boyce," I say. "They're worried about Kenny. They knew we were going to be in town so asked if we could stop by and check on him." I try to peek around him, catch a glimpse of whoever's tee-hee-hee-ing back there.

Doug shifts his weight to block my view and looks at me through the slits of his eyes, but the cynicism still slips out. We have a stare off. I try not to plead with my eyes too much—all *it's up to you if we come in. No big deal.* Doug's grip on his doorknob gets tighter and tighter. I expect it to close right in my face in about two seconds.

"That was a long ride, though," Riley adds. "Mind if I come in to pee?"

I wince at Riley's bluntness. Riley's eyebrows shrug at

me. She's thinking on her toes to give me an in, even if it means embarrassing herself. Doug gives a half smile—partially amused, partially confused. Whoever's behind him speak in hushed voices now and my heart skips a beat. One of those voices seems high-pitched enough to be a girl's. I strain my ear to make out whether or not it's Nic.

"Make it quick," Doug finally says, stepping aside. I push past him and make a beeline for his living room, Riley hot on my heels. I stop in my tracks when I see two black dudes around Doug's age passing a joint between each other. The one with dreads past his shoulders looks up at me and frowns.

"Damn, nigga. Can I help you?" he asks.

His friend across from him breaks out into snickers, teetering like a bird. The same high-pitched voice I heard outside the front door. The one I had thought—no, hoped— was Nic's. But once again, my hope crashed to the floor. It was just two clowns smoking bliss with a fit of the giggles.

"Uh . . . bathroom?" Riley asks Doug, who closes the front door and locks it behind him. Not just once—he makes sure to use the deadbolt. The click of it sends shock waves throughout my limbs. Something tells me this wasn't a good idea.

Doug hitches his head toward the back of his condo. "First door to the left."

Riley nods then gives me a look. *Should I search for clues?* No. Definitely not a good idea. I scratch the back of my neck.

Give a slight shake of my head: *No.* But Riley must just think I'm itchy because she takes tentative steps toward the back.

"Now what's this you said about Kenny?" Doug asks me as I try to follow her. He sits on the barstool in front of his kitchen island. His kitchen bleeds right into his living, all open concept like those fancy homes on HGTV. Homeboy even has a curio cabinet across from his stainless-steel fridge, showcasing all types of shot glasses and crystal bottles of brown liquors.

I glance at his countertops, his couches, his shiny wooden floors. Try to spot anything that might hint that a female's been up in here. That Nic's been hiding out. But aside from all his bougie fixtures, I only find bongs and rolling papers and a pair of nunchucks. Random. "He split town over a week ago," I say. "His parents thought maybe he's been crashing here with you."

Doug scratches at the stubble on his chin. "If they thought that, why didn't they just call and ask me?"

I shrug. "Not sure. You know your people better than me."

"My people, huh?" Doug stands and I notice a huge, black-and-white framed photo of Bruce Lee hanging on the wall behind his head. Guess that would explain the nunchucks. He gives me the same sneer Bruce Lee wears behind him and suddenly I'm the one that really needs to go the bathroom. "So . . . my people is worried about my cousin. But instead of calling and coming by to see me, they send you two doofy motherfuckers—doofy motherfuckers I never laid eyes on in my life—to follow up?"

I swallow down the fear rising from my gut. Riley really needs to hurry up. "Yep," I squeeze out. "So . . . you haven't heard from Kenny?"

"Terrence," Doug calls out, but keeps his eyes decidedly on me, "you heard from Kenny?"

"Naw, man," the guy with the dreads says. He looks over at his friend. "What about you, Ray?"

"Nope," the guy who I'm assuming is Ray responds. He takes another hit from the joint and studies me as the smoke seeps out of his nose. "Haven't seen that nigga since forever ago."

Doug cocks his head at me and shrugs. "There you have it. Did you get the answers you were looking for?"

I try to crack my knuckles, but my hands are too slippery. I don't even know when I started sweating. "Yeah," I say. "Yeah, I'm good. Thanks."

With perfect timing, Riley returns from the back of the condo. She looks at me with her mouth bent downward. She didn't find anything or anyone. Dammit. Another roadblock. But if I can't find Nic, I have to make sure I keep Riley.

"Okay, so we'll let you guys get back to it then," I say. I reach for Riley's hand. She blinks at me, startled, then takes it. I lead her toward the front door when Doug steps in our way.

"I don't know," he says, shaking his head. "Something's just not sitting right with me. What did you say your names were again?"

My heart starts pounding in my ears. I think about giving him a fake name, but then I also think about what he might do to us if he found out I gave him a fake name. "Jay and Riley," I say.

"Jay and Riley?" He shakes his head again. "See, that doesn't ring a bell to me. Never heard Kenny mention either of you before. Why do you think that is?"

"I . . . I don't know," I say. I keep gripping onto Riley's hand as I take a step back away from Doug's accusatory glare. We bump into someone. I look over my shoulder and both Terrence and Ray stand behind us, shoulders side to side. Almost forming a wall. Shit. This is definitely not good.

"I think I know why that is. I think maybe, just maybe, you two are . . . narcs." Doug's hand stretches out to his side and gets dangerously close to his nunchucks. I thought those things were just for show, but his fingers seem to be itching to do damage with them.

"Whoa, chill out, man," I say, panic rising in my throat. "We're not narcs. Far from it. We don't stick our nose in anyone's business."

"But you over here looking for Kenny." He grabs a nunchucks and lets them dangle behind his neck. "I'd say that's pretty nosy."

179

"We're just worried," I try again. "He left with my sister and—"

"Oh, now he magically has a sister?" Terrence says, breath hot on my neck.

Okay, this is not going well. At all. My eyes dart around the room, looking for any other kind of exit aside from the front door. I spot a window behind one of the couches. But Doug lives on the fourth floor. A leap out of there is bound to leave us with a few fractured ribs, if not more.

"Jay . . ." Riley says under her breath, enveloping my hand with her free one. She doesn't need to say anything else. She's scared, just like me—and I'm the one that dragged her into this mess. What the hell was I thinking?

"Don't be scared, darling," Doug says, in a scary-ass tone. "As a matter of fact, let me help you relax. Take a hit."

Riley blinks at him. "A hit?"

The fact that she even has to ask sends Doug and his friends cackling, and only makes me squeeze her hand tighter. I wish my whole hand could blanket her until whatever this is was over.

"A hit from our joint," Doug explains. "Ray, puff and pass, bruh."

Riley sucks in a breath and a noise escapes her. Something tiny and innocent. That's it. I pull away from her and step to Doug. "That's enough."

"Come again?" Doug quirks up an eyebrow.

"She's not smoking shiz, okay? So let us dip. We're not bothering y'all."

Doug shakes his head. "See, that's where you wrong. You come to my place after dark, tapping on my door like a goddamn narc? That's not going to fly, homey. Only way you're stepping foot out of here is if she sucks on this joint."

"Let me do it," I say. I demand. The smell of bliss always scratches my throat, and even the thought of tasting it almost sends me into a hacking frenzy—but I'd eat three whole joints if that means Riley walks out of here clearheaded and in one piece.

Doug scoffs at me. "You probably smoke five of these bad boys a day. The fuck out of here."

Ray and Terrence snicker again and my jaw clenches. It's one thing to have cops look down on me, but to be pigeonholed by actual blissheads? Smoke trickles out of my ears and I haven't taken a hit of anything yet.

"It's okay, Jay," Riley says in a small voice behind me. "I'll do it."

My head snaps back at her. "The hell you will."

"It's our only way out of here, right?" She walks up closer to Doug. "Just one puff, right?"

Doug raises his eyebrows at her, amused, then nods his head to Ray. Ray passes Riley the joint but I grab her arm.

"You don't have to do this," I hiss to her. "I can't let you do this."

She pats my hand before pulling away. "What else are we going to do?" She turns to Ray. "Is this just bliss?"

Ray snickers. "You tell me, little mama."

Riley nods and takes the joint from his hand. I move to swat it away from her, but Doug steps in my way. She places it to her lips and starts making tiny kissing noises on the tip. Doug and his friends fall out, laughing.

"Nah, sis," Doug says. "If you want the full effect, you have to inhale deep. Let the smoke get down in the rib cage."

Riley looks over at me and I mouth *no* to her. She looks back down at the joint and then does exactly what Doug says—inhales so deep that her whole chest swells.

"Now hold it," Doug instructs.

Riley's eyes get wide as she holds her breath. We all watch her on pins and needles, and the seconds drip by. Suddenly, a blast of smoke escapes Riley's mouth and she starts gagging. Doug and his boys laugh it up again. I push past Doug and pat Riley on her back.

"You okay?" I ask her.

She lets out a few more coughs and rubs her chest. "Is that all?" she asks through her phlegm.

Doug snickers. "Oh, you'll be feeling it soon enough. I only mess with the Grade A stuff. But if you want to try it again . . ."

"We're good," I spit out, pull Riley into the crook of my arm. "So, can we go now, or what?"

Doug looks us over then takes the joint from Riley's hand. "Your girl got bigger balls than you, homey." He unlocks his front door and hitches his head out to the corridor. "Don't bring your punk ass back here."

He doesn't have to tell me twice. I pull Riley through the front door, Doug and his crew's laughter floating above us right along with Riley's head.

FOURTEEN

I CAN'T GET TO RILEY'S CAR FAST ENOUGH. MAINLY because I practically have to carry Riley in my arm. She only took one hit, but damn if it wasn't a long one. Her being a lightweight makes for a weighty getaway. I wait for the elevator to open to lead me and Riley to the ground floor. Peek over my shoulder to make sure Doug didn't change his mind about us kissing his nunchucks.

"What kind of car is this?" Riley asks, poking at the elevator door. "One of them foreign, sporty things?"

I grab Riley's hand just as the doors open to make her stop assaulting the elevator.

"Whoa, voice command, much?" she asks.

"Something like that. Come on." We hobble into the elevator with her arm wrapped around my neck. I press the button to make the doors close behind us and the elevator chimes each time we pass a floor.

"Ay, this my jam," Riley says, pulling away from me to pump her arms up and down. She shimmies like an old cat at a cookout, doing a dance my dad used to call "raising the roof." I place my hand near her lower back, ready to swoop in just in case she loses her balance. I can't believe she'd do something this crazy. That joint could've been laced with anything. She didn't even flinch, though. She did what she had to do to get us out of there. In fact, that's what she's been doing since I told her about Nic. Sticking her neck out much farther than she needed to. Doug was right—her balls were huger than mine. I've underestimated Riley all this time.

The elevator door opens and we're on the ground floor. I put Riley's arm back around me and we trek toward her car.

"I see what you're doing," Riley says, poking her finger into my chest. Her and that finger, though. "You're just trying to find an excuse to touch me."

I stifle a laugh. "Come again?" I ask.

"I can walk just fine, Jay Murphy. Matter of fact, I can walk better than fine. I'm floating in air."

"On air," I correct.

"That's what I said. On air." She pauses then cracks up

laughing. "You ever notice how weird that word is? AY-ERRR. Is that one or two syllables? You try."

"I'm good," I say. Thankfully, we're less than a block away from her car. Riley gets quiet and I glance at her, make sure she's still with me. I find her studying my face. "Are *you*, though? Good?"

She keeps looking at me. "Your lips," she says.

"What about them?"

"They're really . . . kissable."

Okay, I can't stifle my laughter anymore. This time it comes out. "Okay, you need to sleep it off."

"I'm not even tired," Riley insists as I dig into her pocket, pull out her car keys. I don't have my license, but I have my permit. No point in going through with the deed when you have no car to drive. I unlock the door and gently place Riley into the passenger seat, buckle her in real cozy. I glance across the street once more at Doug's complex. Thankfully, neither he nor his boys decided to follow us. Guess he figured we really were just harmless, doofy kids.

"Let's get you home," I say to Riley once I climb into the driver's seat. Riley doesn't answer. I look her way and her head is resting against the window, lightly snoring through her nose. I smile at her and pull out away from the curb. Drive slowly over all the speed bumps so I won't wake her.

✳ ✳ ✳

I feel empty once I spot the sign on the interstate that tells me we're back in Newport News. I mean, on the one hand, I'm glad I'm getting us back home in one piece. Not bad for a guy driving in the dark with no license. But on the other hand, I have the same amount of info that I had when I left Newport News: Nic and Kenny blew town together and Javon was far from happy about it. It doesn't make sense, though. Even if Nic suddenly fell hard for Kenny, she wouldn't just leave me and MiMi in the dust like that. Yeah, she and MiMi got into it a few times, but Nic was the one who rubbed lotion over MiMi's feet after a long day at work. The one who washed MiMi's hair in the kitchen sink, then took her time detangling it, and greased her scalp to make sure it glistened the next day. The one who added too much pepper in Deacon Irving's mac and cheese during the Easter brunch because he stared a little too long at Sister Gladys in her new dress.

And then there's me. Nic and I may have drifted a bit after her hookup with Javon, but there was nobody else on this earth who lived what we lived through. Dad dying, Mom basically killing herself with dope. Getting herself locked up because she couldn't handle the single parent thing. We could share a thousand words with one look. Nic could send a text with one or two emojis, and I could transcribe her whole side of the story to MiMi. We just got each other even when we thought we couldn't. So for her to just drop off the face of the planet like that? Something isn't adding up.

I slightly turn up the music on the car radio, let Kendrick Lamar drown out my questions—if only for a few minutes. Riley stirs in her seat and I quickly turn the volume back down. She rubs her eyes then peeks over at me.

"Sorry," I say sheepishly. "You were just so knocked out that I figured a little bass wouldn't bother you."

"Where are we?" Riley asks, peering through the window.

"You're almost home." I sigh. "Not sure if I can hang out with you anymore. MiMi's not too fond of me spending a lot of time with blissheads." I smile over at her.

Riley groans and covers her face with both hands. "I thought I dreamed about that. Ugh."

"Nope, you took that bliss to the head, for real," I tease. "You did a little shimmy for me. Gave me a little compliment."

"Compliment?" Riley drops her hands and looks at me again. "What kind of compliment?"

I feel heat rising to my cheeks. I crack the window some to relieve them. "I don't remember. Something about my lips . . ." I peek over at her. See if the memory will wash over her face. But Riley frowns and shakes her head.

"I don't remember any of that," she says. "I guess that makes me lucky."

A draft comes through the window and what the hell am I doing? It gets too chilly at night to crack the window open even an inch. "Yeah. Guess so," I say. I close the window and shift away from her. It's good that she doesn't remember. It would make this car ride a hell lot more awkward. Still . . . maybe a small part of me liked Riley looking at me like that.

Ugh, stop, Jay. *Stop!* I roll down the window again.

Riley raises her eyebrows at me. "Can't make up your mind, huh?"

I shrug. "I'm just as confused as Virginia's weather."

Riley smiles at me as I pull up in front of her house. "You really didn't have to drop me off first. How are you going to get home?"

I swat my hand at her. "I haven't been driving all my life. I always find a way to get around. Besides, I'm not sure I trust you behind the wheel yet."

"Good point." Riley rubs her eyes again.

"But thanks," I say. For some reason, wanting to prolong these seconds in the car with her. "For getting the car. For driving me to Richmond. For turning into Snoop Dogg back there."

Riley laughs.

"Really . . . not a lot of people have my back like that. So . . ." So what? I have no more words to express how grateful I am for everything Riley's done for me. If she has some ulterior motive, I don't want to know. I just like feeling about her the way I do right now—next to her in the car.

Riley locks eyes with me and she has tiny freckles of green

in her eyes. I never noticed those before. Like tiny flecks of emeralds buried in sand. I blink and unbuckle my seatbelt. "It's late. I should head to the bus stop."

"Jay." Riley's hand is over mine again. Still soft, still the right temperature. "I . . . I remember."

I raise an eyebrow.

"The compliment? About your lips? And . . . I meant it."

My other eyebrow raises, too, along with my pulse. Holy shit. Riley Palmer thinks I have kissable lips. And I think I care about Riley Palmer thinking I have kissable lips. Soon, her body sways toward mine—like a magnet pulling her to me. And my body sways to hers, too, like they both know just what to do without us telling them. Like they were supposed to be doing this all along.

Her mouth comes closer to mine and—holy shit. Holy *shit*. I'm about to kiss Riley Palmer.

A thud on the window sends us both jerking back against our seats.

FIFTEEN

MRS. PALMER GLARES AT US THROUGH THE PASSENGER SIDE window, her face covered with green slime. I'm sure that she'd look just as scary without the face mask—her glare is enough to slice me in two.

Riley takes a deep breath and rolls down her window. "Hey, Mom," she says.

"Don't just 'Hey, Mom,' me. We specifically told you to be home by ten," Mrs. Palmer snaps. I glance over at the clock on the dashboard. 10:03. Guess the Palmers didn't give a damn about traffic. "And why is he behind the wheel?" Mrs. Palmer lasers in on me again and I want to bury myself under my seat. "Do you even have your license, Jay?"

"Yes," I say. Mrs. Palmer's eyes narrow at me. Reminds me of the time she caught me pocketing an extra cookie during Christmas service years ago. "No," I correct. "But I do have my permit." I give her a weak smile. All *see, I didn't* completely *break the law.*

Mrs. Palmer pinches the bridge of her nose, green gunk oozing between her fingertips. "Riley, you know the rules."

"Yes, ma'am. But you know how I feel about driving in the dark, and Jay was kind enough to—"

"You shouldn't even be hanging out with Jay!" Mrs. Palmer flinches, just for a second, as if remembering that I could hear her. Too late. Heat rises to my cheeks again, but not the good kind. This one scorches in a different way. This one feels like shame. "I mean, you shouldn't be hanging out with any boys after dark. You know the rules." Even with her paraphrasing, I get it. She tries making it all about what Riley did wrong, but all I hear is that the wrong is me. I guess I'm good enough to teach Sunday school, but not good enough to be out at night with their only daughter.

"Mom, can we not right now?" I think Riley nudges her head at me. I'm too busy staring down at my hands on my lap. My head feels too heavy to look up.

Mrs. Palmer sniffs Riley then lets out a gasp. "What's that smell? That better not be what I think it is."

"It's not . . . it's incense. The bookstore was having a Caribbean night featuring West Indies authors." The lie comes out of Riley's mouth so smoothly that I should be scared. But nothing's more fearful than Mrs. Palmer at the moment.

"I'm going to stop you right there, Riley Faith, before you get yourself into even more trouble. Get out of the car and get into the house. Now." Mrs. Palmer directs her wrath toward me again: "The Reverend and I will have a word with you tomorrow, Jay."

Great. As if Sunday service isn't suffering enough, now I get to have a private sermon from Reverend Palmer. He'll find some godly way to tell me to go to hell. I nod and get out of the Palmers' car. I don't even say goodbye to Riley because my throat's too tight to let the words come out. Shove my hands in my hoodie's pockets as I trudge down the street toward the city bus stop. Riley and her mom are on the sidewalk behind me, exchanging a few heated words that I can't quite make out. Maybe that's a good thing. I don't know how many more times I can hear Mrs. Palmer tell her daughter how much of a loser I am.

"Jay!" I look over my shoulder and Riley's jogging after me. "Hold up!"

I shake my head at her. "You shouldn't be out here still, Riley. You're in enough trouble."

"It's okay. I told her to give me a minute and that I had to grab the keys from you." She looks behind her to make sure her mom's disappeared into the house, then turns back to me and sighs. "I'm so, so sorry about that."

I shrug, even though it feels as if my shoulders have weights on them. "No worries. I'm used to folks thinking I'm trash. Par for the course when you live in the Ducts."

Riley's face falls as she shakes her head over and over. "No. *No.* It's not personal. Jay, my parents love you. They just don't want me hanging around any guy. They think I'm supposed to live at school and church. School and church. That's it. They're always talking about how they want more for me."

Her words sting more than her mom's glare. "Yeah. Exactly," I say. Of course they want more for Riley. More than Bad News. More than a guy from Bad News. Hell, more than *me*. Period. No matter how proper I speak or how groomed I keep my hair or how I smile at old folks when there's not much to smile about, my own people still look at me like I ain't shit. MiMi's right—can't win for losing. "Look, you've been mad cool, Riley. Way cooler than I deserve. But maybe we should chill out."

If Riley's face went any more slack, it'd be a puddle on the sidewalk beneath us. "Jay . . . don't do this."

"Later, Riley." I turn back around and continue toward the bus stop. I don't check to see if Riley's watching me. If she were, it'd be even tougher to say goodbye. Cutting her loose before she got even more tangled was for the best. Now I just have to find a way to untangle Nic.

✳ ✳ ✳

"Hold on, pass me that mirror," MiMi says, sitting up in her hospital bed. One of the nurses helped her plait her hair into halo braids. Let her borrow some lipstick to make her feel more presentable. Deacon Irving had arranged it so that the local news station would visit me and MiMi in the hospital. Talk about Nic to get the word out. I should be grateful for all his help, but MiMi still hasn't mentioned him paying her an actual visit. Guess he doesn't want the folks in the hospital running their mouths as much as the ladies at church.

I hand MiMi the mirror perched on one of the side tables, buried behind the latest flower arrangement from someone from Providence Baptist. "You look good, MiMi," I insist.

"Like you'd really tell me. One morning you let me go through a whole service with lipstick on my teeth."

"I told you, I didn't notice." Okay, really I was salty about her not letting me go to the movies with Bowie the night before. There had been another shooting so, of course, she kept me on lockdown.

MiMi checks herself in the handheld mirror, then examines me. I had to find one of my button-downs in the back of my closet. The ones I keep on hold for family funerals or Easter service or some other reason that we're in church more than just to see Reverend Palmer prance across the stage. MiMi motions me over then refolds one of my cuffs. "You could've at least run an iron over this."

"I did."

MiMi shakes her head. "I should've shown you better. But you're spoiled, so . . ." She nods, pleased with her fold. "I hope you didn't wear this all day. How was service this morning?"

I chew on the inside of my cheek. Try to keep my face as neutral as possible. "I was feeling under the weather when I woke up. Thought I'd rest up so I could feel better to do this later today." Truth is, I couldn't face Reverend Palmer after getting his precious daughter high last night. Even scarier, though, was seeing Riley again. I didn't know what to say to her after telling her we needed to cool it. And I think it would've hurt even more to see Riley going back to business as usual after the week we had.

MiMi gives me a look, not buying even an ounce of what I'm selling. Thankfully, we're interrupted by a knock on the door. Before I can reach the door to answer, a white older guy with thinning hair and glasses pokes his head through it.

"I'm looking for a Ms. Murphy," he says.

"Came to the right place, darlin'," MiMi says, smoothing out her hair and sitting more upright in her hospital bed.

"Yeah, it's a good thing she was decent," I say to the intruder.

"Excellent." The white guy pries the door all the way open, as if my words didn't reach him at all. A small crew spills into the room, carrying lights and cameras and cases with God knows what, but I'm sure it's needed to make that TV magic.

"Price Bullock," the white guy says, crossing over to MiMi to shake her hand. "Correspondent with WVZY Evening News. Pleasure to meet you."

"Pleasure's all mine," MiMi says, giving her dainty church-lady chin tilt. "Especially if it means you'll get my baby back home."

Price breathes loudly through his nose and clutches his heart, like he's just been struck by an arrow or something. "I have to tell you, Ms. Murphy. Your story's completely compelling. When Deacon Irving called our station and shared it, I just knew I had to be the one to help tell it. We're going to get thousands of pairs of eyeballs out there looking for your Nicole."

For some reason, the way he says Nic's name makes me want to gag. Her name sounds hollow in his mouth, like one of them dud plastic Easter eggs that has jack-squat in it after cracking it open. This Price dude must feel me burning a hole in the back of his head, because he swivels on his heels and plasters on a smile for me.

"And you must be the grandson . . . Jackson, right?" He extends his hand.

I just look down at it. "Jayson."

"Jayson—that's right." Instead of leaving his hand dangling, he reaches out and slaps me on the arm. "That's great for you to support your grandmother like this."

I shrug. "Didn't really have much choice." It's true. MiMi

gave me the time to be at the hospital, then reminded me that she wasn't too weak and I wasn't too old to take a switch to the butt.

Price throws his head back and laughs. His voice bounces off the walls. "I love your community. The toughest-looking guys are always afraid of their moms and grandmoms."

I look down at my button-down shirt, navy slacks, and black loafers I got from Goodwill. If this is tough, then I don't even want to know what he'd think of me in my dad's hoodie.

"Okay, let me give you the rundown," Price continues. "I'll start off in the hall—give my brief intro. Then we'll cut to you and your grandmother sitting together in here. We'll pull your chair right up next to her bed, make the lighting just right for both of you. Then I'll cue you to talk about the last time you've seen Nicole, as well as share some endearing stories about her. I'll be asking the questions but won't be in the shot with you, so make sure you both look straight into the camera. Sounds good?"

"What kind of questions are you going to ask?"

Price stops midway as he heads for the door. I guess he wasn't figuring that I'd actually need clarification. Me just being a tough guy and all. "You know, standard stuff about your sister."

Standard stuff? That seems mighty vague—vague enough to make my stomach jazzy. "All good things, though. Right?"

The rare times that I've seen stories about black youth on the news, it's never really been in a positive light. Even when they're talking about a black kid winning the state science fair, they have to show a picture of him with his pants sagging a little too low.

"Jesus, Jayson, of course." He presses his whole palm against his chest, almost like he's trying to shock his heart back into action. "By what the Deacon says about your family, you have strong values. A lot of love for each other even through thick and thin. I really want to shine a light on that. Appeal to everyone's heart to see if we can't get her home."

"I think that sounds lovely," MiMi says, then swats a lady's hand away from her face. "Baby, I told you. I already put on makeup."

"It's just a little powder, Ms. Murphy," Price explains. He cradles one of MiMi's hands with both of his. "Your spirit and beauty just shine so brightly, we don't want to blind the camera lenses, that's all."

MiMi giggles and gives Price a playful tap on the arm. Price chuckles then winks his eye at me. That wink sends me a thousand red flags, but before I can get through them all, the cameras are ready to roll.

SIXTEEN

AS SOON AS I ENTER YOUNGS MILL HIGH THE NEXT MORN-ing, the air feels different. Thicker almost. Like a dark cloud hangs so low in the halls that I can barely breathe. Students walk through the halls with trepidation, like they're wading through honey. Not the usual Monday morning blahs, but something else. Something that makes it seem painful for most of them to take a step. Punctuate that with the group of girls sobbing and hugging across from my locker, the teachers whispering all solemn-like to each other with their hands folded across their chest. Something's off. Something's way off.

"Yo, what I miss?" I ask the lanky dude pulling out books from the locker next to mine. He told me his name once. Twice, maybe. But I had no need to remember it since we didn't have any of the same classes and he never was a customer.

The lanky guy closes his locker and shakes his head. "A former student got popped over the weekend, I think."

I raise my eyebrows. "Damn, another one? Who was it this time?"

"No clue, man. I just transferred here this year." No wonder I didn't really remember him. At least, that's the excuse I'll give myself. He gives me a subtle head nod before walking away, because that's what you do when you pay respect for the dead—even when you don't know who they are. I think about asking one of the somber-looking teachers for deets when the sound system beeps everyone to attention:

"Morning, Lions," Principal Gilbert begins, speaking slowly like he just downed a couple of Benadryl. "As some of you might know, we lost one of the Pride recently. The counselors will be available in the media center all day if you need extra support. You will not be penalized for missing some of class to grieve. In the meantime, let's all pause and give a moment of silence to our dear friend, Kenny Boyce."

Something thuds at my feet. I look down expecting to see my heart, but it's my books instead. The fick. The *fick*? Kenny is dead? Kenny is DEAD. How is Kenny dead? He's supposed to be off somewhere frolicking with Nic, stealing kisses in some car with the top down like they do in music videos. Kenny is dead?

Wait.

Wait.

Nic left with Kenny. If Kenny is dead, like really dead, then did that mean . . . ?

I run over to one of the trash bins in the hall, but nothing comes up. Just snot and air. Once again, I forgot to grab breakfast this morning, but my stomach doesn't care. It clenches over and over, trying to push anything out. Every time I think it's done, it socks me again. It won't be satisfied until Nic's completely out of my system.

"Are you okay, son?" A teacher's hand is on my back. I stumble away from the trash bin, away from the teacher. I need to find answers. I need to find out what happened to Kenny.

"Do you need me to take you to the nurse?" the teacher asks again. I ignore him and charge down the hall. Don't even know who I'm looking for, but I have to find someone. People talk way too much to not know what went down. Maybe someone tall. Tall usually means basketball player and everyone knows that Kenny played basketball.

Wait—the basketball team.

I book it toward the gym. The coaches' offices are located in the same hall. The team's probably congregating around Coach Dunn. They have to be. My sneakers squeak as I reach the gym's corridor—the faster I get there, the faster I'll get answers. Just as expected, most of the basketball team are in a sad huddle outside of Dunn's office. There's too many of them to fit all the way inside. Dunn is in the doorway, red-faced and sober. Saying something to his team. Probably something sweet about Kenny. Probably something to keep up their morale. It's a tough balance and I certainly don't envy him at the moment.

I crack my knuckles, wait for a way in to get information but don't want to come across as a complete asshole. I needed to find Nic more than anything, but I give them the same respect that I'd hope someone would give me if this was Nic.

I squeeze my eyes shut: please don't let this be Nic.

There's weeping away from the huddle. I open my eyes and spot DeMarcus folded up on the staircase, digging his fist into his open palm. I sneak over to him.

"DeMarcus, man," I force out, throat so tight it's like I'm learning to speak again. "I'm really sorry—"

DeMarcus climbs to his feet and before I can back up, pulls me toward him. My face slams against his chest as DeMarcus weeps again. He wraps his arm around me and weeps, as hiccupy and raw as a child leaving his mom on the first day of school. You could hear the pain in every sob. DeMarcus put on a good show on the court the other day, but it's clear as day now. Kenny meant something to him.

Kenny was his boy. All I can do is wrap my arms around him and give him that moment.

Finally, he pulls away from me, wipes his face on his forearm. "It's all just so jacked up, bruh," he says.

I nod. He's totally right. I wish I could be the guy he needed right now. Give him my shoulder and ear as he told me all his memories about Kenny. And I want to be, but first: "What happened to him?"

DeMarcus blows out breath through his mouth. "They're not even sure yet. The cops found his body down at Deer Park last night. But from what I heard, he's been dead for a while. They took forever to identify him. His parents had to . . . his parents had to . . ." Something guttural leaves DeMarcus's mouth and he strikes at the air. I reach over, pat his back as he tries to get himself together. But I get it. No parent should have to see their child like that.

"We told him," DeMarcus continues. "We told him to keep away from Javon, but that nigga's always been stubborn as hell."

My hand drops. "Javon did this?"

DeMarcus smirks at me. "Like we'd ever know."

I grit my teeth. He's right. About both things. I saw the rage in Javon when Kenny and Nic first took off. I felt what he wanted to do to them if he ever got his hands on them. What if he finally did? But if Kenny's dead then what did that mean for Nic?

My feet take off running. I had to pay another visit to someone. The only person who could probably make sure Nic is okay.

✳ ✳ ✳

"Didn't see you at church yesterday." Officer Rick Ross didn't even bat an eyelash when he spotted me waiting for him in the lobby of his precinct. But after that bomb dropped about Kenny, of course I'd be here.

"I think you and I both know that I have a lot going on right now," I say.

Officer Hunter gives me a nod: *Fair enough.* He then hitches his head toward the back, beckoning me to follow him. But my feet stay planted.

"I don't want a snack," I say. "I want some answers."

"We're in a station, kid. Everyone wants answers." He raises his eyebrows and motions at all the business of the precinct. I had been too laser-focused to scope out anything or anyone else. But now? I spot the nosy officer at the front desk. I spot the guy waiting to be booked on the bench, leaning forward for intel so he could cop a deal. Too many ears out here. And those ears are attached to mouths that might spill wax to Javon.

I give in and follow Hunter back to his break room. "Don't you have school?" he asks. He doesn't ask if I want to take a seat and he doesn't take one, either. He and I both know that there's too much going on for pleasantries.

"Free period," I lie. "So, you weren't going to tell me about Kenny?"

Hunter blinks at me. "I don't believe you have a badge, son. That's the only people I need to bump gums with."

I huff, full of irritation. "Yeah, but you know my sister is missing. You know Kenny used to live in the same neighborhood. And you know who they both have in common. Plus . . ." I brace myself for what I need to say next. " . . . Nic took off with Kenny. They were . . . together."

I can't read Hunter's face. His mouth just quirks to one side as he leans against a vending machine, crosses his arms over his chest.

I throw my hands up as if I can use the force to hitch him into action. "Do I need to spell it out? Javon obviously popped Kenny! He could do the same to my sister unless you guys stop him! I know Nic's not high on the priority list, but someone's dead now. Aren't you guys supposed to stop that from happening again?"

Hunter looks at me as if he's waiting for me to say more. When he realizes I won't, he pushes himself off the vending machine. "We're questioning Javon now."

The words ring so loudly in my ears that I almost think I imagined them. Javon Hockaday is at the station the same time as me. The guy who I know deaded Kenny. The guy who might try to do the same to Nic. "Where is he?" I scan around the breakroom as if he'll magically appear. "He's a pretty slippery guy. He got away with all his crap for this long, you can't let him do the same for this."

"Jay." He clasps a heavy hand on my shoulder. "We have guys in this precinct that've been on the force since before you were born. We've questioned guys even slicker than Javon Hockaday. Now . . . are you going to keep telling me how to do my job, or are you going to *let* me go do my job?"

I step away from his hand. "If you and your guys were doing your jobs, Kenny wouldn't be dead in the first place." I almost wince. Almost. After all, I need him to get Nic back. But because of their casualness about Nic in the first place, another brother is a statistic. Kenny could've been something great. Not anymore. How many Kennys do there have to be in Bad News?

Hunter's jaw clenches as my words sink in. I expect to see his hand flying down to the back of my neck, pushing my face down against the card table to slap some cuffs on me. All because I talked smack. All because he can.

Instead, he opens the door for the breakroom. Motions for me to leave. "Get to school. Your grandmother has enough going on without worrying about your grades."

I pry my feet off the floor, make them move toward the

exit even though there's so much more I want to say. To do. I pause at the threshold, turn back to Rick Ross.

"We got this," he reassures before nodding me out of the station.

I don't return the nod. I can't force my head to agree with something when my heart doesn't.

SEVENTEEN

RETURNING TO SCHOOL TODAY WAS A BIG MISTAKE. IT'S hard to concentrate on sonnets and solution sets when Kenny's no longer breathing and Nic's . . . I don't even know. And it's the not knowing that leaves me edgy, that makes me nod along in class when I can't hear the words coming out of my teachers' mouths. That makes me bump into classmates in the hall because I can't see what's two feet ahead of me. But what the hell else was I supposed to do? Officer Hunter made it clear that I wasn't wanted at the station, and one of the ladies from the church was supposed to bring MiMi home from the hospital at any moment. Last thing she needed to do was catch me cutting class and all up in my feelings. So, school it was.

I at least try to avoid the tears and grief during lunchtime. I don't go to my usual stairwell—Camila had already busted me, so I'm sure others could find me there too. Instead, I retreat to the media center. The counselors had moved their grieving circle to one of the rooms closer to the cafeteria, which meant the people who were here were the usual nobodies that didn't want anyone else to see them sitting alone. My people.

I grab a pack of Doritos out of one of the vending machines to munch on but get so wrapped up on the computer that I barely remember to eat them, pulling up every article I can find about Kenny. Some of them only call him "a body." At least two of them give Kenny's full name and an old yearbook picture of him. Those are the ones that provide more details. The articles describe how some white woman playing Frisbee with her dog found Kenny's body. She had tripped over what she thought was a tree root but was actually Kenny's hand poking out of the ground. Sounds like one of those horror movies. A guy buried alive and tries to crawl his way back to the surface but loses air right at the last moment.

But this isn't the movies. According to the police, it's believed that Kenny had been dead for a few days, but an autopsy would confirm it. Even before the autopsy, though, foul play is suspected. No shit. I highly doubt that Kenny would take a stroll in Deer Park to off himself, but somehow managed to dig his own gravesite, too. I wonder if Riley heard the news. She'd know just what to say to ease my mind before it got too uneasy. I wanted to text her as soon as I left the precinct, but figured she was in class. I already got her into enough trouble with her parents—and I didn't want her teachers to look at her any differently.

I scroll back up one of the articles, stare at Kenny's yearbook picture. It had to be a couple of years ago—maybe when he was in tenth grade. He shows all his teeth with his smile. His eyes don't focus in on the camera lens. Instead, he's looking somewhere up. As if he's thinking about all the things he can't wait to do after taking that picture. Now, he won't be able to do most of them. It's not fair.

"Hey, Jay." A hand clamps down on my shoulder and I yelp, swivel in my chair with my fists raised. Bowie raises both hands, lets me see they're empty, as he takes a step back. "Relax . . . it's just me," he says.

I breathe out through my mouth, try to get my pulse to slow down, then turn back to the computer. "How'd you know that I'd be in here?" I close out the browser, hope Bowie didn't scope out what I was scoping.

"Missy Johnston spotted you."

I smirk. "She's forever in somebody's business."

"And she's forever trying to pull somebody in hers. Remember how she made that whole dance last year about her missing handbag?"

"But it's FEND-I," Bowie and I both mock, giving our best valley girl impression. The guilt sets in before I can even laugh. Kenny's dead, Nic's God knows where, and I'm throwing jabs at an entitled classmate.

Bowie gets the guilt memo, too. He lets out a laugh through his nose that's about five notches below his usual volume and pulls up a chair next to me. Great. Somehow our Missy bashing turned into an invite for him to join me. "Messed up about Kenny, huh?"

Dammit. Maybe he did catch my snooping. I shrug, play it off. "Just another day in Bad News."

"Still, it has to be weird for you. Wasn't he tight with Nic?"

I almost forgot how aware he is about everything. Even though he's never been in my crib, he knows my family like they're his own. Guess all those late nights playing videogames, he actually listened to my bitching. He leans forward in his seat now to do more of the same, ready to be an open ear for me. But we don't have a videogame to distract us. And Nic has done more than just leave her dirty dishes in the sink overnight. She's gotten herself missing. The more I tell Bowie, the more he'd stack me up as another hood horror story. Plus, now that I know Kenny's wound up dead, I have to keep Bowie an extra arm's length away.

"Yeah." I open up the internet browser on the computer

again, click on one of the bookmarked pages to keep myself busy. TMZ? Sure, I'll roll with it. "But the police are on it. It's all good."

Bowie blinks at me. "All good? Jay, she's been gone over a week, right? What if she's seen what happened to Kenny? What if she—"

"They're on it, Bowie." If I could say the period aloud, I would. He needs to drop it, and he needs to drop it now.

Bowie slinks back in his seat, finally catching my drift. "Well, I want to help out. Maybe we can put something up on The Gram. People do it all the time. I saw one up there the other day about this old dude that wandered off. He had dementia or something. Anyways, I think they found him like twelve hours after posting his pic. He was chilling in a Hardee's. What's up with old people and Hardee's?"

Bowie laughs but it sounds like static to me. He wants to put Nic's business all up on social media? Like anybody's going to pay attention to some missing black girl in between posts of someone's dog napping on their lap and a sepia-toned pic of a homemade cheeseburger.

"I don't know, man," I say. "We got enough going on as it is. Last thing I need is hundreds of fake comments on every black chick with braids. You know how some people can't tell us apart." I wince as soon as I say it. Bowie's in my grill so much that it's hard not to group him with "us"—even when

I try to keep him at a safe distance.

But Bowie shrugs like he's helping water roll off his back. "A false lead is more than you got now, though, right?"

I sigh. Bowie's the type of guy who needs to feel needed. Always the first to volunteer to pass out papers for teachers. Always the last to get back to class after a fire drill for helping out the students with special needs. It's like he dyes his hair all these crazy-ass colors to remind us he isn't a saint. So yeah, he won't let this social media thing go. And maybe he has a point. Even though he doesn't have the most followers, there'll still be more eyeballs on Nic than what the cops currently have.

"Okay. Sure," I mumble. Don't want to be too enthusiastic because I'm not a thousand percent in.

That's good enough for Bowie, though. He claps his hands together like he finally killed a gnat that's been bugging him. "Awesome. I'll get right on it. Oh, and I know you have a lot going on right now, so take this." He digs in his pocket and pulls out an envelope. I peek inside and find a couple of folded up twenties. "It's our take over the week. I took care of all the transactions—even was able to knock out a paper on Napoleon. I never want to do that again." He laughs again. "But yeah, I didn't take my cut this week. It's all yours."

He taps me on the arm and I immediately flinch. I know Bowie means well. He always means well. But the last thing

I need right now is to be his damn charity case. "Thanks," I say through gritted teeth. If I open my mouth farther, something might slip out that I'll regret later. "But now I really have to get back to this." I nod to the computer.

Bowie glances over at the screen and spots breaking news about some Hollywood A-list couple breaking up. He and I both know I could give a damn, but he catches my drift with both hands. "I'll post something before the next bell." He gives me one last look before leaving me with my celebrities. I think about dumping the money somewhere in the media center, but MiMi's coming home today. And she needs to retire.

✳ ✳ ✳

I barely get an hour home with MiMi before the Old Lady Gang from Providence Baptist steals her away. It's for a good cause, though. They want to make her a home-cooked meal to celebrate her return. But while everyone's stuffing their faces, the Old Lady Gang puts folks to work. Making more flyers for Nic, making phone calls for Nic. Anything they can do to find Nic. Plus, me and MiMi's news clip is premiering tonight, so the gathering also triples as a viewing party. Since the congregation was rallying for the family this much, MiMi said I needed to tag along. Pay my respect. So here I am. Sitting on Sister Gladys's plaid living room couch, poking at a plate of baked ham and mac and cheese. Any other time I would tear this plate up, but now? With Kenny lying on a slab and Nic still floating in the wind, this food looks about as appetizing as roasted roadkill.

My phone pokes at me inside my jeans pocket, begging me to go on and pull it out. Text Riley. I haven't spotted her yet at Sister Gladys's—not like I can blame her. I told her we needed to put whatever we were doing on ice, so I couldn't just ask her to thaw and save me from the prying eyes of our congregation. Still, having her sit right next to me would make this whole meal—hell, this whole scene—way more appealing.

"Scoot on over." MiMi taps my leg. I snap to my feet, hold MiMi's arm to help her take a seat. "I got it, baby." She adjusts the pillows behind her, sits all the way back. After catching her breath, she looks over at my plate. "I know Sister Kathy goes a little light on the pepper, but her mac and cheese isn't that bad."

I laugh. "It's not that, it's just . . . it's a lot . . ." I don't even know how to finish. It's a lot of everything and nothing all at the same time. But all of it together is so much that it turns my stomach into a fist.

MiMi pats my knee like she gets it. "It certainly was nice for everyone to make us all this food. There's too much of it. I think I might stop by the Boyce's. Bring them a plate. Lord knows the last thing they need to worry about is cooking right now."

I swallow even though I haven't taken a bite of my food yet. I remember the look of disappointment on Mr. Boyce's face when he talked about all the things his son could've been but wasn't. The hope across Mrs. Boyce's when I spat her some lie about Kenny and a job prospect. I can't imagine what either of them looks like now. I don't think I want to know.

"We're planning the funeral at Providence," MiMi says. "I told the Reverend I would help set up."

"MiMi, you just got back."

She nods. "I know. That's why I said you'd help, too."

I give her a look and she dishes it right back.

"Now you know that's the least we could do for that family. I didn't like who he started hanging around with, but he was a good kid. A *good* kid. And he was always so sweet to Nic. Whenever she'd come storming into the house after some nonsense with Javon, I'd find her on the phone late with Kenny. It's like he wanted to make sure she was okay. That she was home. But now . . ." MiMi's voice breaks and I rest my hand over hers. She blinks back tears and I squeeze her hand, try to help her fight them. But the harder I squeeze, the more I push out more of my own. Without even saying it, MiMi says it. With Kenny gone, what did that mean for Nic? He was the one who made sure she got home safe. If he wasn't here to tether her, where did she drift off to? And is she even able to still drift?

I use my free hand to pinch the bridge of my nose. Try to stop the tears and the thoughts. MiMi rubs the back of my head.

"It's okay," she says. "It's okay. Look around us, baby." She waves a hand at the older ladies making calls at the dining room table. The young kids drawing on flyers at the coffee table. The hustle and bustle of everything. "This is all for us." She pulls my head closer to hers to make sure I look at her. I do. "This is all for Nicole. We're going to find her, baby. We're going to bring her home."

I let out a shaky breath, then peck MiMi on the forehead. I want to believe her. I do. But each time I make traction, I lose my footing. Soon, I'll have nothing left to tread on.

"Hush, everyone!" Sister Gladys calls out, rushing into the living room. "The program's on!" She grabs her remote and unmutes her TV. The intro to WVZY Evening News blares through the speakers, and moments later, we're greeted with Price Bullock's insincere face.

"Imagine this," he says, taking measured steps through the hospital corridor. I'll be glad to never see that place again. "A young girl, a church-going girl, preparing to graduate high school this spring. She has her hopes and dreams lined up in front of her. Will I be a teacher? Will I be a doctor?" I frown at him. Nic never mentioned either. "Now, those questions linger in the air—feared never to be answered. Because this young, beautiful girl, Nicole Marie Murphy, has vanished— just like that." Price snaps his finger and I wait for a rabbit to hop across the screen from his theatrics.

"She's a good girl," the MiMi on the TV screen says

while rocking back and forth in her hospital bed. I sit next to her in my chair, a vein bulging at my temple from chewing the inside of my cheek so hard. Do I walk around looking this pained all the time? "Always has been. Of course, she's made a few bad decisions in her life, but what teenage girl hasn't?"

The screen pauses on MiMi's shrug and the angelic music they were playing screeches to a halt. "But what exactly were those bad decisions?" Price's voice-over asks, all deep and ominous. "Sources say, they have to do with Kenny Boyce—the young man who was just found in Deer Park . . . MURDERED."

Several of the women in the living room gasp as the TV now shows footage of presumably Kenny being wheeled out of the park in a body bag. "Sources also reveal that Kenny was a well-known drug dealer in Newport News, selling, quote, unquote, 'party favors' to all the high school parties. Maybe even selling them to one of your children."

I grit my teeth as the TV now shows a series of the most unflattering pictures they could find of Kenny: him in the background shot of some dude with his face blurred out getting arrested. Him throwing up a peace sign with one hand and holding a can of beer with the other, like it was pulled from someone's social media account. A close-up of his face grimacing, looking as if he was ready to bite's someone face off. I know that last one. It's from the yearbook years ago. If they'd shown the full picture, you'd see him blocking a pass at one of his basketball games. Those bastards.

"So, what does Nicole Murphy have to do with this?" Price asks, now sitting in a newsroom on the screen. "That's what everyone wants to know. My same sources reveal that Nicole and Kenny were dating, but that she was also his biggest customer."

"That's a lie!" Sister Gladys cries out. Then peeks over at MiMi. "Right?"

MiMi's eyes remain glued to the TV, either too stunned or too pissed to comment.

"Sadly, it would be a cycle of drug abuse. Nicole's mother is currently serving a sentence in Northern Virginia for crashing into a police car while driving under the influence." One of my mom's mugshots pops onto the screen. The worst one. The one where her eyes are barely open and her hair's all crinkly with clumps of grease at the roots. She had just taken out braids when she decided to run to the store, pick up another bottle of wine—although she already had a full one in her. Even though the mugshot was awful, she only got a slap on the wrist that time.

"Nicole's father passed away ten years ago from cancer. There is no clear indication of how involved he was with the family prior to his death."

At that, a small noise escapes MiMi's mouth and she clasps a hand over it to muffle the sound. I want to reach out and comfort her, but my skin feels like it's on fire. I'm afraid I'll sear her if I touch her. I'm afraid to touch anything. Even my own leg as it bounces up and down in front of me.

"As for Nicole, all the family can do is pray for her safe return—and answers."

I'm back on the screen again, holding MiMi's hand in the hospital bed. "Yeah, I want her back home," I say. "I'm tired of taking over her dish days." The screen cuts back to Price in the newsroom and I leap to my feet.

"That's not what I meant," I cry out to the screen, knowing damn well Price can't hear me. "He knows that's not what I meant." He left out the part where he told me to tell a joke, something that would get her attention. He left out the full half hour before that, where MiMi and I shared stories about her helping me with homework or her helping MiMi make dinner or how she was on the homecoming court during her freshman and sophomore years. He left out the part where I said I text her every single night, praying that I'll get a response, encouraging her to cut her phone back on.

That asshole made Nic look like some common hood rat, or us some common hood family. I scrub my head in frustration as everyone else passes each other glances and whispers. I hear weeping behind me and MiMi's still on the couch, wiping her eyes. Thankfully, Sister Gladys swoops into my old spot, wraps her arm around MiMi's shoulder. As much as I want to do that, I can't right now. I'm on fire. Good thing I didn't have Price Bullock's address—or else they'd be showing my mugshot across the screen right now. Looking as haunted and warped as my mom.

Some of the ladies' eyes return to the TV, in awe, so I glance at it—both out of fear and fuel. Almost like I want a reason to hunt this Price prick down. The screen shows the yellow tape around the spot in Deer Park where they found Kenny's body.

" . . . and Kenny Boyce's murder is still an open case," Price continues. "The police released a suspect from custody earlier this evening. Anyone with information should contact . . ."

The number he recites turns to humming in my ears. The only words that linger: *released a suspect. Released a suspect.*

Javon Hockaday slipped through the cracks. Again.

EIGHTEEN

WHEN WE GET HOME, I GET MIMI IN THE BED IMMEDIATELY. It's enough that she had to socialize as soon as she got out of the hospital, but then she also had to deal with the emotional exhaustion of watching that smear campaign Price Bullock called news earlier tonight. And to be embarrassed like that in front of the women of her congregation? Sure, they were all hugs and well wishes while we were over at Sister Gladys's, but I know that as soon as we hit the bricks, those gums started bumping. That's what they do.

"It's not right," MiMi says again as I pass her a glass of water to swallow down her medicine. "He promised me he'd get my baby back home. The way he painted her up there? Nobody's going to care if she makes it home in one piece."

"We care, MiMi," I say. "*We're* going to make sure she gets home in one piece." By we I mean I, but I'm not about to add extra worries in MiMi's head right now. "Now go ahead, get some rest."

MiMi takes her pills and I help her lie down. Pull the blanket up to her chin. "I just hope she knows I'm not mad," MiMi says, eyes halfway closed.

"She knows, MiMi. She knows." I peck her on her forehead. By the time I walk over to switch off her light, I can hear her lightly snoring—the day taking its toll on her.

Good.

I grab my bike just as my phone buzzes. I smirk, already knowing what it is. Right after that fake-ass news hit the airwaves, Bowie's post about Nic started blowing up. Only it wasn't leads. The trolls came out in full force. People with no profile pics calling Nic ghetto . . . or worse. Folks posting phony stories about seeing Nic and Kenny strung out together. These assholes even had the nerve to start tagging me in their insults—hence, my buzzing phone. I finally cut off my alerts and push my bike out the door.

Now here I am. Camped out behind a tree in front of Javon's building, waiting for him to make his next move. His Dodge Charger is parked in its usual spot, so I know he's still here. Slim and Quan aren't posted on the stoop. With Javon being released from the police and all today, he probably thinks he needs to lay low for a bit.

But I know Javon. Or at least I know Javon through Nic. He's too antsy to stay in one place for too long, especially when he feels the heat on him. It's just a matter of time before he cracks up and does something stupid. He might've gotten over with the cops again, but he's not pulling the wool over my eyes. He's going to lead me right to Nic.

I glance at the clock on my phone. It's after ten. I've already been out here over an hour and Javon hasn't as much as cut on his bedroom light. What the hell could he be doing? Riley would have something witty to say about the possibilities. Hell, Riley would find some clever way to get into Javon's building to get answers, like dressing up as someone from DoorDash or something. I pull up my contacts and my thumb hovers over her name. I wonder if she saw that trash on the news today. I wonder if she thinks differently about me or my family. Even if her parents feel validated, she wouldn't believe that nonsense. Right? Maybe I should call her just to be sure . . .

There's a loud clatter as the front door of Javon's building flies open, knocks against the brick. I duck farther behind the tree as Javon scurries down the steps of the stoop, face all twisted like somebody's about to get the ass whooping of a lifetime. You'd think a man who got off scot-free for murdering his best friend would be happier—unless he feels like the walls are closing in on him.

He hops in his car and speeds off. I hop onto my bike and

take off after him. I may not have an engine, but the steam in my head is enough to keep me going.

✳ ✳ ✳

I died about five minutes into chasing after Javon with my bike. Thankfully, I had enough strength in my lungs to order an Uber when Javon stopped to gas up his ride. I type a random destination in and get the driver to meet me across the street from the gas station. I tell him to follow Javon. That he's my friend and I'm worried. I'll change the route and pay him for wherever we end up. The driver nods and does what he's told. As long as he gets paid, he'd follow Javon to Arizona. Hopefully it won't cost me that much.

Javon zigzags through lanes, floors it on yellow lights. Only pausing at stop signs. It's like he doesn't care that the cops have their eyes on him. He's a man on a mission, but so am I. And so apparently is Yusef, my Uber driver, who keeps up with Javon as if he reenacts car chases as a side gig.

We reach the outskirts of uptown Newport News—closer to the Yorktown or Williamsburg area of the city lines. The part of Newport News where the houses get bigger, the cars get sleeker, and the residents get whiter. Javon finally turns into a neighborhood where a wrought iron gate holds up a sign in fancy cursive lettering: Feather Fork Homes. Feather Fork? Why does that sound familiar?

"I'll take it from here," I say to Yusef from the back seat.

"You sure? I don't think he's spotted me yet." Yusef's eyes dance in the rearview mirror. I guess I'm the highlight of his evening, but his bright yellow Toyota doesn't necessarily bleed into the night. If I needed to see what Javon was up to, I had to be stealthier.

Yusef pulls up alongside a curb and I yank my bike out of his trunk. Take off behind Javon before my ass is even on the seat. He finally slows down a bit and my legs thank him for the break. I ease up on them, make sure to keep a safe distance so he won't spot me. Javon turns down one more street until he reaches a cul-de-sac, pulls his car alongside the curb of the house on the end. I park my bike behind an SUV about half a block away. Massage my legs a bit while I wait on Javon's next move.

Javon doesn't leave the car. Just flicks on his interior light as he punches something furiously into his phone. I glance over at the house and take it all in. Columns near the front entrance. Wooden stairs leading to a second-floor deck at the side of the house. A birdhouse in the front yard in the same style as the main home. I suck in a breath. I know exactly where we are. I rode with MiMi over here a few times before, picking up a reluctant Nicole after not telling MiMi she decided to spend the night.

The front door opens and Sterling spills out of the house,

wearing a sweatshirt, tiny cotton shorts, and some fuzzy bedroom slippers. I duck lower as she looks around the neighborhood. Finally, her eyes laser in on Javon's car.

"What the hell are you doing here?" she asks, flailing her arms behind her toward her house.

"Get your ass in here!" Javon barks from inside the car. Sterling folds her arms across her chest and holds her head up high, just like a blonde girl that's been handed everything in her life. Javon leans forward and pushes open the passenger door. Sterling peeks back at her house again, then sighs and enters the car, closing the door timidly behind her.

Javon's arms thrash around as he says whatever he says to Sterling. Her arms respond in the same fervor, going at it in some manic dance battle. I don't get it. Why the hell is Javon so pissed at Sterling? Sterling's tagged along with Nic to a few of his parties or whatever, but Nic never mentioned them saying more than two words to each other. Almost like they had some unspoken agreement that they only tolerated each other because of Nic. Just like me and Javon.

Javon leans over and gets right in Sterling's face. His words come out more hushed, but his anger hasn't muted. I can tell by the way his head seems to bob after every other word. I need to get closer. I have to find out what's going on. If Nic is the only thing these two have in common, there's only one thing they both could be arguing about right now—and that's wherever the hell Nic could be.

I peel off my bike, squat down real low even though my quads scream at me. I do some strange duck shuffle toward the back of Javon's car, keeping my head down so I can't be spotted in Javon's rearview mirror.

"I know, Von," I think I hear Sterling say. Von? That sounds rather friendly for people that were just acquaintances. "You really think I'm that stupid?"

I can't make out what Javon says, but by Sterling's gasp, I'm guessing the answer is yeah. He thinks she's pretty damn stupid.

"I can't believe you," Sterling continues. Thankfully this girl hasn't learned the art of whispering. "After all this, you really think that about me?"

Javon makes a noise. A cough. A scoff, maybe? Damn, where's Riley when I need her? She'd MacGyver her way into picking up sound from Javon's end. Maybe if I called him, he'd pick up. Be too pissed to hang up the phone on me and I could catch the rest of the action. Wait, did I even have Javon's number?

Sterling's front porch lights cut on and I scurry away, dive back behind the SUV. My chin scuffs across my tire and I clutch my mouth to stifle my groan. I look down at my hand and a few droplets of blood have gotten on the sleeve of my hoodie. Dammit.

I hear tires screech, and I look up through the SUV window in time to see Javon speeding off. Sterling's left in her front yard, literally eating Javon's dust. I watch her watching him until his taillights fade away. Finally, she lets out a sigh and hurries back inside her house.

"It's just me, Dad!" she shouts before she closes the front door behind her, and the house swallows her whole. I climb to my feet, stare at her house. Nic might not be in there, but the person who knows her whereabouts definitely is. And the other one just left.

NINETEEN

I THOUGHT I MIGHT BUMP INTO STERLING IN THE HALLS at school the next day. Sure, she'd probably ignore me—probably have Meek draped around her like an angry shawl—but maybe I could pull her aside. Get something from her that would tell me what the hell is going on. But I never saw her. Word in the hallways is that she was out sick. How convenient.

I won't get my chance the following morning, either, because today I'm taking the day off. Though, I must admit, I'd much rather be stuck in the classroom than do what I have planned today. MiMi parks her car in the parking lot of Providence Baptist, lets out a heavy sigh. It was tough to find a spot since there were so many other folks here already.

And sitting front and center at the entrance of the church is a black hearse. The vehicle that will be transporting Kenny to his final resting place after the service.

I look down so I won't have to stare too long at it. As if avoiding eye contact with the car would make Kenny's death less real. Less certain. Instead, I adjust a button on my shirt. A similar button-down to the one I described to the Boyces—dishing out fake promises about their son and his future. I don't know what to even say to them today. Hell, I don't even know how I can look them in the eyes today.

"You ready?" MiMi asks me.

"Not really," I say. I button and unbutton, then button the same spot again. Just to keep my hands busy. MiMi places her hand over mine to relax them.

"Me neither," she says. "But it's important that we be here for his family. For Nic." She squeezes my hands then opens her door, in a rush to get out of the car before things got too heavy inside. As if things were lighter out here. I get out, too, and we trudge toward the entrance. There's already a line of Kenny's loved ones trickling toward the door. Some weeping openly, some wearing shades to mask their grief. I don't see Mr. and Mrs. Boyce. They must already be inside. Taking a quiet moment to be with their son one last time before they have to share him with everyone else. Near the start of the line, I scope out Doug. He wears all black. His hair is cut so short that he's almost bald. An older woman muffles her face inside of his shirt while he rubs her back. His mom, maybe. Doug looks straight ahead, his face stretched into stillness. As if he's trying to hold back anything he could possibly be feeling at the moment. His eyes land on me and I almost look away. Like maybe that moment between him and his mom was too intimate to witness. But Doug gives me a soft nod. A thank you for representing. I return the nod and tap my fist against my chest: *Of course.*

"Did any of you get a program yet?"

My eyebrows automatically hitch up. It's been too long since I heard that voice, but I know it like a favorite song now. Riley makes her way down the line, passing out programs to all the attendees while they wait to be seated. Every now and then she pauses to give someone a comforting rub on the arm, or a gentle hug. And you can tell by the way she lingers with either act that she's not just doing it because she's the Reverend's daughter. She's doing it because she's all light inside, and she wants to share it with others on their darkest day.

"She looks lovely," MiMi says, watching Riley make her way over to us. Riley locks eyes with me and I don't look away.

"Yeah," I say, not even able to play it off. It's not like she's had a makeover for Kenny's funeral. Her hair is still slicked up into a ponytail. She wears a long black dress that hits just above her ankles. She does, though, trade her Converses for a pair of low heels. But even though every feature looks the same on Riley, it's like I finally got all the sleep out of my eyes and am getting the full picture. Every elegant curve and angle.

"Hey." Riley smiles when she reaches me and MiMi. Passes MiMi a program. "Wow, you look great, Ms. Murphy. I'm so glad you're doing better."

"Thank you, baby. The good Lord wasn't ready to take me." MiMi's mouth quirks as soon as the words leave it. Wrong time, wrong place. Riley gives her an understanding smile before leaning over to hug her.

"It's certainly nice for you to help out like this," MiMi says to her.

"Well, I figure it's the least I can do. This whole situation is so sad." Riley looks over at me. "How are you holding up?" By the way her forehead crinkles in the middle, I know she's not just talking about Kenny.

"As much as I can," I admit. It feels good not to dish out lies to that question. I couldn't do that with Riley. Not after the week we've had. "Hey . . . let me help you with that. I'll be back, MiMi."

MiMi gives me a knowing eyebrow raise. "Mmm hmm," she practically sings.

I step out of the line and Riley and I walk toward the parking lot, away from the prying ears of Kenny's friends and family.

"I wanted to call you when I found out," Riley says, once we're at a safe distance. "I really wanted to. I just didn't know if you wanted me to."

"I shouldn't have wanted you to call, but . . . it felt weird each day you didn't."

Riley flips through the programs, obviously embarrassed.

"But that's on me, though," I quickly add, touching her hands to calm them down. Thankfully, she doesn't pull away. "I'm the one that told us to cool it. So, I should've been the one to pick up the phone to ask if we could thaw out."

Riley gives me another smile, but then blinks it away. Again, wrong place. Wrong time. "Did the cops say anything to you and MiMi after they found Kenny?"

I roll my eyes. "Just that they had Javon in for questioning. But nobody had the decency to let us know that he was released. I had to find that out on the news." I clench my teeth, remembering that smear job Price Bullock pulled on my family. What I would do to run across him in a dark alley.

Riley sighs and shakes her head. "That was a disgusting piece," she says. Knowing that Riley watched that trash makes me want to crawl in a gutter. Right where pricks like Price think I belong. "Even my parents thought so."

That should give me some peace, knowing what her parents thought about me. But still, I can't help but wonder how much of it they thought was true. "But check this," I say, trying to push the thought out of my head, "I followed Javon the other night."

Riley's mouth drops. "You *followed* Javon? Do you know how crazy that sounds?"

I shrug. "I learned from the best." If Riley could blush, she would at that moment. "And guess who he paid a visit to late at night?"

Riley leans forward, hungry for my response.

"Sterling—Nic's bougie best friend. They had some kind of heated exchange in Javon's car."

"Whoa. What do you think that was about?"

"I don't know. Sterling went MIA on me, and it's not like Javon's going to give me a straight answer. But you should've seen them, Riley. The way they were going at it . . . it was almost like they were trying to hide something they don't want getting out."

"Then we'll get it out of them."

Just as I'm about to shake my head to protest, Riley reaches out and grabs my arm.

"You can't get rid of me. I got your back through this. You know that, right?"

I sigh. I want to push her away, but Riley is right. I can't shake her off. She was already in too deep. She needed answers just as much as me. Not for herself, but for *me*. I know I can count on her. "Yeah," I say. I take her hand, lace my fingers through hers. We stare at each other just as a car horn honks. Riley and I both jump as an angry arm waves at us out the window of a Cutlass Classic. Apparently, we're in the last available parking space.

"I should get back to this," Riley says, pointing to the growing line of attendants outside of the church. "Catch up with you later?"

I smile at her. "Don't have a choice, right?"

We head back to the line as it slowly makes its way inside the church. As soon as I get back to MiMi, she weaves her arm through mine. Takes a breath to ready herself. I do the same.

It's beautiful inside, but the Palmers always do it right for their funerals. There are huge flower arrangements anchoring either side of the stage. Two large pictures of Kenny set up on easels. Nice ones, ones that look like him—not those trashy ones on the news painting him as some kind of Bad News thug. One is the younger picture of him with the missing teeth I saw on the Boyces' coffee table. The other a more recent one of Kenny. He's hugging his mom tightly, bending over to kiss her on the forehead while she beams at the camera. So proud to have a son who's not embarrassed to still show her love like that.

But my heart really hits the floor when I spot the casket. A silver one, just underneath the pulpit. It's closed, which makes sense based on how DeMarcus described Kenny's remains. A velvet cover and another flower arrangement sit on top of it, right at the center. Kenny's underneath all that pretty dressing. Sleeping but not, peaceful but not. Kenny won't be able to rest in peace until his murder is solved. Hell, none of his family will be able to either.

I take in a shaky breath as MiMi and I slide into one of the pews. I finally spot Mr. and Mrs. Boyce at the front of the church, already seated in the first row. Mr. Boyce's shoulders shake violently, the sobs leaving his body in angry bursts. Mrs. Boyce tries to be the strong one, rubbing his back and shushing him. I know that role must be tough for her to take on right now, but she plays it for her husband. For her son. This service is going to be too much to handle.

It starts off beautifully. One of Kenny's female cousins goes on the stage to sing "His Eye Is on the Sparrow." Her voice soars in all the right places, and breaks when everyone else is just about to, as well. But it's the good kind of sorrow. The kind that makes mostly everyone in the congregation leap to their feet and raise their hands up toward the sky, as if they're trying to send Kenny to the place we all hope he's going. Reverend Palmer and I aren't the best of friends, but the man also knows how to bring down the house. He shares some of the Boyces' memories about Kenny before leading into a sermon about forgiveness. How we needed to forgive Kenny during his moments of weakness and forgive those that took advantage of his weakness. At that, MiMi climbs to her feet with others, shouts out an "Amen!" loud enough for Kenny to feel it.

Reverend Palmer wipes the sweat from his brow as he invites people who want to say a few kind words about Kenny to walk up to the pulpit. Some of the guys from the Youngs Mill basketball team walk up to the front, with DeMarcus and Rico leading the charge. Rico really cleaned up for today's service. He still has beads in his hair, but the colors are more muted. Mainly clear and black, all out of respect for Kenny. DeMarcus unrolls Kenny's team jersey and lays it across his casket. I ball my fists, try to stab what little fingernails I have into my palms—preferring to feel physical pain instead of grief.

"Kenny was our boy," DeMarcus says, clearing his throat so that he can continue. "We all knew that he was the best on the team, but he'd never let anyone say it. 'We're a team,' he'd always say. I remember the time when he could've broken a district record for the most three-pointers in one game. But instead, he used that opportunity for himself to pass the ball to me. I hadn't gotten much floor time that season, so he wanted to—"

There's a loud clank in the back of the church as the door swings open. Sunlight spills into the room and just as my eyes adjust, I see Javon strolling in—wearing a button-down with black jeans. My nostrils flare and I can feel the heat pouring out of them. The hell is he doing here? He's like one of those creepy killers in the movies. The ones that like to return to the scene of the crime to gloat. The gasps spread through the congregation like wildfire once people realize who it is.

"Oh, hell naw!" Doug leaps to his feet, ready to take action, but other family members rush over to him. Speak in hushed tones as they sit him back down. Doug rocks angrily back and forth in his seat but doesn't turn back around.

Javon seems unfazed by the whole exchange. He blinks a few times at Kenny's pictures, then squeezes into an empty space in one of the back rows.

"Uh . . . yeah. Kenny will be sorely missed," DeMarcus stammers. He and the rest of the team awkwardly return to their seats. Javon's presence has thrown a wrench in everyone's grief. And the clumsiness continues throughout the rest of the service. Others that come up to share their stories pause, sneak glances to the back of the church. Even though I don't follow their eyes, I know who they're scoping out: Javon. At the end of the service, the choir stands up to send us out with "Take Me to the King." The vocals are just as rousing as Kenny's cousin's from earlier, but there's a new-found heaviness in the air. When we rise to our feet now, it's not to celebrate Kenny's life—it's to wait for our turn to head out to the cars. Follow the procession to his gravesite.

Kenny's family trails down the aisle first. Mrs. Boyce and someone else have to hold Mr. Boyce up, his sorrow making it impossible to walk in a straight line. As Mrs. Boyce wipes away tears with her free hand, she gives a gentle nod to some of her loved ones as she passes their pews. I look down at my shoes. I'm not ready to exchange glances with her just yet. For some reason, even though I'm not the one that ditched Kenny in Deer Park, I can't help but feel like I helped put him in there. If only I let his parents know the real deal, that Kenny took off and no one knew where to find him, maybe they'd have an opportunity to get him back home.

MiMi gives me a tiny nudge to let me know that it's our pew's turn to file out of the church. I help her out to the aisle and we wade our way to the door. Unfortunately, Mrs. Boyce and some older gentleman stand by the exit, hugging and shaking hands with other mourners. Mr. Boyce probably finds this moment too painful to participate. I can't really blame him. I take a deep breath. What am I supposed to say to Mrs. Boyce? Do I just shake her hand, peck her on the cheek like nothing's happened at all? Or do I apologize and risk explaining to her and MiMi why I'm apologizing? As we near the exit, my body jerks and I step out of the line. MiMi blinks at me.

"I have to tie my shoes," I say to her. "I'll catch up with you." I pray that MiMi doesn't look down at my tightly tied shoes. But she nods and makes her way over to Mrs. Boyce, ready to say and do all the right things. I sigh and lean forward to at least poke at my shoe, make it seem like I'm busy to anyone that caught wind of my explanation. Suddenly, I feel a pair of rough hands clamping down on my shoulders, dragging me backward. Before I can even cry out for help, I'm being hurled into the bathroom.

My side slams against the tiled wall. Just as I catch my breath, Javon steps forward with a frown tattooed across his whole face. Makes me grateful that we're already in the bathroom. Still, my body acts on instinct. I ball up my fists, lift them close to my face. I'm not going to let him get a hold of that again. Javon smirks at me and slaps my hands down like he's batting away a mosquito. Well, damn.

"You think I'm blind?" he snaps at me. "I saw you trailing me the other night."

Well, *god*damn. I clench my fists again and stand up straight, try to get as tall as him. "I don't know what you're talking about. I was just out riding my bike. It's a free country, right?"

The air gets knocked out of me and I crumple at my waist. Grab onto my stomach that burns like it just ate a bullet. Only when I peek up at Javon through teary eyes do I see that his fists are also clenched. This mofo punched me in the stomach.

"Don't get cute," he warns. He pulls me up so that I'm eye-level with him. Gets so close to my face that I smell his aftershave. "And don't pull that shit again. Back. Off." He pokes me in the chest with enough fervor to send my back against the wall again. Then he's out the door in a second like nothing happened.

I hobble over to the sink, catch my reflection in the mirror. My face all crooked in pain. Kind of like Javon's when he ambushed me just now. There was some discomfort behind that rage. No wonder folks like Price Bullock always group us together. We both have a way of hiding our angst with anger. I splash some cold water on my face. Wash away the fear. Only it seems like I'm not the only one that's afraid. Javon must know I'm close to something . . . but what? Sterling definitely knows.

And I think I know how I can get to her.

TWENTY

"JAY! I'M SO GLAD YOU DECIDED TO JOIN US!" MRS. CHUNG greets me in front of her classroom. The final bell has just rung, but you couldn't tell from all her pep. As if seven and a half hours of dealing with teens wasn't enough, she signed up to be an advisor for the lit magazine after school. I almost feel bad that I'm here under false pretenses. *"Run of the Mill* can certainly use some fresh ideas," she continues, escorting me into her class as if I wasn't in here all last year for tenth-grade English. She waves her hands toward the four students already camped out in desks. "Everyone, this is Jay Murphy. I'm sure most of you know each other."

I nod to the group. "Yeah. What's up," I ask, but I laser in on just one of them. Sterling. She looks up at me from her phone, her eyes widening for a brief moment. Like it just hits her that I'm really here. It's going to be tough to not have a conversation with me now, even though she's been avoiding me like the plague all day.

"We were just talking about our upcoming winter issue," Mrs. Chung explains. "It'll be the first one this school year. We're off to a late start, but quality is better than quantity, am I right? We were working in small teams. Brooks and Tasha were reviewing some of the early submissions. Evan was helping me take a look at some potential covers—"

"And what are you doing, Sterling?" I ask. Sterling and Mrs. Chung both glance at me. I give a shrug. "I know Mrs. Chung was thinking about us being co-editors. Figure we get on the same page, right?"

Sterling doesn't respond. Just sets down her phone and returns to her open laptop on her desk. Brooks and Tasha look at each other and snicker. I'm coming across as one of these thirsty dudes trying to get at Sterling, but I don't care how I look right now. Sterling and I are going to have a chat one way or another.

"I think that makes perfect sense," Mrs. Chung answers for Sterling. "She was getting started with the letter from the editor. You both should take a crack at it." She motions for me to join Sterling but I'm already two steps ahead of her. I push another desk right up against Sterling's until they're kissing, then plop down next to her.

"Hey," I say, all calm and casual like we chitchat every day. "One of the first things we need to do is change the name of this lit mag. I mean, we can't have other schools thinking that we all rock Uggs and Aeropostale while sipping high-end cappuccinos, right?"

Sterling ruffles in her seat some and pulls a document up on her laptop. "So, I was thinking about using the theme 'Chill.'" She gets right into it. Doesn't even look at me or exchange any pleasantries. It's clear she doesn't want to *talk* talk with me, so I have to play this real slick. "You know, this being a winter issue and all. Maybe we could get into all the iterations of the meaning of chill. Like cooling off, or hanging out with your friends . . ."

I nod, smile. Catching everything she's throwing. "Or relaxing. And make some kind of mention about how one of the best things to do when it's chilly outside is to get real cozy with something warm to drink and something good to read."

Sterling finally glances over at me, her face glowing. "I like that. That's good." She makes a note of something in her laptop.

"You do? You know, I could take a look at what you have so far. Maybe give some feedback on where we could fit that in."

Sterling rubs her thumb against one of her fingers, as if she's trying to read my bullshit meter through touch. She gives a nod and shifts her laptop to my desk. I scroll through her rough draft, but my eyes shift to her menu bar below. It'd be so easy to click on her browser. See what she's searched for before. Filter through her email and type in Nic's name. Log in to her social media accounts to see her private messages. But Sterling hovers over me so close that her hair tickles my forearm. She may be willing to work with me, but she damn sure's not leaving me alone with her top-of-the-line laptop. After all, Nic's only her token black friend. That doesn't mean she has to trust Nic's black brother in a hoodie.

I force myself to concentrate on the words in front of me until I can read them as full sentences, and not just words floating in front of my eyes. I point to a spot in her paragraph. "See, right here. You mention something about fireplaces. This would be the perfect segue."

Sterling leans even farther over me to review the sentence, then nods. "You're right." She takes her laptop back and my heart drops. "You know, you might be actually good at this." One side of her face lifts as she begins to type. Not exactly a smile, but all she's willing to give me for now.

"Yeah . . . that used to be me and Nic's favorite thing to do during winter break," I say, cracking my knuckles so my voice won't crack instead. "We'd go to the bookstore, the one with the Starbucks inside of it? Sip on one of those holiday drinks while we'd flip through pages. I think one time we sat in the café for so long that I finished an entire book without paying for it. Felt bad for the author, though." I force out a small laugh.

Sterling's fingers pause and hover over the keyboard. Her mouth shifts slightly as if she's primed to say something, but then her fingers fly over the keys again.

I sigh through my nose. Let's try being just a little more direct. "It's crazy she's been gone so long, right?" I make sure I really make it sound like an innocent question, raising my voice so high near the end I could pass for Mickey Mouse. "I mean, this doesn't really seem like her."

Sterling chews on her lip. Her eyes remain on the screen but at least she stops typing. *Let me push a little more.*

"She hasn't reached out to you recently, right?" I ask.

Sterling's eyes snap over to me. "You'd hear from her more than I would. You're her brother."

I nod. "That's what I'd assume. But you two seem so close. Sometimes it's easier to talk to friends than family."

Sterling sighs and shakes her head. "Sorry. Haven't talked to her in ages."

I search for a tell. A muscle twitch, a wandering eye. Something to let me know that she's not being one hundred percent truthful. I get nothing, though. "What about Javon? Has he heard from her?"

Any sympathy coming from Sterling's face has morphed into something bitter. "How in the hell would I know?" she asks.

Holy shit. I hit a nerve. Tread lightly, Jay. "I don't know. I thought you all kicked it or something."

"Ew, no." Sterling looks around the classroom, but everyone is busy doing what they're supposed to be doing at their respective desks. "Not like that. I'd see Javon when I had to see him, and that was through Nic. You think I'd hang around a guy like that?" She scoffs to make a point.

Wow. Whatever she and Javon were talking about in the car was so intense that she can't even admit that she speaks to him when Nic's not around. What in the hell is going on? "Of course not," I say. "I just figured that—"

"Look, I'd like to get as much of this done as possible. I have to leave exactly at three thirty. How about you work on something, I work on something, then we combine them later. Sounds good?" She doesn't wait for my input. Just digs her foot into the floor to push her desk away from mine, then buries her face into her laptop. Conversation over.

I rub my forehead in frustration, knowing I've rammed into another wall.

✳ ✳ ✳

I give a wave to Joshua Kim as I make my way out of Taco Bell. He gives me a distracted smile before fiddling with the cash register. As soon as I step out of the door, my wave mutates into the middle finger. Not necessarily to Joshua, though he can take some of it, too. To coming home smelling like refried beans. To minimum wage. To wasting hours in the evening here when I could be finding out what's going on with Nic.

Not like that would be any more productive, though. I got nowhere with Sterling. I got nowhere with Officer Hunter. Kenny's friends and family were just as lost as, well, Nic. And the guy with all the answers likes pulling sneak attacks on me in church bathrooms. I keep failing Nic. I'm officially the worst brother in the world.

As I cross the parking lot toward the city bus stop, a dark car pulls in front of me. A Lincoln Continental. A smile crawls over my face as Riley pokes her head out of the driver's side window.

"I officially have forty-two minutes," she says to me, then holds up a Chinese food carton. "And I figured you might be a little tired of eating leftover cheesy gorditas for a late supper."

I sniff the air. "Do I smell shrimp fried rice?"

"You're actually smelling house special fried rice. A whole smorgasbord of meat and seafood. Not to mention some greasy egg rolls and a warm Diet Mountain Dew to wash everything down."

I sigh extra loud. "Sorry. I only drink Mountain Lion."

"I'll keep that in mind next time." She gets out of the car and unfolds a blanket over the hood. "After you, sir." She motions for me to take a seat.

"You first. I insist," I say. I grab her hand and help her

climb onto the hood. I sit next to her and she passes me my food and chopsticks. She even hands me soy sauce packages for extra seasoning. I look down at my food, at her blanket . . . at Riley.

She stops pinching at her rice with chopsticks then smiles up at me. "What?" she asks.

I smile back. *This is really nice,* I want to tell her. *You really went all out for me,* I want to add. "I take it your parents don't know where you're at," I say instead.

"Not true. I told them I was picking up food." She pokes at her food again. "Granted, I told them I was picking up food to bring to Bible study, but still . . . I'm eating."

I shake my head and laugh.

"Also," Riley continues over my laughter, "my parents only told me not to have boys *in* the car. Technically, I'm following directions."

"Something tells me you're going to end up in law school."

Riley makes a face. "Ugh. Could you imagine me as a lawyer? I'd either always want to throw the book at people or get them off with a slap on the wrist. There'd be no gray area with me. I'm extreme like that."

"You don't say."

Riley nudges me with her arm. "What about you?"

"What about me?"

"What do you want to be when you grow up, Jay Murphy?"

I take a huge gulp of my food—enough to keep my mouth busy for a few extra seconds. Enough to make Riley want to move on to another topic. But she peers at me, patience all over her face. I swallow. "I'm going to manage a Taco Bell."

Riley rolls her eyes at me. "Ha. Ha."

"Being extreme's not so bad," I say, wanting the spotlight back on her. Exactly where it should be. "It would make you a dope-ass detective. You have more skills than any of the idiots working in the stations around here. There would probably never be any cold cases in your precinct."

Riley blushes. "I wouldn't say I have the skills. It's just easy to pick up on information when everyone ignores you. They talk around you as if you're not there."

I blink at her. "Riley, anyone would be crazy to ignore you."

Riley tilts her head at me. Gives me a look. "Remember that time back in, like, fifth grade? The church had that Trunk or Treat event the night before Halloween?"

I frown, trying to remember which specific Trunk or Treat she's talking about. I didn't like any of them. I didn't see the point of wasting my Halloween costume with some lames at church when I could be hitting the streets in the bougie neighborhoods, collecting at least two pillowcases filled with candy.

"I was Mal from *Descendants*. You were a Ninja Turtle. Michelangelo."

I snap my fingers, the memory suddenly hitting me. I had wanted Nic to be April that year, since April was a girl. She wasn't having it, though. Wanted to be Donatello instead since he was the "smart one." When I told her she couldn't be him because he was a boy, she asked me to show me where his "pee pee" was. Shut my ass up with the quickness.

"You and Nic had been coming to Providence, like, full-time for almost two years at that point. I was so excited to see you guys there. I had some more kids close to my age to talk to, especially cool ones that knew all the words to Drake songs—and not just the radio edit."

I smile. Nic and I did go hard on old Drizzy. We would sneak onto the family computer in the kitchen while MiMi was at work to find the unedited versions of his songs on YouTube.

"And I really, really wanted to talk to you." Riley looks down at her lap, getting shy on me all of a sudden. "I spent all afternoon getting my makeup just right, so you could tell me how cool my costume looked. And I thought about the questions I could ask you about yours to get you talking to me. When I saw you, with your half shell and your plastic nunchucks, I knew exactly what to ask you." She raises her eyebrows to see if I remember. I give a sheepish shrug, completely clueless. Riley sighs. "Where'd you get your mask from?"

I pause. The moment hits me like an ice bath. I had lost

the orange mask that came with the costume. MiMi, Nic, and I had spent a full hour ransacking the apartment, trying to find where I might've dropped it. MiMi gave up, said we couldn't be late. Cut some holes in her orange bandana and made me wear that instead. I never felt so embarrassed, so ghetto, in my life. Then the Reverend's daughter walked over to me and pointed out the one thing on my costume that made me want to disappear.

"You told me to shut up," Riley continues, poking at her rice. "You told me to shut up, then didn't speak to me for the rest of the night. Which was partially my fault, since I spent half of the evening crying in the bathroom afterward."

I wince, wanting to punch that big-headed ten-year-old in the face. "Riley, I—"

"It's okay. Your sister found me. Apologized for you." She smiles now at the memory. "She apologized a lot for you over the years, then would tell me some embarrassing story about you to make me feel better. But that was the first time. We developed a silent thing after a while. Whenever one of us would do or say anything to make you snap or make this face . . ." She scrunches her nose and forehead up until they look like origami. "She'd cross her eyes at me and I crossed them back. Something silly just to make us not take you too seriously. I know you were going through a lot then. I know you're going through a lot now."

Now I poke at my food. My throat feels too swollen to swallow anything at the moment.

"I know you probably thought that I was all up in your Kool-Aid about the Nic thing at first but, I don't know, I guess in a weird way, I feel like she's my friend. One of the few that paid attention to me. I just wanted to return the favor." She gets real quiet and so do I. We just listen to the cars whiz by on the street behind us. Something about the chaos back there calms me. Like everyone keeps moving, but I get a moment to be still with Riley.

She finally cracks another smile at me. "You're not so smooth, Jay. You never told me about your dreams. What are you doing when we graduate next year? JRU? I know you probably wouldn't want to be that far from Ms. Murphy."

I scoff at her suggestion. John Ratcliffe University is one of the few colleges right in our backyard that the smart, uppity students in our schools usually wanted to attend, and not as a backup choice. It was as close to an Ivy League as we could get in this area—the admissions requirements included a high GPA, high SAT scores, and fair skin.

"Yeah. College is not really my cup of tea," I say.

Riley looks at me, wide-eyed. Kind of like Mrs. Pratt when I tell her about my future plans, or lack thereof. "I don't get it," she says. "You're so smart."

My cheeks get warm from the compliment. "I can't afford

it. And I farted around too much to get a long list of extra-curriculars going. Every dollar I make is going to MiMi. It's the least I can do for her after taking me and Nic in."

"Jay, she's your grandmother."

"Exactly. She's already raised her children. She didn't ask for another set during her golden years. That's the only reason why I'm putting up with this." I tug at my Taco Bell polo shirt.

Riley looks down at my shirt then back up at me. "Okay, I get where you're coming from. I really do. But . . . don't you think that the best way you can repay Ms. Murphy is by going to college? For her to see that all her hard work actually gave you a better future?"

I open my mouth, ready to give the same rebuttals that I give all my teachers, that I give Mrs. Pratt. But . . . damn. She got me. She got me good. College is all MiMi has been talking about with me lately—at least it was before Nic's disappearance. Though I know she'll be geeked about seeing me walk across the stage getting my diploma, she'd about jump out of her skin to see me doing the same with a college degree.

I look at Riley. Cock my head to one side so I can really take her all in.

"What?" Riley asks, smoothing down her ponytail. "I got something in my hair? Shrimp in my teeth?"

I smile and shake my head. "I just want you to know that

I see you, Riley. I really see you. I couldn't stop seeing you if I tried." Maybe that's what Nic needed to hear, too. That she was seen for her inside, not just her outside. That she mattered. Maybe that's what would've kept her next to me.

Riley takes a breath and her shoulders rise, like she knows exactly what I mean. I slide closer to her so she can feel it too. She doesn't move away. She leans over to me, gives me permission to get even nearer.

So I do. I touch the side of Riley's face. Tilt my head toward hers, then pause. "Can I kiss you?" I ask.

Riley smiles and grabs the back of my head, pressing her mouth against mine. Our lips move in and out of each other's, speaking a language that they'd learned forever ago but only get to use now. And every time I think one of us gets tired, Riley presses the back of my head or I squeeze her lower back, and our communication continues. Hell, I could speak to Riley like this all night long.

Tires screech in front of us, snapping Riley and me back to reality. Javon thrusts his head out of his driver's side window.

"Get in," he demands.

TWENTY-ONE

RILEY AND I FREEZE IN TIME, WATCHING JAVON WATCH US with a slight crease in between his eyebrows.

"Hello?" Javon snaps his fingers a few times at me. "I said get in."

"Why . . . why should I go anywhere with you?" I remember how my vocal cords work. "You told me to stay away from you. To back off. Remember?" I sure as hell didn't forget—and neither did my stomach muscles.

"I also told you to stop getting cute. So get your ass in the car. Now."

Maybe this is how it was when he confronted Kenny. If I get in that car, that might be the last car ride I'll ever take.

I cross my arms over my chest, stand my ground. "I'm good right here."

Javon's nostrils flare, but then he squeezes his eyes shut. Takes a deep breath. Like Javon Hockaday is suddenly practicing mindfulness. He reopens his eyes and his face is now more still. "It's about Nic."

At that, my arms go slack. Nic? So this mofo finally wants to come clean about Nic. He must be broiling from all the heat on him, so now he's ready to do something right. I slide off Riley's car. "I need to go with him," I say to her, almost apologetically. Even if he does spill wax about Nic, it still might be the last thing I hear. But maybe I can at least send a message to MiMi, give her some answers.

Riley hops off the car. "I'm going with you."

"What?" I shake my head so many times I get dizzy. "No way in hell. Your parents are expecting you home. It's okay—you've done enough for Nic."

"If I had, she'd already be here. Now let's go." Riley walks past me and straight to Javon's car.

I curse under my breath then glare at Javon. "Look, if you even think about hurting her—"

"Nigga, I ain't got time for empty threats. Let's go."

Riley opens the door to the backseat and slides in. I follow her. Before I can even close the door all the way, Javon speeds off.

259

"Whoa." I scramble to click on my seatbelt. "What's going on?"

"Nic's phone's back on," Javon explains as he pumps the gas and grazes under a traffic light just as it turns red. "I got an alert on my Find My Friends app. Check it."

Javon hands me his phone and, sure enough, Nic's picture pulses on the screen. My heart almost jumps out of my mouth. I slap my hand over it just to keep everything in. Could it be? After all this time . . . every call going straight to voicemail. Every text message going unanswered. Every lead leading to a dead end. Finally, this is something we could hold on to. I blink away tears when I notice it: Nic's picture is *moving*. Wait . . . if Nic's phone is moving, that means *she's* moving. Which means . . .

"She's alive!" Riley says, then wraps an arm around me to squeeze me in a hug.

Holy shit. My sister's alive. I rest my head on top of Riley's and close my eyes. Take a moment to take this all in. Nic's alive. I get to go home and tell MiMi that Nic's alive. Hell, I get to go home with *Nic*.

Javon snatches his phone back. "I need this to track her."

I nod. Lean forward in the space between the two front seats to keep my eyes on her picture. To make sure she's still moving. And she is. Two weeks of silence and now she's letting us know she's okay. She's okay. Wait, if she's okay, that also means . . .

"You didn't kill her," I say to Javon.

Javon smirks and gives me a side eye. "Nigga, are you crazy? Of course I didn't kill her."

I want to believe him. Hell, I have to believe him—the proof is on his phone. "I don't get it, though," I say aloud. "Why were you and Sterling arguing in front of her house? Why does she get all cagey whenever I mention you or Nic around her?"

Javon takes a deep breath but shifts his eyes back on the road. "Sterling's my alibi."

Riley and I look at each other, confused.

"What does that mean?" Riley asks for both of us.

"The last time I saw Nic or Kenny was about two weeks ago. Slim was throwing one of his Friday eve parties."

"Friday eve?" Riley asks.

Javon shakes his head. "Some stupid shit to get ready for the weekend. But Slim comes up with stupid shit all the time to find an excuse to party."

Friday eve? That would be Thursday. The last time I heard from Nic was that phone call from two Thursdays ago. I lean forward again, ready to put together the pieces.

"Sterling came with her. Homegirl got white girl wasted. And when she gets like that, she also gets a little . . . touchy-feely. Particularly with me." He scratches something on his face, clearly embarrassed. "Anyways, Nic wasn't feeling it, but took all her anger out on me. Broke up with my ass in front of everyone then took off with Kenny. Straight clowned me. So, I took off, too."

I take in what Javon tells me, but there still seem to be holes in his story. "If you took off, too, then who's to say you didn't go after them? You knew you couldn't hurt Nic because she's your girl, but Kenny's fair game, right?" I knew firsthand what he could do when he was pissed about Nic. I still have a scar on my chin to prove it.

Javon huffs, his patience running thin with me. "I ain't sweating Kenny. He presses up a little too hard on Nic sometimes, but that nigga isn't my competition." He pauses, winces. "*Wasn't* my competition. Yeah, I wanted to rough him up some, but I couldn't do whatever they think I did to him. Toss him out like garbage? Not my style." At that, he punches the steering wheel. "Not my fucking style."

Riley and I give him his moment. The pain for Kenny is still close to Javon—raw like an open sore. And if he's putting on a show for us, he could give Denzel Washington a run for his money. I want this all to make sense for me, but everyone knows Javon's a bad guy. We heard the stories about what he'd do to guys if they were short with his money, or even short with him. Aside from our tussles, I've never seen him exact revenge firsthand—but there's always truth in rumors, right?

"I went home after I left the party," Javon says after getting himself together. "Sterling came over to . . . check on me."

Riley scoffs. "Wow," she says.

Javon frowns. "Look, Nic knows how I roll, okay? But she also knows I got love for her."

Love? *Love?* He's kidding me with this. I think about all the times I had to cover for Nic when she was off doing who the hell knows with Javon. All the arguments I had to break up between Nic and MiMi when MiMi found holes in my stories about Nic. How Nic went from honor roll student to barely a student over the course of kicking it with this clown.

"You have a funny way of showing it," I spit out.

Javon looks at me through his rearview mirror. "Come again?" he says—almost warns.

I'm too fired up to take a hint. "Nic turned into a whole-ass other person after getting with you. Suddenly, all she ever wanted to do was get high and cut school. Forget college. Forget leaving the Ducts. She's never going to be able to put our hood behind her with you holding her back."

"Jay." Riley touches my arm, begs me to calm down with her eyes, but I'm on a roll now.

"But you don't even give a damn. You got your stoop. You got your paper. Hell, you probably have some chick on rotation just in case Nic never made it back." The words tumble out of my mouth, too quick for me to keep up. Like they've been aging on the back of my tongue. And it feels good letting it all out. Not just for Nic, but for me. Hell, even for Javon. He needs to finally get it. All the bullshit he pulls is why Riley thinks she can make jokes about me knocking someone up. Why Joshua Kim doesn't trust me to handle the cash. Why Officer Hunter doesn't blink twice when I tell him my sister's missing. My dad warned me about The Man even when I was too young to know who the hell The Man was. But Javon's almost a grown-ass dude. Why can't he see he's doing exactly what The Man wants by slinging shiz in his own hood? To his own people?

"Oh, you got me all figured out, huh?" Javon's hands clench around his steering wheel, so tight that his knuckles grow pale. Probably imagining wringing my neck. "Know my social security number, too? The pin to my ATM card?" Okay, maybe Riley was right. I should've dropped this a long time ago. If Javon gets too pissed, no telling what he might do. He probably wouldn't even give a damn that Riley's in the backseat. On instinct, I reach over and grab her hand.

"Since you know me so well, answer this. How many times did I tell your sister to carry her ass to school? How many times did I tell her to get home so she wouldn't have to hear her grandma's mouth? How many times did I tell her to lay off the bliss?" He lets out a long sigh and finally detaches one hand from the wheel to pinch the bridge of his nose. "Look, I know you and your grandma and everybody else think I'm a piece of shit. Ain't no thing to me—my dad told me that before I even learned how to ride a bike. Nic's the first person to look at me like I'm a king. Not because she's scared of me or anything, just because. And, shit, I want to feel good sometimes, too. So, fuck me for not pushing her away hard enough."

Riley takes in a breath and squeezes my hand. She gets it. Nic had done the same for her. Saw something in her that others didn't. And if I really think about it, she's done the same for me, too. I wouldn't have survived all this shiz we've been through if she hadn't been beside me. Putting her arm around my shoulders, telling me everything was going to be fine because we had each other. "Me and you against the world," she'd say to me. That's why I've been working so hard to get her back.

Javon's car stops moving. I blink, look around.

"This is where the tracker says she is," he says.

His headlights spill over a sign: Deer Park.

Holy. Shit.

TWENTY-TWO

RILEY, JAVON, AND I STUDY THE DEER PARK SIGN IN SILENCE. By the way Javon's breaths come out, all jagged like he's about to implode, I can tell he hasn't been here since news broke of Kenny's body being found. Why would Nic come out here? Is this her way of paying her respects to Kenny, especially after missing his service?

"Stay right here." Javon's voice slices through the air and causes Riley to jump. I guess she's just as on edge as I am about being so close to where somebody spotted Kenny.

"Naw, man," I say. "If Nic's out there, then—"

"Damn, I see what Nic was talking about when she called you hardheaded." He shoves his phone inside his pocket. "I'm not going to repeat myself: you both stay put. No telling what's out here this late." He slides out of the car and goes running down the path toward the sign. Soon, he gets out of reach of his headlights.

My knees bounce up and down, up and down. Nic's so close but still so far away. I can't believe I have to wait even longer to see her.

"You heard him before," Riley says, placing her hand on my knee. "As hard as it is to believe, he loves your sister. He's going to get her back to the car safely."

Riley has a good point. But there's only one thing she forgot: I love Nic, too. I unbuckle my seatbelt. "Lock the door behind me."

Riley sighs. "Jay . . ."

"I mean it. Call me if you see anything funny, and I'll come back running." I squeeze her hand. "I have to do this."

Riley pulls away from me, but nods. Of course she gets it. She's seen what I've been through over the last two weeks. I close the door behind me and dart in the same direction as Javon. The park gets dim as soon as I'm a few feet away from Javon's car, but thankfully I remember my surroundings from the time Dad used to drive me here for peewee football. As soon as practice ended, we'd sit out on one of the benches and sip on slushies. Watch people play with their dogs. I'd always ask Dad why we didn't have one of our own, and he'd wave a hand across the park and say, "We get a new one every week." He'd laugh each time like it was the first time he told that joke and I'd roll my eyes, all while hiding my smile behind my slushie. The park hasn't changed much since then. Physically, at least. Knowing that Kenny was buried a few feet away from where five-year-olds toss footballs gives the place a gloomier vibe.

I hear scuffling close by. I blink, adjust my eyes, and spot Javon pushing down some other guy right by one of the bike trails. I rush over to them as the other guy tries to scurry to his feet. He wears a Dallas Cowboys jersey with Tony Romo's name fading away on the back.

"Pooch?" I say, my feet screeching to a halt once I'm close enough to them. "What the hell are you doing here?"

"This motherfucker had your sister's phone," Javon says, holding up another phone. The case is striped with purple and turquoise and glistens from all the tiny crystals embroidered on it. I once joked with Nic that a unicorn must've sold her that. This was definitely her phone.

My pulse tries to punch its way through the side of my neck. It's only Nic's phone here, not Nic herself. I don't understand. "Why do you have Nic's phone?" I ask.

"I told him already," Pooch says, scrambling to his feet. "I found it."

"Lies!" Javon hisses, then jumps at Pooch. Pooch stumbles back onto his ass, tries to scoot away but Javon grabs hold of his feet. Drags Pooch back toward him.

"Jay!" Pooch cries out. "Jay! Help me!"

My stomach does the Harlem Shake as I watch the scene unfold in front of me. Any other time, I would've stepped in front of Pooch. Explain to his assailant that Pooch never means any harm, that Pooch is just being Pooch. But . . . he has Nic's phone. Which means he might know what's going on with Nic. Or maybe he even hurt her . . .

"Just tell him the truth, Pooch." The words shake out of me.

Pooch looks up at me, wide-eyed, like a deer staring at the headlights of his impending doom. Javon steps toward him and I spin around. I can't watch whatever it is Javon plans on doing to get some answers. I hear Pooch grunt and plead, and the rubble underneath him and Javon screams for mercy. My hands tremble so I shove them into my hoodie. *Just talk, Pooch*, I beg. Hope my words get to him. *Please. Just talk.*

"All right!" Pooch cries out.

I suck in a breath, turn back around. Javon still hovers over Pooch, fist cocked and ready to fire. Pooch cradles his head with both arms, his body trembling from pain and fear.

"I didn't find it—I stole it!"

"From who?" Javon demands. "From Nic?"

"No!" Pooch drops his arms and looks up at Javon. "I would never steal from any of the Murphys. I didn't know it was Nic's phone!"

"Then who?" Javon's voice explodes through the park,

sends birds scampering away out of trees. Didn't even know birds kicked it this late.

"I don't know his name," Pooch says. "I went to Mickey D's to grab something off the value menu. Some cocky white guy trashed it in the dumpster outside. I thought I could sell it."

Javon smirks, then pauses. Drops his raised fist to his side. His face gets real still, like he's programming a computer inside his head. Finally, his face twists in anger again. "I'm gonna *kill* them!" He steps over Pooch, storms toward the park's exit.

Pooch lies back onto the trail and curls up into a fetal position. I should check on him. I should at least call for help, but somebody who wasn't Nic had Nic's phone—and Javon seems to know who it is. I shoot an apologetic glance at Pooch, then jog after Javon, though my legs are heavy with guilt.

"What's going on?" I ask Javon in between breaths. Even jogging I can't keep up with Javon's gait. He's walking with determination. He's walking like he wants to *kill* someone.

"I fucking asked them," he shouts, more to himself than to me. "I asked them if they knew what's what. 'Nah, Javon, bro.'" His voice morphs into something that sounds like a surfer dude. "'He never showed up at the spot. We haven't seen him, bro.'" Javon barks out something I can't translate and punches his fist into his open hand.

"Javon," I try to speak calmly, even though it seems like Javon's past the point of no return. "I don't know what's happening. Tell me what's going on and I can help."

Javon laughs at me. The laughter comes out harsh and quick, like a stab. Before I know it, we're back at Javon's car. He swings open his back door and nudges his head at Riley. "Ay, come on out of there."

Riley blinks as she gets out of the car. "Is everything okay?" Then to me. "Where's Nicole?"

I shake my head at her. Another dead end. But I'd have to explain that to her later. Right now, Javon looks like he's about to jump from a cliff.

"What are you doing, Javon?" I ask him.

"I need to take care of something." He gets back into his driver's seat. "Y'all going to have to find your own way back home."

"Wait, you're just leaving us out here?" I ask.

Javon's tires answer me, screeching at high volume as Javon speeds away. He leaves with Nic's phone—and leaves me with a shitload of unanswered questions.

TWENTY-THREE

"WAIT . . . IS THAT HIM?" RILEY ASKS, PULLING BACK the curtain of my living room window.

"Riley!" I tug the curtain back down. "We can't be too obvious."

"Why not? Javon filled us in on everything. It's obvious we'd want to know where he ran off to. Especially you."

Once again, Riley makes a good point. The night's just been so jumbled that I can barely keep my head on straight. After Javon ditched us at Deer Park, we ordered an Uber. Dropped Pooch off at the closest emergency room to clear his head, then made it back to Riley's car. Riley drove me home and wanted to wait with me for word from Javon. Wouldn't take no for an answer. Now we're posted up on my living room couch, peering out the window to see if anyone drives up to Javon's building.

"Okay, so what did he say again?" Riley asks me.

I sigh. "Told you . . . he had some kind of dialogue with himself. With voice changes and everything. He seemed like he was pissed at someone but didn't tell me who."

"It has to be someone who he thinks might have had Nic's phone." Riley taps her chin in deep thought. "But who?"

Those are the questions of the night—the ones that Javon disappeared with. The ones he'll hopefully answer for us once he returns to the Ducts.

"You both know it's a school night, right?"

Riley and I swirl around from the window and MiMi stares at us, tying her house robe around her waist. I figured she'd be so knocked out that she wouldn't hear us, but this night has been full of surprises.

"Yeah. Riley was just helping me with a project," I say. "She's done something like it at her school already."

MiMi frowns at me then shifts her eyes to Riley. "Your parents know you're here?"

"Yes, ma'am," Riley lies. "I told them I'd be a little late. As long as I'm home by eleven, they're fine."

MiMi studies us as if waiting for one of us to pop so the truth bursts out. I hold my breath. Finally, she shakes her head and walks toward the kitchen. "Well, sure you can't concentrate on an empty stomach. Let me fix you both a PB&J sandwich."

"MiMi, you don't need—"

"Sounds delicious," Riley says. I give her a look and she shrugs. "What? We never finished dinner, remember? You try calling Nic's phone again?"

I point at her. Good thinking. I tried ringing up Nic's phone a couple of times, hoping that Javon would pick up and fill me in on everything. I press her name when there's a sharp knock at the door. Riley and I look at each other, eyebrows raised in hope.

"Who in the world is that this time of night?" MiMi calls from the kitchen.

"I got it, MiMi." I jump to my feet and rush to the door. I had been so caught up with selling fake news to MiMi, that I didn't even see Javon pull up. Maybe he's dropping off the idiot who took Nic's phone to demand some answers. Wait— maybe he's even dropping off Nic herself! I'm so jittery with the possibility that my hand slips from the doorknob before I'm able to take a proper hold to swing it open.

Javon doesn't stand at my door with answers. Instead, Rick Ross, aka Officer Hunter, stands there, his mouth turned down at the corners like somebody's tugging at it.

"Hey, son," he says to me. "Mind if I come in?"

I blink, taking in the fact that he's really there. "For what?" I manage.

He breathes through his nose. "You said before that I never fill you in on anything. I think it's time that I did." His eyes shift past me. "Evening, Ms. Murphy."

I turn and MiMi stands in the living room, holding on to a butter knife slathered with peanut butter. "What's going on here?"

Hunter looks back at me, raises his eyebrows as a request to enter. I take a step back so he can come in, close the door behind him.

"We arrested your neighbor, Javon, tonight," he says. He takes off his hat and holds it in his hands like an old-school gentleman.

Arrested Javon? I don't get it. Javon was on the way to get me answers. He didn't have time for any nonsense that could've gotten him pinched. "For what?" I ask.

"One of our patrolmen caught him speeding. When he pulled him over, Javon got mouthy, which led to him getting handsy with the officer. While restraining him, the officer found your sister's phone on him. It was the missing link we needed to arrest him for Kenny's murder."

I shake my head. No. No, this isn't right. Javon didn't hurt Kenny. He told us himself.

"Wait, this is a huge misunderstanding." Riley stands, speaking up for both of us. "Javon didn't have Nic's phone all this time. He found it tonight . . . on Pooch. Jay saw it all."

"Wait—what?" MiMi frowns at me. "What were you

doing hanging around Pooch or Javon? You were supposed to be working."

"I'll explain it all to you, MiMi. I promise." I give her my best attempt at a reassuring nod before turning back to Hunter. "Riley's right. I saw everything go down at Deer Park tonight."

Hunter sighs and looks at me like he's about to break the news that the Tooth Fairy isn't real. "Did you actually see the phone on Clyde Thompson?"

It takes me a moment to realize he's talking about Pooch. I haven't heard Pooch's real name in a minute. No one around here ever felt the need to call him that. I think about the scuffle between Pooch and Javon. How Javon hovered over him with Nic's phone already in his hand.

"I mean, no," I say—then remember another piece of the puzzle. "But we saw him tracking Nic's phone. That's how we ended up at Deer Park. Javon couldn't be in two places at one time."

"Right, Deer Park," Hunter repeats. "The place where you so conveniently found Mr. Thompson, a known frequent customer of Javon's." He shakes his head. "Mr. Thompson's unemployed. No way he was able to pay for all that product he's gotten from Javon's boys. But pretend to hold on to Nic's phone for him? That'll be a way to clear up all debts."

I scrub my forehead with the heel of my hand. Yeah, Pooch is pretty hard up. Everyone in the neighborhood knew that. He'd even run out behind cars pulling out of parking lots at the last minute just to embezzle a quick buck. Maybe taking a hardcore ass whooping from Javon to even the score wouldn't be so out in left field for him. Then again, did I ever actually see Javon put his hands on Pooch? My back was turned—those sounds could've been anything. But still, something seems off.

"What about Sterling?" I try. "Javon was with her that night Kenny and Nic took off."

"Of course, she'd say that. Those two have been secretly hooking up for months. One of her friends even told me she scored party favors off Javon for some of her get togethers. As long as she keeps Javon's nose clean, hers will stay clean as well."

I look over at Riley, wait to see if she has another rebuttal. But she stands there hugging herself with a slight crease in her forehead, looking like she's solving a riddle in her mind.

"To make matters worse," Officer Hunter continues, "word is that Kenny owed Javon money. He kept pocketing some after every deal. So, Kenny took off with Javon's loot, as well as his girl. What do you think someone like Javon would do once he caught up with Kenny? I'm sorry, kid, but Javon played you."

His words drop at my feet. I fight the urge to look down at them. I want Hunter to see me with my head held high— show him that I'm nobody's fool. "Why would Javon care enough to play me?"

Hunter rubs his fingers across his eyebrow, almost massaging it. As if he's trying to take his time before saying whatever it is he needs to say next. "Because . . . we have reason to believe that your sister is dead, and that Javon's the one who killed her."

There's a shriek behind me—something primal and full of pain. I turn and MiMi's crumpled on the floor, sobbing and slapping her palms against the carpet. I want to go to her. I want to peel my grandmother off the floor and hold her up while she cries. Rub her back and tell her we'll get through this together. But my feet are cinder blocks. I couldn't move them if I used every muscle in my body. I clutch my chest, try to feel for a heartbeat. And it's there, pumping so hard it feels like it's in a boxing match with my fist. It would stop, right? My heart wouldn't be working this hard if my sister were dead.

Riley's on the floor next to MiMi, rubbing her hair and shushing her. Officer Hunter crosses the living room to them.

"I'm so sorry, Ms. Murphy. I really wish I had better news for you." He bends over and rests a hand on her shoulder.

At that, my chest sets on fire. "Don't touch her," I shout to him.

Hunter blinks, looks up at me. "Jay, I'm just trying to comfort her."

Comfort her? By coming to our house and telling her

that her granddaughter is dead? He can't be for real. "Get out," I say.

"Jay, I know you're—"

"Get. The fuck. Out!" The words explode out of me, finally jarring my feet from staying planted to the floor.

Officer Hunter takes a step back from MiMi. Takes two steps back from me. He looks across the living room, surveying all the damage he caused. Finally, he nods and leaves the apartment without saying another word.

I rub my chest again, hope the burning relieves itself now that Hunter's gone. But it doesn't matter. His words are still there: *Your sister is dead. Your sister is dead.* Yeah, I know that people have already thought that. I see the way heads tilt when they ask me about Nicole. When they give me tiny smiles at my latest updates. Now, though, someone's said it aloud. And hearing the words aloud is the same as someone reaching through my ribs and squeezing my heart until it turns to mush. I close my eyes—imagine that I'm in my bed. When I open them, it'll be morning and Nic will be in the kitchen burning waffles and all of this'll be some anxiety-riddled nightmare about us going off to college. Has to be.

"Jay?"

I open my eyes and Riley's in front of me, her eyes wide with concern. I look around and MiMi's nowhere to be found.

"I got her into her bed," Riley explains. "Gave her some Benadryl so she could wind down."

"I . . . I have to go check on her." I shake out my legs. Make sure they're still working.

Riley grabs my arm. "I think you need to check on yourself first."

I pull away. "It doesn't matter how I am right now."

"Yes, it does, Jay. I get it. You're hurt." Riley sighs. "And I'll give you the time to be hurt, but then we need to get back to action."

I frown at her. "What are you talking about?"

"Didn't you hear Officer Hunter? He never said that Nicole was dead. He said they believed she's dead—which means they don't have full proof. Which means that there's still a chance to—"

"Stop!" The word comes out much louder than expected. Good, though. Maybe the louder I am, the more she'll listen. "Enough with the games, Riley. I have to take care of my grandma."

Riley blinks at me. "What games? What are you talking about?"

"This!" I point back and forth between me and her. "We're not playing Clue, okay? We're not acting out the plot of your favorite mystery novel. This is my actual life. With a locked-up mom and dead dad and now a dead fickin' sister to top it all!"

Riley shakes her head. "I never said this was a game, Jay. I told you, I care about Nicole, too."

"Why? Because she wiped away your tears when a boy was being mean to you? Big deal! Nic was never your friend, Riley. She never even mentioned you. So, while you're chasing after this imaginary buddy, I have to go talk to my grandma about funeral arrangements." I walk over to her. "That part of your game, too? How many points do you get for picking out the casket? What kind do you get when you don't even have the body?"

"Stop," Riley says, blinking back tears. But I can't. For some reason, I want her to hurt as much as I do.

"What about burial plots? Do you get bonus points if you find a spot right next to my dad?"

"Jay, stop it! Why are you being this mean?" One of the tears spills from her eyes but she doesn't wipe it away.

I look down—even in my rage, I can't watch her cry. "Why don't you go home and tell your parents how much of an asshole I am. I'm sure you'll hear a couple of told you so's."

Riley sniffles and pushes past me. She opens my front door but doesn't slam it behind her. Even if she hates me, she respects my home. Goddamn her.

I look down the hall toward MiMi's bedroom door. Hear her muffled cries behind it.

Goddamn us all.

TWENTY-FOUR

I'M ALREADY AT THE DOORS WHEN THE CITY BUS PULLS UP across the street from Taco Bell. As soon as they open, I spill out onto the curb. I'm almost a half hour late. I try to go right into a jog, but my whole body aches. Not sure why. The only amount of exertion I've done all day was roll over from one side of the bed to the other. I couldn't make it to school, and MiMi couldn't make it out of her own bed to tell me to go to school. I think both of us knew it would be too soon to go into our usual routine. It would be tough to eat fried eggs and discuss our To-Do Lists for the day while staring at Nic's empty spot at the kitchen table. Yeah, it's been empty for over two weeks, but now that we know she's never going to fill it, breakfast would be hard to swallow.

I thought twice about not showing up for work. Okay, I thought more than twice about not coming here. But with Nic gone and MiMi still recuperating from her stroke, I have to step up. Bring home some cash until we catch our breath—though I don't see that happening any time soon.

I push my way through the doors of the restaurant and get smacked in the face by the smells of shredded chicken and chili powder. One of my coworkers at the cash register gives me a slight nod before getting back to work. I can hear some of the others cracking jokes in the kitchen. It's business as usual here. Not sure why I thought that time would freeze because my world turned inside out.

I make my way toward the breakroom to clock in, when Joshua Kim appears out of thin air and steps in the middle of the hall. "You're late," he says. Crosses his arms across his chest like a big shot.

"I know," I say. I'd like to not be even later, but he's standing in my way. "I have a lot going on right now, but it won't happen again." I shrug my shoulders at him, ask for permission to pass.

"We all have a lot going on, Jayson," Joshua says, not budging a muscle. "Cars that won't start, babysitters canceling at the last minute. Heck, even Carmen had to recently put her ferret to sleep. But guess what? We all still make it here on time."

I blink at him. A ferret. A fickin' ferret? He's going to

compare my shitty-ass life to having to part ways with a weasel? I cough out a laugh and shake my head. "I win," I say.

Joshua frowns at me in confusion. "Excuse me?"

"I win the woe is me card," I say. "Your Honda Accord needs work? Try riding your bike or catching public transportation just to pick up a carton of milk. No babysitter? I don't even know what a babysitter is. I've had to warm up dinner plates after school since I was nine years old if my grandma ever ran late. And a dead . . . *ferret*?" I bark out another laugh. "You think I give a damn about a stretched-out rat? I buried my dad in elementary school. Gonna bury my sister in the next few days. My grandma is barely hanging on, and I might end up in the fickin' system because my mom's serving a fifteen-year bid. So yeah, I win!"

There are more eyes on me than just Joshua Kim's. My coworkers stop cracking jokes. Customers in the dining area stop ordering. Hell, the flies buzzing around probably stop being annoying. But I don't care if I'm disturbing anyone because Joshua Kim's complaining about scuffing his diamond shoes while I take thirty minutes out of my shift to mourn my goddamn sister.

Joshua finally clears his throat and shifts his weight to his other foot. "Okay, I understand now that you're going through it, but I can't have you causing a scene at work."

"Causing a scene?" I repeat. "All I was doing was trying to clock in. I haven't even started to cause a scene. But *this* is

284

causing a scene . . ." I swipe at a stack of trays at the end of the counter, send them plummeting to the floor. Joshua jumps but I'm not done. "*This* is causing a scene." I yank out as many napkins from a nearby dispenser that I can. Ball them up in my fists, then make it rain in the dining area. "THIS is causing a fickin' scene!" I intercept an order of tacos from an unsuspecting customer and pitch them to the floor. I step on them for good measure just to make sure the tacos are dead. The crunch underneath my feet is oddly satisfying, so I keep stomping and stomping until I turn those tacos into powder.

Soon, I'm out of breath. The eyes that stared at me with amusement now look at me with concern. I even see fear from some people—including Joshua Kim. Good.

"If you haven't caught on by now," I say in between breaths, "I'm not cleaning any of this shit up. I quit." I snatch the apron over my head and toss it to the floor. Step on it just to prove an extra point before pushing out of the doors. I never want to eat a burrito again.

✳ ✳ ✳

I get home with one thing on my mind: crawling back into bed. But as I trudge down the hall, I pause outside of Nic's bedroom door. I think about all the times I popped my head in to see if she made it home. I think about all the times before then, when she'd let me pile my blankets at the foot of her bed after a night of watching too many Saw movies. I think about Father's Day five years ago, when I caught Nic crying into her pillow, so I sat on her floor. Resting my head on her legs until she was ready to speak. Willing to still sit there even if she didn't want to speak at all.

My hand reacts before my brain does. It turns her doorknob, pushes her door open. Everything's still slightly askew from me and Riley's snooping, but Nic's bones are still there. All her scents are still there. I walk over to her bed and plop down. I wonder when's the last time Nic actually slept in here. Maybe a little over two weeks ago. Did she fall right asleep, or did she fart around on her phone to pass time? And when she did fall asleep, what did she dream about? I hope it was something nice. I hope it was something about Mom and Dad and me before all the storms came. I hope we were piled up in Dad's car, listening to Mom and Dad sing along to their oldies. Groaning every time they kissed or held hands, but passing secret smiles to each other because our parents still wanted to kiss and hold hands. Our parents loved each other. Our parents loved us.

The first cry comes out like a hiccup. I touch the pit of my throat to make it stop but the levees have already broken. The tears come out in steady streams now, like they've been backed up for far too long. Nothing I think or do can make them stop from overflowing. I fall back onto Nic's bed, bury my face in her pillow like I saw her do all those years ago. I let out a rumble that doesn't even sound like me. It's deep and hoarse and sounds like it came from a man who lived through years of pain. Who doesn't know how he'll ever pull himself out because the sorrow feels too deep. So deep it's swallowing him whole.

There's a hand on my back. I peek up and MiMi stands over me, blinking back tears. I choke up again and MiMi sits down, rubbing my back so hard to help me get all of them out.

"I . . . I quit . . . my job," I barely get out.

"It's okay, baby." She shushes me, keeps rubbing.

"I quit my job . . . because I think she's really dead." My voice breaks even more and I slap once at my face. Pissed at the tears that won't stop leaking. "She's gone, MiMi. She's gone."

MiMi's hand moves up to the back of my head and she strokes my scalp. "I felt that way at first, too, baby. Up here." She taps her forehead. "But I still don't feel it here yet." She taps at her chest. "I'm putting all my hope into Him. Until He tells me your sister is gone, I'm going to believe she's still out there."

I want to shake my head but it's already spinning. One more move and I'll forget where I am.

"The church is going to have a prayer vigil for your sister tomorrow night," MiMi continues. "Everyone in the congregation believes she'll come back home. And with all those prayers happening at once, I know she'll hear them. They have hope, baby. We just have to have it, too."

Hope? She's talking as crazy as Riley did last night. If the last two weeks have told me anything, it's that hope can be snatched away from you as quickly and unexpectedly as a loved one. Hope is just a four-letter word. But I let MiMi continue to rub my head and tell me fairy tales like she did when I was a kid.

TWENTY-FIVE

I DON'T KNOW WHICH IS WORSE: PICKING OUT AN OUTFIT for a funeral or finding something to wear for a prayer vigil. Right now, standing in front of my bed, choosing between two identical black shirts, I'd have to say the latter. At least with a funeral, you get finality. A period after the universe's longest run-on sentence. But with a vigil, you're just dishing more lies to yourself and adding semicolons. What's the point of praying for someone you already know is long gone?

I sigh through my nose, snatch up the shirt with the least amount of lint on it, just as my phone rings. I stare at the screen. Definitely a number I don't recognize. I wait for the person on the other line to realize their mistake, but they're persistent as all hell. Finally, I answer.

"You have a collect call from . . ."

I suck in a breath as the automated voice on the other end lets me know that Javon Hockaday is calling me from the city jail.

"Would you like to accept this call?"

My thumb hovers over the red phone icon, itching to hang up. But it won't cooperate. Neither will my vocal cords as the word "Yes" scrapes up from the pit of my throat. I don't know, maybe I'm a glutton for punishment. This day has already gone to shiz with that vigil looming. At least I might get some kind of satisfaction from hearing Javon wallow to me from behind bars.

"I didn't think you were going to pick up," Javon says. He's only been in jail two nights, but he already sounds hardened. Hoarse. Like he has enough stories to tell that would keep any black guy up at night.

"You have two minutes," I say. I don't even squeak the words. Remember how Officer Hunter said Javon played me. I can't let him do it again.

He takes a breath. "I know you heard some crazy shit about me. Especially because I took off like that the other night. Left you and your girl in the dark."

I wince at Javon referring to Riley as my "girl." Whatever she was, she isn't anymore. Especially after all those awful things I said to her.

"The cops, though. They wouldn't listen to me. They

never do. So, I'm hoping you can pick up where I left off. We both owe it to Nic."

I put a chokehold on my phone. "*Owe* it to Nic?" Repeating his words makes them sound even crazier. "You know what Nic deserves? To sleep in her own bed tonight. To finish high school. To go out and change the world. Or not. Maybe she wanted a regular nine-to-five, but guess what? She no longer has that choice because she had a jealous-ass boyfriend." I sling out every syllable with so much fervor that I imagine each one clocking Javon right across the head. I want him to feel my rage. I want him to feel Nic's pain.

There's a pause on Javon's end. I try to imagine what he's doing. Rubbing his forehead with regret? Wiping away a tear? But that's impossible. The cops finally arrested Javon— which means they have to have something on him. Which means that he killed Kenny and did God knows what to Nic. If he's crying, it's because he's finally caught.

"I get it," Javon says finally. "And look, you can think what you want about me, but at least hear me out. I think I know where she is. I think . . . I think I know who has her body."

My stomach tugs at Javon's final word. Body. Nic's body. That's the closure I need. That MiMi needs. Hearing it, though, doesn't make it go down any easier. Javon's throat makes a noise on the other end and, for a moment, I think he laughs. But the snort is too guttural, too harsh. Almost like he's fighting against his own body. Wait—*can* Javon be really crying?

I swallow even though my throat is dry. "I'm listening," I croak. I grip the phone tighter. Brace myself for whatever Javon has to say.

"These white guys. Punk-ass frat dudes who think they're down with the culture because they listen to Childish Gambino or some shit. They've come by my stoop a few times to . . ." Javon takes a breath, like he's catching himself before he stumbles. ". . . hang out. The night Kenny and Nic went missing, I sent Kenny to their spot to hang out with them."

I frown, confused, but then everything hits me in the face like a shovel. He sold drugs to these dudes, but he doesn't want to out himself on a recorded line. Even when he tries to help me, he can't help but help himself.

"What the hell does this have to do with Nic?"

"You know Nic rolled with Kenny after she got pissed at me that night. So, they went to the spot together and then I didn't hear anything. Which means something went down with those boys. The night I was arrested, I was heading to them to find out what."

He played you, kid. Officer Hunter's words slice through our conversation again. Shakes the fog out of my head until I see Javon clearly again. Is he seriously saying some doofy frat guys attacked Kenny? *Killed* him? For what? Talking shit about Donald Glover on a bad bliss trip? And what about Nic?

She always knows to steer clear of any deals. Though Javon got her all twisted most of the times, she kept her head straight enough to never be around for any of those exchanges. At least MiMi did something right with raising her.

"And you told the cops all this?" I ask.

"Come on, bruh. Without evidence, they don't listen to guys like us."

My jaws clench. Javon boxed me in with him, too. But I'm not the guy who tried cracking another dude's nose against the pavement or jacking me up in a church. I'm not the guy who let a blisshead score in exchange for an alibi. I'm definitely not the guy who won't admit I sell drugs in order to do right by my girlfriend.

"I'm not like you, Javon." I don't even shout. I speak clearly, calmly, so he takes in every word. "And your two minutes are up."

Javon tries to say something else but my thumb twitches and I hang up. I hang up on Javon with a million questions floating above me, but one answer. Javon seems certain that Nic is dead.

I toss my black shirt on the bed. Grab the one with the most lint. Need to save the better one for Nic's funeral. My fingers tremble as I button up my shirt. I go all the way up to my neck until the collar chokes me.

✳ ✳ ✳

It had only been a few days since Kenny's service, but the dreariness lingers at Providence Baptist Church. Makes sense since we're not here for a joyous occasion. Reverend Palmer and some of the congregation went all out for Nic's prayer vigil, though. Damn near every candle they could find lights up the aisles of the nave. Maybe if the prayers don't work, Nic can find her way back home from all the flames. That is, if she's still alive.

I know I should be grateful for all the support. For all the faces from the church and even from the Ducts that came out to show us love. Man Boo ushers people inside, helps them find a spot to park their prayers. Mrs. Jackson from the next building brought us a freshly baked apple pie to go along with her hope. The Armstrongs from upstairs wanted MiMi to hold on to their Bible because apparently it brought them good luck after praying over it every night when they were trying to conceive a baby. Now they have three. Even Lil Chuck showed up with his parents, giving me a solemn high five as his parents greeted MiMi and me. Told me he hoped Nic comes back because she's nicer than me. Can't argue with that one.

Javon's phone call eclipses it all, though. He sounded so sure about these mythical white dudes having something to do with Kenny. With Nic. There were moments when he even sounded sad. Broken about everything that's happened.

But Officer Hunter had seemed sure, too. The cops were never able to pin anything on Javon, even when everyone and their mama knew what he did to make ends meet. Now he was finally behind bars, so that must mean something. Right?

Deacon Irving slides his slithery self next to MiMi in our pew. He grabs one of her hands and massages it. Because that's what MiMi needs right now. A fickin' masseuse.

"How are you holding up?" he asks MiMi.

MiMi nods. "Better now—especially after seeing all this love that Nicole has. Warms my heart. Isn't that right, Jay?"

I look up from my hand, which holds on to my phone. I keep glancing at the clock. Seeing how long this vigil will last. "Uh huh," I say.

Deacon Irving leans forward over MiMi to get all up in my business. "You're taking care of your grandmother during this time, right?" It's like he took a bath in mouthwash and aftershave. His rigorous hygiene regimen assaults all my senses.

"I always take care of her. No one does it better than me," I say. Hope he feels my not so subtle dig for him not making an appearance at the hospital. By the way he quickly leans back in his seat, I know he catches my drift.

"I'm going to lead the next prayer after the Reverend says a couple of words," Deacon Irving says to MiMi, conveniently avoiding eye contact with me. "You want me to grab some-thing for you in the meantime? Cup of water? Deviled eggs?"

I make a face. Nothing like mourning over a plate of stinky boiled eggs.

"You've done enough." MiMi smiles and pats his hand.

Deacon Irving squeezes MiMi's shoulder before sliding out of the pew, slithers his way over to the Reverend to talk about his prayer, I guess. He's probably requesting a spotlight, a wireless microphone, and anything else to make his prayer extra and all about him. Reverend Palmer nods at Deacon Irving, then turns to pass along a message to . . . Riley.

I suck in my breath when I see her. I don't know why I'm surprised she's here. Why wouldn't she be here? It's her father's church. Plus, she said that Nicole was her friend. Nicole was her friend and I mocked her about that. What kind of friend was I? We lock eyes for a few seconds. Finally, Riley blinks and makes her way behind the pulpit. I wait for her to peek back at me, but she doesn't. I can't blame her. I wouldn't give me a second glance, either. Not after I took everything out on her. I'm not sure if she'll ever forgive me.

"Hi, Ms. Murphy."

My eyes pull away from Riley's direction and Pooch hov-ers over us. My head snaps back at his appearance. He isn't wearing his trusty Cowboys jersey. Instead, he tucks a black T-shirt into black, holey jeans. He has his same dusty white Keds, though. I still have to applaud his effort. He put some thought about showing up here tonight. Looking decent for MiMi.

MiMi scans him over. "How are you feeling, Pooch? Everything going well with you?"

Pooch shakes his head over and over. Looks like he's malfunctioning. "Don't even worry about me, Ms. Murphy. This is all about you guys tonight." He peeks over at me, then looks down at his hands. Almost like he's embarrassed at something. Proves Officer Hunter right—he did take a payoff from Javon to pretend like he had Nic's phone. The nerve of him for showing his face tonight.

"I just wanted to say that . . . that I'm really sorry about Nic. That's a sweet girl right there. Never let anyone rag on me. Never let me go hungry. Always willing to loan me some change to grab some nuggets or something."

"Yeah," I say, raising a skeptical eyebrow at him. "She really deserved better."

At that, Pooch chews on his bottom lip. "Didn't mean any disrespect," he mumbles. "Just wanted to send my well-wishes, that's all."

"And we appreciate your well-wishes, Pooch," MiMi says, nudging me with her elbow. "Why don't you sit down and join us for the next prayer?"

Pooch shakes his head again. "I gotta . . . you know . . ." He grunts something else that doesn't sound like it belongs in the English language and then scurries down the aisle.

The guilt really seems to be eating away at him. Good.

MiMi nudges me again. "What did you say to that man?"

I shrug. "Nothing. You heard me."

MiMi smirks at me as she stands. "Sit here and fix your face. People went out of their way to be with us tonight."

"Where are you going?"

"I'm going after Pooch."

I roll my eyes and groan. "But MiMi, he—"

"Needs just as much prayer as Nicole." She pinches my chin. "When I get back, you better be a brand-new Jay." She shuffles out of the pew and heads in the same direction as Pooch.

A brand-new Jay? That's what got us all in the situation in the first place. I pushed Nic away when she called, thinking that this New and Improved Jay would stand his ground. Stop covering for his big sister so she could grow up and get on track. Help her be more than what others expected her to be. But I didn't think I was pushing her away forever. Now the last thing Nicole probably remembered about me was that I hung up when she needed me the most.

I clutch my phone again. Maybe if I try hard enough, I can squeeze out the minutes to make the time go by faster.

"Hi, Jay."

Sterling stands over me, a sniffling, sobbing mess. Her face is pink and soggy, and her mascara drips down her cheeks, leaving dark trails of sorrow.

"Hey," I say, though it comes out more like a question. She has some nerve stepping foot into our church after covering for Javon. She's supposed to have been Nic's best friend, but she probably just used her to get closer to him.

"I just wanted to tell you that I'm so, so sorry." Her voice breaks as she pulls out a handkerchief, blows her grief into it. "You came to me about Nic weeks ago and I kept shooing you off. I just figured she was going through the motions, you know? Had I known . . ." She cries into her handkerchief again. I would reach for her hand . . . but that handkerchief looks mighty damp. And so does her attempt at sorrow.

"I'm sure she knew you cared." The words come out flat. My throat won't even allow me to lie for Sterling.

"Oh God, you're speaking about her in past tense?" Sterling flinches. "Oh God, and now I'm saying the Lord's name in vain in a church. Ugh, I did it again!" She pops herself on her hand. "I'm sorry. I really don't know how to do this."

I sigh. "Neither do I." It's the most truthful thing I've probably said all night.

Sterling gives me a sympathetic nod as she points next to me. "Can I sit with you? I really don't know anyone else here."

Before I can even say no, Sterling slides next to me. Trapping me inside the pew just as Reverend Palmer takes center stage again. I peek behind me. Pretend to search for MiMi, but really I'm just looking for an escape. Some place close enough to show MiMi I'm supporting her, but far away from phonies like Sterling.

"Such a beautiful turnout," Reverend Palmer says into the mic. "But that's how our community has always been— *beautiful*. Black and beautiful. Our black is what makes us beautiful, can I get an amen?"

Several folks give him what he wants at full volume. Sterling looks at me, eyebrows raised. Asking permission for something I didn't have a right to grant her. Instead, I turn back to the Reverend and try to give him my full attention. So at least I didn't have to explain the rules of a black church for Sterling.

"And this is despite what the mainstream media tells us," Reverend Palmer booms, his voice trembling in all the right spots like a fine-tuned instrument. "This is despite how they want the world to see us. Fatherless. Motherless. No future. No direction." Between every example, every beat, the crowd shouts out in agreement. His words driving them home. "They tried to turn us against our sister. Our daughter. The beautiful Nicole Marie Murphy. But everyone in here knows everything they need to know about that young lady. She's smart. She's driven. She loves her MiMi." *Yes!* "She loves her brother." *Yes!* "She loves God! And she is black . . . and beautiful!" *Amen!*

Feet start pounding throughout the nave as people catch the spirit, rejoicing in agreement. Even Sterling presses a hand to her chest, as if all the joy and hope in the room is too much for her heart. Reverend Palmer goes on and on about Nicole defying the odds. Defying the stereotypes. But my head is on the phone call I had with Javon again. He wanted me to pick up where he left off, he said. And I dismissed what he had to tell me. Because all I saw in Javon is what everyone else wanted me to see about him. Fatherless. Motherless. No future. The same shiz people probably think about me. I know how I feel having the doors close on me, and I basically did the same thing to Javon.

My guilt makes me leap to my feet. Sterling blinks and copies me, like she assumes I have the Holy Ghost so she should too. And I do catch something, but it's not the spirit. It's the need for clarity. I squeeze past Sterling, push past the celebrating until I find who I'm looking for. Pooch is in the corner of the room, going to town on a dinner roll. He pauses midchew when he scopes me heading his way.

"Your grandma left with Sister Gladys," he tells me, crumbs spewing every direction. "She told me I could take a plate home."

Pooch could take ten plates home, for all I cared. There were more pressing issues at hand.

"We need to talk," I say to him. Get up close enough to smell the gravy on his breath. "About that night in Deer Park."

Pooch swallows down the rest of his roll. Stares down at the plate in his hand like he plans on stuffing more in his mouth just to keep it full and busy. "Nothing more to say," he says instead.

"Be honest . . . did Javon pay you off?"

Pooch's head jerks back like I just shoved it. "Pay me off? For what?"

"To pretend like you had the phone on you."

"But I really did have the phone on me. And after that clown shoved me around in the park, now I don't." He pushes the food around on his plate with his finger. "Really, though. I wouldn't have tried to sell it if I knew it was Nicole's."

The way the words leave his mouth all slow and measured makes me believe him. "So, where did you find it?"

Pooch shrugs. "I don't know, man. Some white boy."

White boy. Just like Javon mentioned. "Yeah, but what white boy?" My voice is shrill. Desperate.

Pooch tries to take another bite of his roll, but I cover it with my hand.

"Pooch, please," I say. I beg. "Whatever you remember. Just let me know."

Pooch sighs but then twists his mouth to one side. Puts on his thinking face. "Never really saw him around or anything. Him and his friends wore these corny sweatshirts with Greek letters. Oh, and he got out of this really sweet Escalade. Guess with a car like that, you can toss an iPhone out like leftover takeout, know what I'm saying?"

My hand automatically covers my mouth. I did know what he was saying. I knew exactly what he was saying. I've seen those corny sweatshirts before, too. I've seen an obnoxious Escalade eating up the entire Taco Bell parking lot. Those frat boys. Just like the ones Javon said over the phone. The ones that swing into the Ducts, looking to score . . .

I dart past Pooch and scurry up the rest of the aisle, only to collide right into Bowie.

"Whoa!" he says, steadying me. He carries a bouquet of flowers in one hand. "I knew I was running late, but is it over already?"

"Gotta fade," I say, pushing past him. But Bowie grabs my arm.

"Hey. I know you're pissed at me. I mean, I'd be pissed at me, too," he says.

I blink at him until his words connect and make sense. They never do—and my patience is getting skinny.

"I didn't know all those idiots would come out and talk trash about Nic like that," he continues. "Obviously, none of them knew her. I deleted all the comments. Doesn't fix everything, but it's a start."

Everything snaps into place. He's talking about his Instagram post. With everything starting to come to light, that post seems a thousand years old.

I nod more times than needed. "Yeah. It's all good."

Bowie tries to say something else, but I pull away from him. No time for apologies when you're on a mission. I think he calls after me. I think MiMi does, too. But the exit has answers and it calls me even louder, so I listen.

TWENTY-SIX

I TAKE AN UBER TO JOHN RATCLIFFE UNIVERSITY. SCROLL
through Greek letters on my phone to shake my memory.
Triangle with horns . . . triangle with horns . . . Those jack-
asses were wearing DU hoodies at Taco Bell. Delta Upsilon.
The driver has no clue where the DU fraternity house might
be, so I get her to drop me off at the student union, hope to
bump into someone that could point me in the right direction.

My head's so full of steam as I storm through the campus
that my eyes get foggy. Why did these white guys have all
of Nic's stuff? Did they know she was my sister when they
showed up at Taco Bell, or were they in their usual douche
mode? It's not adding up. But the answers were so close right

now that I could end a drought with all the sweat I have pouring from me.

I bump into some white guy with a bun. He tells me where to find the DU house. All the frat houses are throwing "major ragers," he says, to raise money for the Special Olympics. Because nothing says altruism like a bunch of frat guys playing beer pong. As I make my way down what the students call Frat Row, I hear the competing bass lines from the houses creeping their way up the pavement.

Thump-a, thump-a, thump-a.

The throb gets louder with every step I take, the bass sending tremors to my soles. I check the pulse in my neck just to be sure. It could definitely rival whatever's going on in those DU Douchebags' house, but it's not the culprit of the loud tempo. I finally reach the spot. Some kids fart around in the front yard—dancing to the music leaking out the house, laughing at some guy who spits up his liquor in the bushes. All just living their best lives on a Saturday night.

I lose some of my steam as I reach the bottom of the porch steps. If these guys were bold enough to have a "rager" with drunks throwing up in the front yard on campus, why the hell did I think they'd give me any easy answers about Nic? If Riley were here, she'd know how to tap-dance around the topic. Ask just the right questions to get exactly what we needed. I'd even take Javon. His methods are a bit more barbaric than Riley's, but still, all our questions would be answered. But I didn't have Riley nor Javon. Just me. I came this far to find out what's going on with Nic, so I can't turn back now. I shake my hands out to ready myself, then climb the steps.

When I slide through the front door, the pulse from the techno music almost jolts my newfound nerves out of me. I swivel, try to head back out to regroup, but a cluster of guys whooping and hollering like it's their first college party comes barreling through the door, pushing me farther inside. Crap. But maybe that's a sign.

I look around, search for one of the clowns that came to Taco Bell—but most of these guys look like the clowns that came into Taco Bell. Most of the guys here are tall, tan, and look like they go sailing on the weekends. I definitely stick out. I spot a JRU ballcap lying on one of the speakers. I swipe it, place it on my head, nod along to the song playing like I requested it. I see two girls giggling and dancing with each other in a corner. They look happy enough to help out. I nod my way over to them. Do a little two step beside them before I make my move.

"'Sup," I say over the music.

The girls look at me, then each other, then giggle again. "You're cute, babe, but we're together," the one with curly black hair says. She grabs the other girl's hand to prove her point further.

I hold up both hands and take a small step away. "Congratulations," I say . . . because I'm a dorky eleventh grader who has no business being here. "I was wondering if either of you knew where I could find someone."

"We're all looking for someone, babe," the same girl says.

Okay then. Maybe I should get into specifics. "He drives an Escalade," I say. "Dark brown. Killer rims," I add, just in case all these assholes drove Escalades.

"You're talking about Tyler," the girlfriend says.

I nod. Tyler—now we're getting somewhere.

The girl with the curly black hair shakes her head. "That's not Tyler's car. He's in it so much that he probably thinks it is. You mean Liam."

Tyler? Liam? Both sound like they have money in their checking accounts with more digits than my social security number. "Yeah . . . yeah, I meant Liam. Know where he's at?"

"Last I saw him, he was checking out the liquor supply to see if he needed to make a run."

I don't get to ask where the liquor supply is because the girls return to their giggling and dancing. If I interrupt to ask more questions, I'll paint a bull's-eye on my back. Best to keep it moving. I decide to follow the trail of discarded red Solo cups. Maybe the end of it will lead to the liquor. Hopefully this Liam guy is still there. I continue to bob my head along to the music. I even throw a wave at some random guy just to give off that I belong here. That I come to the DU house every weekend. My confidence pays off—the guy pulls me in for a hug, lifts me off my feet for a moment. I adjust my cap just as I hear a loud bang on a door down one of the halls.

"I told you—just don't cause a scene!" Some tall, macho guy barks at his almost as tall friend, pinning him up against the door. For a guy that doesn't want to cause a scene, his actions say otherwise. He then leans over and whispers something in the other guy's ear with so much rage that I see the spit flying from his mouth.

The other guy nods as if he gives in, then knocks his aggressor's hands off him. He spreads out all ten of his fingers and says something I can't quite make out. Ten minutes maybe?

"Yeah, no shit!" The macho guy broods back toward the living room. He sideswipes me as he pushes past and that's when I catch a whiff: Pine-Sol. Mixed with a couple of beers, but obnoxious and spruce-y nonetheless.

My heart catches in my throat as the guy continues to push his way through the dancing crowd. Okay, it's time to do something, Jay. If you lose him, no telling when you'll find him again.

"Liam!" I call out.

Liam pauses in his tracks, looks back at me. Holy shit. I didn't expect that to be so easy. He stares at me, his mouth pinched in annoyance. I need to keep moving mine before he disappears on me.

"Cool party, dude." *Shit.*

His annoyance switches into disgust as he curls his lip. "Do I know you?" he asks.

I push past a couple who bumped and grinded their way between us. "Yeah. I think we have first period together." *Shit again.* "I mean, first class. Of the morning. On Mondays . . . yeah."

Liam cocks his head at me. "You're in poly sci?"

I nod. "Yep." But please don't ask me what the hell that is.

"Bro." His jaw finally slacks. "That test last week. Like what the fuck, yo?"

I force out a small laugh. "I know, right? Like was the professor in the same class we were?"

"But Tiana, though . . ." Liam holds out both hands in front of his chest, squeezes imaginary breasts. I gnaw my bottom lip so I won't gag. He looks at me, waiting for a response. So I nod. "I see why they call them TAs, know what I'm saying?"

I keep nodding. "Yep," I manage. "Just like an hourglass."

"But wait . . ." Liam scratches his chin, studies me. "Or is her name Brittany?" His eyes trail over the cap on my head, back to my face. Back to the cap. He's trying to place me in his class, and this is my quiz.

I crack a smile. "Does it matter?"

Liam laughs then points at my hand. "Where's your drink?"

"I just knocked back a brewski," I say, not even understanding the words leaving my mouth. "Told my moms I'd take it easy this weekend. Last time I was home, she claimed she could smell the Budweiser coming out of my pores."

Liam laughs again. "Moms are always so dramatic." He slaps me on the back. "But at least you still have yours." This mofo, though. "I'll catch you Monday morning." He begins to head back the way he was going.

"Man, speaking of T and A, you got some lovely ladies up in here," I say to him, making him pause again. "Feels like I'm at a buffet. Only thing, though." I step closer to him and smile. "I like a little dark meat, know what I'm saying?"

Liam studies me again, then lets out a smaller laugh than before. "Sorry to disappoint," he says.

"Really, though," I continue. "You don't ever get any sisters around here?"

Liam's jaw clenches as he glances somewhere over my shoulder. I look behind me at the same hall where he fought with his friend. When I turn back around, he's staring at me with narrow eyes. "I mean, we don't discriminate. Anybody could come through here."

"That's what's up." I snap my fingers like I suddenly remembered something. "I saw a dope one around here about two weeks ago. Skinny braids, light eyes. A little thin in the waist. Know who I'm talking about?"

Liam is silent. Too silent. Almost makes me forget the bass line throbbing all around us. I keep my face as still as possible. Don't give him anything before this all goes to hell.

"What you say your name was again?" he finally asks.

"I didn't." I extend a hand. "Bowie," I say, because it's the first name that comes to my mind.

"Bowie?" He raises an eyebrow. "Your parents named you Bowie?"

I shrug. "What can I say? They loved the movie *Labyrinth*."

"Yeah . . ." He scratches the back of his neck. "Weird, though. I definitely would remember a black guy named Bowie in my class."

I ignore the spinning in my stomach. The spinning in the room. This guy knows something, so I have to be even until I find out what. "I like to chill in the cut. Philosophy's never been my thing."

Liam's head cocks to the side. "Philosophy?"

Fick. *Fick*. Did I say the wrong class? "I'm so lit." I laugh. Liam looks around and I have to reel him back in. "But yeah, that honey I was talking about earlier—"

"Nah, bro. Don't know who you're talking about." His jaw clenches. Adam's apple bobs up and down.

I give a slight frown. "You sure? Pretty sure she'd be hard to forget since you don't have that many sisters that come around here."

Liam's eyes graze over my shoulder again and he shakes his head. "Nope. I'll let you know if she swings back again.

Look, man. We're about to clear people out of here. Why don't you stick around, though? Seems like we have a lot to catch up on." He slaps me on the back again. This time a little too hard. I nod at him as he pushes through the crowd, not even responding to someone else that calls his name. He moves as if someone's life depends on ending this party at a reasonable time.

I look behind me again. What was going on back there that kept Liam's attention like that? Then I spot it. A closed door near the end of the hall. Not like the other rooms—this one had a dead bolt on it.

Nic.

Something tugs at my chest, almost pulling me to that door. Something's going on in there. Nic could be down there. Question is: Is she dead or alive? I'll need backup to get past that lock. I reach for my phone. No way Officer Hunter will be able to hear me through all this chaos. I search for an exit. But everyone's searching for an exit. One of the frat guys stood on a couch, got on a megaphone to tell everyone to peace out. They usher us out now in droves, even though I can still hear the music from neighboring houses. Either the DU house is the most responsible fraternity on Frat Row, or they have a reason to get everyone the hell up out of here. Something tells me it's the latter.

I decide against the front door in case I bump into Liam again. He's onto me. I just know it. I reach the kitchen and find a screen door leading into the backyard. Perfect. I'll run about a block or two away. Wait until I hear the sirens before coming back. No matter how they find Nic, I know I needed to be there when she's found.

I grab the handle of the screen door and pull it. The cold night air hits my face . . .

And something else hits the back of my head. Before I can reach to feel the damage, I tip forward and the night eats me up.

TWENTY-SEVEN

THE BACK OF MY HEAD THROBS TO A STEADY BEAT:

Thump-a, thump-a, thump-a.

Feels like my head's about to explode. I groan. Blink until
my eyes fully open. I'm greeted with darkness. I blink some
more, force my eyes to adjust. The thumping continues. I
touch my head to make sure a vein's not about to punch out
of it. Pain sears from my scalp as soon as my fingertips graze
it and I wince. Pain is good, though. Pain tells me that I'm
not dead.

"Jay?"

My heart catches in my throat. That voice . . . that voice
sounds familiar. The same one that would shake me awake
in bed to make sure I didn't miss the bus. The same one that

would whine at me when I had to shake her to make sure *she* didn't miss the bus. The same one that would reassure me of its presence when everything got too much: "You and me against the world, right?"

I push myself up to all fours. The dark room starts spinning, and I search for the voice. Search for something to keep me steady.

Again: "Jay!"

"Nic!" Her name explodes out of me, eclipsing any thumping going on.

My eyes catch on to an outline of my sister running toward me. Her gait is so strained, so jagged, that I almost think she's a ghost. But then she pulls me in for a hug, and she's so warm and real that the tears burst out of me.

"Nic," I choke out. I touch her braids. Make sure she's still real. "Nic?"

"It's me," Nic sobs and squeezes me tighter. "I promise. It's me."

We cling to each other with all the strength we have left. When one of us buckles, the other lifts us back up. I bury my face in the space between her neck and shoulder. Can't remember the last time we hugged each other like this. With so much sentiment. Maybe it was right after MiMi explained to us that Mom was going to be gone for a long, *long* time. Nic pulled me to her chest, let me bury my face in her shoulder so nobody else had to see me cry. I left a puddle on her new sweater, but she didn't care. She looked out for me like that. She's doing the same for me now, even though she's the one that's probably been through hell. Doesn't matter. She'll be my big sister 'til the end.

Finally, Nic pulls away. Cups my face in her hands. "You're real."

I choke out a small laugh. "I'm real." I touch her face, too. "So are you."

Nic smiles and rests her cheek more into my palm. Then she blinks as if suddenly remembering she left the oven on. "Did they hurt you? What are you doing here?"

Here? Where's here? I wipe away the rest of my tears with the back of my sleeve and scan the room. It's dusty, dank. Cluttered with a tattered plaid couch and old foosball tables and paddles and flags with Greek lettering on it. DU. Delta fickin' Upsilon. The bass continues and I realize it's not coming from my head—it's coming from outside. Somewhere above us. The music on Frat Row. I'm still in the damn frat house. The basement, maybe? This must be the room with the locked door that Liam kept sweating about.

Against one of the walls is a mattress on the floor covered by a thin sheet. A tray lies next to it with discarded pieces of fruit and a sandwich. The sight makes me want to gag. I really take Nic in. Her braids hang limp from her head, almost like they've given up. Her jean skirt has a tear on the bottom, and her shirt is wrinkled and covered in dirt. Now my stomach clenches even tighter.

"Have they been keeping you in here?" I ask Nic.

Nic's bottom lip trembles as she nods. She rubs her eyes furiously with the heels of her hands, like she's refusing to let herself cry about it.

"Nic." I hold on to her arm. "I don't understand. What happened?"

Nic blows breath out of her mouth, puffing some of the braids out of her face. "Javon and I got into it a few weeks ago at a party."

I nod rigorously. I knew this part. The party a little over two weeks ago, where Sterling was being a bad friend and Javon was being a worse boyfriend.

"I took off. Kenny was already outside. He had to make a deal for Javon. He said he'd take care of that first, then take me wherever I needed to go to cool off. He pulled up . . . here. Told me to wait in the car." Nic hugs herself, rubs her arms up and down as if she caught a chill. "But he was taking a long time. Longer than I expected. So, I finally got out of the car and came in here to check on him. They were having some get-together. Nothing huge like tonight. The guys didn't even want to have this thing tonight, but all the frats had to . . ." The *guys*? She talks about them like they're old friends. Nic shakes her head as if she suddenly remembers who she is and the assholes she's talking about. "But people were dancing, giggling. Feeling lovely, you know? I searched around for Kenny—then heard shouting coming from one of the bedrooms. I think they were trying to stiff Kenny. I kept hearing them yell, 'We don't have your money!' And then one of them called Kenny a nigger."

My fists clench on autopilot. That word coming from these boys' mouths was something more than them just copying off their favorite rapper. When they used it, they did it with intention. And their intention was to make Kenny feel like a lowlife.

"I heard scuffling," Nic continues. "I'm sure Kenny took a swing at the guy who said it. I mean, who wouldn't? But then the scuffling got louder and louder. I ran to the door, peeked inside . . . ." Nic closes her eyes and the tears begin to pour. "They were all on top of him, Jay. And it happened so quickly. By the time I got there—" She lets out a sob. I reach to rub her arm again, but she shakes her head. Lets me know she needs to keep going. "When they got off him, he wasn't moving, Jay. And I just knew . . . I knew immediately. He was gone." She wipes the tears from her face and her lips purse in anger. "They caught me staring so I ran. Couldn't leave out because too many people were in the living room. They would've ratted on me. So, I ran up the stairs. Hid in one of the bedroom closets. Then I tried calling you." She peeks up at me.

I chew on the inside of my cheek. Crack my knuckles over and over until they burn. But I want to feel pain right now. I deserve it.

"I couldn't talk too loud because I didn't want them to hear me," she continues—and keeps pouring salt into my open wounds. "After you hung up, I tried calling you again. You didn't pick up and then . . . they found me. One of them took my phone. Texted something to you to throw you off."

I stumble back, fall against a wall behind me. I'm such an idiot. I'm such a fickin' idiot. If only I'd paid attention, if only I'd been a good brother—Nic would've been home all this time and Kenny's parents would have answers. Not to mention those racist pricks upstairs would've paid for what they did to him.

"I'm sorry, Nic." My throat clenches as the words come out, but I keep going. I have to. I'll keep apologizing to Nic until the day that I die. "I'm so sorry. If I wasn't being stubborn. If I didn't think you were—"

"High on bliss?" Nic asks, then sighs. "Let's not do this right now—play the whole blame game. That's not important. Besides . . ." She gives me a weak shrug. "One of them has a conscience. Tyler, I think. He makes sure I eat. Brings down food. Even gave me some soap and deodorant."

I scoff. "A conscience? If that mofo had a *conscience* he'd let you go free a long time ago."

"Well, maybe not a conscience, but he's definitely cracking or something. I don't know. If the others weren't here, I think he *would* have let me go."

I pause as the words sink in. If the others weren't here. But they were. A whole group of them, spiraling enough to keep her cooped in here for weeks while having parties over her head. Hell, they were disturbed enough to beat Kenny to death and then dump his body at a park. These frat guys were long gone in the head—so what the hell did that mean for me and Nic now?

The door swings open and the music gobbles the basement. It dissipates as the door slams closed and footsteps come barreling down the stairs. Liam leads the charge with his two lackeys from Taco Bell behind him—one of them the same guy he roughed up in the hallway. I pull Nic behind me, puff out my chest. These dudes killed Kenny with their own hands. I know they could do the same to me. But, like Kenny, I wasn't going down without a fight.

Liam looks me over, his eyes racing like they're trying to keep up with the deranged thoughts racing through his head. He chucks a roll of masking tape at my feet.

"Tie each other up," he says.

Nicole sucks in a breath behind me. I resist the urge to do the same and puff my chest out even more.

"No," I say.

Liam rolls his eyes, not buying my tough guy act. "Tie each other up, or we'll do it for you."

"Liam," the guy from the hallway scuffle says. "Maybe we should just let them hitch it. If this guy came looking for her, who's to say nobody else will? Everyone's gone now. They didn't see us bring him down here. And I doubt Nicole would say—"

"Shut the fuck up, Tyler!" Liam barks. "Just because you gave this chick a goddamn ham sandwich doesn't make her your best friend! I don't trust her . . . and I don't trust this idiot with her." He glares back over at me. "Tie each other up. I won't tell you again."

My heart pounds so fast that I think it's ready to box all three of these guys in front of me. Still, I can't give in. If I struggle long enough, loud enough, one of their brothers upstairs is bound to hear us. Maybe a sane one that could call for help. I ball my fists. "And I won't tell you again," I say. "No." I spit at his feet to punctuate my refusal.

Liam's eyebrows lift at me. I can't tell if he's impressed or surprised. Maybe both. We have a stare off. Finally, he hitches his head and the nameless lackey rushes to my side. Before I can even throw my hands up, he swings out a right hook and his fist collides against the knot on the back of my head. The last thing I hear before greeting darkness again is Nic shouting my name.

✳ ✳ ✳

I'm jostled awake by a bump underneath me. My eyelids snap open and one of Nic's braids pokes me in the eyeball. I try to push away from her, but everything's too cramped. Too tight. I try to use my hands to sit up but they're bound together in front of me.

"You awake?" Nic asks. She lies on her side with her back turned to me.

I don't answer. I'm still trying to figure out where the hell I am. I shift my head and I stare up at a metal covering. More bumps underneath me and I realize we're moving. I can barely stretch out my feet and the scents of gas and rubber tires trickle into my nose. We're in a car. Worse, we're in the trunk of a car. Holy shit.

"Holy shit," I say aloud. I swing my legs over Nic's and start kicking at the fabric lining. I've seen that in the movies. Kick hard enough and the backseat would push forward, provide a small space for us to slip though.

"I've tried that already," Nic says. "This car's too old. Plus, I think someone's back there, keeping it in place."

Too old? Of course this douche didn't want us dirtying up his fancy Escalade. I kick one more time to be sure then wiggle around again. "What about a latch?" I say. There has to be a latch. Something to yank on and pop the trunk.

"I told you. The car's too old. It doesn't even have that feature." She sighs. "We're going to have to wait until they pop the trunk themselves."

Yeah, but what do they plan on doing when they open the trunk themselves? "How long have we been driving?" I ask her.

"Not sure. A couple of minutes. Maybe ten?"

Ten minutes. I try to think of everything around the JRU campus. The shipyard was just a few minutes out. The hospital was down the street, but I highly doubt they were being Good Samaritans. Huntington Beach was close by. Shit—were they planning on dumping us in the ocean?

My nerves go into overdrive as I feel the car stop, park. "Nic," I say, breathless. "Nic, I'm going to get us out of here. I promise."

I hear Nic sniffle as the trunk pops open. Liam's hands come flying down at me as he yanks me out of the trunk, throws me on the ground. Tyler grabs hold of Nic, but his approach with her is gentler. My eyes scan around the area. A bike trail in the distance, skirting along rows of trees. A field perfect for throwing frisbees—or peewee football practice. They brought us to Deer Park. The same spot where Javon and I found Nic's phone. The same spot where they buried Kenny.

I swallow, try to push my heart back down. "What are you going to do with us?" I demand.

"Get up and start walking," Liam says.

I climb to my feet. "Why don't we just solve this man to man?" I try. "You take me down, all good and well. I take you down? You have to let me and my sister go."

"Jay. No," Nic pleads.

Liam and the nameless lackey chuckle. Tyler just keeps ahold of Nic's arm, looks down at the ground.

"Seems like your sister knows what's best for you, homeboy," Liam says. He spits out that last word like tobacco. Like it wasn't even a good enough term to use for the likes of me. My blood is on fire. "Now turn around and walk. Don't even think about running." He yanks Nic away from Tyler and pushes her toward me.

I use my bound hands to make sure she's steady, then reluctantly begin walking deeper into the park. Nic right next to me. My eyes dart everywhere, searching for my next move. I knew this park so well when I was a kid. There has to be some place where Nic and I can shake these guys. Some path that we scurry down, hide out until morning when visitors might arrive. Maybe we could even sneak out to the convenience store about two miles away and get hold of a phone.

"Stop right here," Liam orders, interrupting my escape planning. "And drop to your knees."

Nic and I freeze in our tracks. I spot a trail that leads right into the trees maybe a few feet in front of us, but Liam steps forward and eclipses my view.

"Drop to your knees. Now!"

Nic whimpers and falls to her knees. But my knees won't buckle. I already let Nic down before. I can't do it again.

"I said, drop to—"

I launch forward, slam my entire body into Liam's. A grunt oozes out of his mouth as he tumbles to the ground. I collapse right on top of him.

"Nic, run!" I cry out just as Liam pushes me off him. I'm on my back and he crawls over to me, lifts his fist to show me what's what. I take my bound hands and deck him on the side of his head. Scurry away from him enough to climb back on my feet. Nic and Tyler watch me in horror, their eyes as round as clocks.

"Run, Nic!" I demand again.

Nic snaps out of it before Tyler does. She darts toward the trail I scoped out earlier. Just as I take off after her, I'm tackled from behind. The air puffs out of me as my chin smacks against the ground. Again. At this point, that scar will never go away. I'm flipped over and Nameless Lackey's over me, punches me right in the mouth before I can dodge it. My tooth pokes into my upper lip but I can't scream. I have to survive.

I hitch my knee up and collide it right in between this asshole's legs. He cries out, grabs his crotch. Frees his face. I smack my forehead against his to get him off me. Damn if I don't see stars, but it works. It fickin' works.

I scramble onto one foot just as Liam cuts through the night and sends his shoe right to my face. I fall back again. So much ringing in my ears that I almost think about answering my phone. Where the hell is my phone?

I don't get to feel for it because Liam's shoe comes at me over and over again. I shield my arms over my head as much as I can, but his foot rams against my chest. My stomach. I cough up something sour as another shoe rams against my shoulder.

"Stop! Stop, please!" Nic screams from somewhere behind me. She didn't get away. All of this and she still didn't get away.

The kicks keep coming and I roll to my side. Curl up in a fetal position. Try to find some comfort until this ends the way it's supposed to end.

"Enough, guys—enough!" Tyler. I think.

The kicks finally stop and I attempt to pull in a breath, but my ribs feel like they've been in a blender. I hear someone coughing up something thick and wrong, and then a wad of something wet plops right on my cheek. I let out a yell that sounds just like a growl. My body may be broken, but dammit, they'll feel my rage.

Liam grabs me by the shoulders and drags me next to Nic, who's back on her knees right in front of Tyler. She reaches for me, but Liam smacks her hand away.

"Don't you fuckin' touch him!" he demands. Then kicks hard at the ground as if he's imagining my ribs again. He balls his fists and shouts into the sky. This dude is losing it and I'm the cause. Good. At least I can own that.

The nameless lackey walks over and passes Liam a bat. Nic whimpers. Inches closer to me.

"Wait," I strain. My tongue even hurts at this point. "You don't have to do this. We won't say anything!"

Liam scoffs at me and shakes his head.

"Maybe he's right." Tyler steps forward and holds up both hands to his friend. "You said so yourself, this chick's nothing but a blisshead. Who the hell would believe her? And then him?" He juts a thumb at me. "You think a cop is going to take his word over ours?"

Liam shakes his head again. "I told you already. They know too much. And if we would've gotten rid of this bitch when I wanted to, he wouldn't even be a problem. This is the only way. Now back off!"

"But Liam . . ."

The other frat guy pushes Tyler away from Liam. Liam must have this guy's balls all up in his hand. Nicole cries again and looks down at the ground. I look over at her, hang my head in defeat.

"I'm so sorry, Nic," I say again. I want those to be the last words she hears. The last thing she remembers. Not her brother trying and failing to set her free. I need her to look at me and be okay and know that I did all this because I love her. "I tried. I really tried. I'm sorry." The final words hiccup out of me.

Nic shakes her head at me and forces out a smile. "You and me against the world, right?"

A tear falls from my eye. Me and her against the world.

Even 'til the end. This is the period, the finality, I've been searching for. Liam lifts his bat, ready to do damage. I inch ahead of Nic. Close my eyes and hope he strikes me first. I wait for the pain to come. Hope it's quick and that I won't feel anything soon. I just wish MiMi knew about the money. Knew how much I love her. Hope she tells Mom how much I tried to put her family back together.

"Hands up! Freeze!"

My eyes fly open and Rick Ross stands a few feet away from us, pointing his gun at Liam and his frat brothers. I blow out a breath and try not to pass out.

TWENTY-EIGHT

LIAM DOESN'T GIVE UP WITHOUT A FIGHT. HE DROPS THE bat and gets booking in the same direction Nic tried to escape earlier. A path that would lead him into the trees. But a police car with sirens blaring skirts in front of him, blocks his way. Two uniforms spill out of the car. One pins Liam against the car to slap cuffs on him. The other runs over to take care of Tyler, who raises his hands in the air.

"I'm not resisting! I'm not resisting!" Tyler insists.

The officer yanks his arms down, slaps cuffs on him, too. Officer Hunter has the other lackey pinned to the ground, secures him with handcuffs as he reads him his rights. The guy cusses Hunter out. Throws a few angry words at Hunter's mother, too. Hunter ignores him and keeps right on doing his job, finally peeling the guy from the ground and shoving him toward the squad car.

"You kids okay?" he asks us. He rushes over to Nic first and removes the tape from around her wrists.

"We've both been better," I admit.

Hunter smirks at me, but it's a soft one. Kind of like he knows I'm being a smart-ass, but I've earned it in this moment. He pulls the tape off me a little rougher than he did for Nic. Nic and I pull each other into a hug again. Every muscle, every bone in me groans, but I can't let go. I squeeze her tight, peek over her shoulder at the frat guys being shoved into the squad car. Liam catches me looking at him and throws me a scowl. So, I throw him the middle finger in return.

"Wait." I pull away from Nic and turn to Hunter. "How did you know where to find us?"

Hunter smiles and helps us both to our feet. "You can thank your friends," he says. "Some kid with purple hair. Bowman, I think. And little Miss Riley Palmer."

I frown. Bowie and Riley? I had kept Bowie in the dark—so dark, in fact, that I didn't think twice about explaining anything when I ran out of Providence. And Riley couldn't even look at me at the prayer vigil. How did either of them know what was up?

"Come on, let's get you both checked out," Hunter says, placing a hand on Nic's shoulder. He's right. We need to make sure Nic's good first. I'll get my questions answered later.

✳ ✳ ✳

I sit in a chair next to Nic's hospital bed. I don't need to shift because my butt remembers what to do to get comfortable in these vinyl-covered seats. Hours of keeping MiMi company. I made a vow that I never wanted to see this place again, but tonight is for a good reason. Tonight, my sister is home.

She makes a face as she swallows some of her sugar-free Jell-O. The doctors had poked and prodded and tested her, so she was finally allowed to put something in her stomach. "Damn, you'd think after weeks of suffering, they'd let me have something with sugar in it."

I laugh at her. "Can't be that bad." She shoves a spoonful in my mouth and I gag.

"See?" she says.

I force the bland gelatin down. "They just want to make sure you're okay. To take it easy."

Nic pokes her spoon inside the clear cup. "Can't I take it easy with chocolate chip cookies? Or a donut? Ooh, or cake? Yellow cake with chocolate buttercream frosting." She closes her eyes and smacks her lips like she can just taste that cake.

Cake. I remember Riley finding that cake pop wrapper from Nic's bedroom. Something didn't add up.

"So, you and Kenny never made it up to Richmond before the frat house? Doug really didn't see y'all that night?"

Nic opens her eyes and frowns at me. "Richmond? What are you talking about?"

"Me and Riley found that wrapper in your bedroom. Kee Kee's Goodies? That bakery's only in Richmond."

Realization covers Nic's face and she nods. "Kenny and I never stayed in Richmond. We always passed through there . . . on our way to visit Mom."

My head rocks back at her revelation. A small part of me feels that Mom had been buried alongside Dad, so hearing her mentioned sometimes took me out of my skin.

"Kenny would give me a ride during some of her visitation days. I didn't want to tell you because you always get so weird when I bring up Mom. I just figured you never wanted to come with us."

I wait for the anger to set in. The betrayal to wash over my body and ruin this happy reunion. But those emotions never surface. I'm sitting here right next to a miracle. Nic shouldn't still be alive, but she is. So is Mom. Now that I know how it feels to think I've lost one of them, I don't want to feel that anymore.

"Maybe we can get MiMi to drive us there next time," I say. "Go visit Mom together."

Nic's face lights up. "Really?"

I nod just as the door swings open. MiMi clutches her

mouth in the doorway, tears streaming out of both eyes. Nic's face crumples when she sees MiMi, and her whole body jerks as she sobs. MiMi rushes over to her and cradles her with both arms.

"My baby," she says into Nic's hair. "My baby's finally home." They cry into each other's arms, spreading so much joy throughout the room that when I breathe in, my chest feels lighter, despite the bruises. MiMi peeks up at me. She peels one hand off Nic and clutches onto my arm. "See?" she says to me. "Prayers work."

I smile at her and rub her hand. She squeezes my arm one last time before pulling away and wrapping both arms around Nic again. I want to take a picture of this moment, but something's missing. There's so much happiness in my heart that it spills over, and I know just who to spread it to. I stand and head for the door.

"Jay." MiMi looks up at me. "Where are you going?"

"I'll be back," I say. "I have to go thank someone."

TWENTY-NINE

I STAND OUTSIDE OF RILEY'S BEDROOM WINDOW WITH MY phone held high over my head. The theme song to *Teenage Mutant Ninja Turtles* pours out of its tiny speaker. Sure, not the most romantic song choice, but hopefully Riley gets it. Hopefully she'll hear it and realize that the kid who told her to shut up all those years ago was just insecure about everything. Had his guard up. Hope she knows that the kid is a young man now, and that he thinks it's fickin' awesome that she cared enough to notice anything about his costume.

"Riley!" I call out over the music. "Riley, talk to me. Please!"

After a few seconds, the window slides open and I hold my breath. *This is it, Jay. Say everything you practiced in your head*. Mrs. Palmer pokes her face out of the window with a satin bonnet sitting on her head. She frowns at me.

"Jayson Murphy, what in the heck are you doing?" she shouts at me.

I quickly lower my hand holding the phone and the phone almost slips out of my grasp. "So sorry, Mrs. Palmer. I was just looking for Riley."

"Do you have any clue what time it is? Where is your grandmother? She know you out here?"

"It's okay, Mom!" Riley comes jogging out of her front door toward me. She looks up at her mom. "I'll take care of it!"

"Riley, don't you be wandering off anywhere! Weekend or not, it's late!"

"Mo-ooom." Riley raises her eyebrows at Mrs. Palmer.

Mrs. Palmer smirks at the both of us. "Five minutes, Riley. That's all." She clicks her tongue and disappears back inside of the house.

Riley sighs then turns back to me. Nods at my phone. "Is that your new jam?"

I forget that the song is still spilling out of my phone. I quickly stop it. "My bad. I just wanted to get your attention."

"I think you got everyone's attention."

I wince. "Sorry. I figured your parents' bedroom was that room downstairs."

"Guest bedroom." She looks me over and her mouth

drops open. The same expression I gave myself when I scoped out the mirror at the hospital. Huge gash on my chin that peeked out of my bandage. A swollen lip. The dawning of a black eye. She reaches for me, but then pauses—her fingertips only centimeters away from me. "Are you okay?"

I swat a hand. "Solid. The hospital gave me the all clear. Nothing a bath with Epsom salt can't fix."

Riley hugs herself. "So . . . I hear you have good news?"

My face breaks into a smile. "Yeah. Nic's home. MiMi's happy. I'm happy. It's all good . . . mainly thanks to you."

Riley looks down at her feet and tries to hide her smile.

"How did you know?" I ask her. "How did you know where we'd be?"

"Bowie told me you ran out of the vigil like your you-know-what was on fire," she explains. "Of course, we were concerned. I figured it had something to do with Nic. Then Sterling told us she saw you talking to that guy from Deer Park. Pooch, right?"

I nod along, urging her to continue.

"Pooch told me how you kept asking about Nic's phone. Kept asking about the guys with the fraternity hoodies who had it. White guys in frat gear in this city could only come from one campus—JRU." Riley's hands dance in the air, detailing how she tied everything together. I watch in admiration, enjoying the moment. "So I filled Bowie in and we took our intel to Hunter. He had just shown up to the vigil with his wife. Of course, I made Bowie start the story because . . . you know." She gives me a smile and I get it. Sometimes, when a clue comes from someone with fairer skin, cops are quicker to listen. Even cops from your own community. "Plus, Bowie had gotten a new reply on his Instagram post. Someone had spotted Nic at a DU party a few weeks ago. Next thing I know, Hunter takes off and I held my breath. I just hoped I wasn't too late."

All the words blend together and paint a full picture. Bowie seemed like he wanted to tell me something else at the vigil. Probably this new tip. Hunter and his guys must've gone to the frat house. Heard from one of the guests that Liam and his friends took off. Put two and two together that they might be headed to the same place where they dumped Kenny's body. Nic and I got lucky. All because of Riley. And Bowie. The same Bowie I've been pushing away and who kept bouncing back.

"Thank you," I say to Riley. "Things were looking real grim for me and Nic at first. I couldn't save us."

Riley swats her hand at me. "Stop. You found your sister before anyone else could. You would've found a way to save her, too."

I take her hand and hold it. "No, Riley. Listen to me— thank you." I push the words out from somewhere deep. Somewhere that hasn't felt warm in a long time . . . until

338

I started spending more time with her. "Thank you for tonight. Thank you for the past two weeks. Thank you for the last eight years."

Riley chews on her bottom lip and snorts. Then covers up her mouth like she's embarrassed. I want to pull down her hand. She should never feel embarrassed about anything again. "Well, that's what friends do, right?"

"I was hoping we were more than that." I take a deep breath. Play with her fingers and try to find my nerve. "Riley . . . I . . . I want to try this. For real. I want us to be an *us*." My whole body exhales, like releasing those words makes me feel lighter than anything I've ever felt in my whole life. Like I was always supposed to say them.

Riley's hand turns rigid in mine and she stares at me like I've just returned from the dead. Shit. I'm too late. I said some terrible things to Riley the other night and she's had enough. She's amazing. Probably the most amazing woman I've ever met aside from MiMi. She wants to find a guy that's known how amazing she is all along and didn't try to push her away.

But Riley doesn't push *me* away. In fact, she grabs the back of my head and pulls my face to hers. She kisses me and I kiss her . . . then pause.

"Did I hurt you?" she asks, concern spilling out of both eyes.

"I'm good. I'm better than good. But . . ." I take a breath. "What about your parents? They don't want you fooling around with—"

Riley puts a finger on my lips. "I'll work on them. I can be pretty convincing."

I smile. She's never said truer words. I lean in for another kiss, and we both float and dance next to the moon.

THIRTY

SLIM AND QUAN ARE AT IT AGAIN ON JAVON'S STOOP—
despite Javon just getting released after being falsely accused
of murder. Even despite it being the Lord's day. It's a lazy
Sunday for me. MiMi felt that we had a good reason to skip
out on service. She's still at the hospital with Nic, getting her
all squared away before signing her out. She told me to take
it easy today, even though the doctor cleared me and said
I didn't have a concussion after all those head bumps the
night before. I take advantage of it, though. Lying in bed and
sending all these cutesy emojis to Riley to distract her from
Sunday school. Yeah, I'm that guy now. The guy who sends
hearts and kissy faces to his girlfriend.

Riley Palmer is my girlfriend. Man, a lot can happen in two weeks.

I peeled myself out of bed, though, when Officer Hunter called to tell me about Javon. Guess he feels so guilty for not believing me so many times—wants to make sure I stay in the loop. He hasn't made it up to me completely yet, but I'm having fun watching him try.

I stand at the foot of Javon's stoop, nod at Slim and Quan.

"Javon home?" I ask them.

Slim leans forward and rests an arm on his chubby thigh. "Who wants to know?"

I blink at him. "It's Jay. You guys know me. I live right over there." I point to my building.

"Yeah, but what's the password?" Quan asks.

I frown. "Since when do we need a password to speak to Javon?"

"Have you ever rolled up here asking to speak to Javon directly, nigga?" Quan says.

I pause. "I mean . . . no," I say finally.

"Exactly." Slim leans back in his seat. "So, if you don't know the password, we can't help you, bruh."

Quan stifles a laugh just as Javon strides through his building's main door. "Man, y'all two motherfuckers need to stop screwing around," Javon says. At that, the laughter fully erupts from Slim and Quan.

"Ha ha," I say, smirking at them.

Javon walks down the stoop and toward the mailboxes. He doesn't say a word, but I assume I'm just supposed to follow him. So, I do. He takes a seat on the bench next to the mailboxes, right underneath the trees. I sit right next to him. Lil Chuck and his friends toss a football in the street in front of us.

"You have to stop letting dudes clown you all the time," Javon says to me but keeps his eyes on the kids. "You too gullible."

I nod then shrug. "I guess. But it's good to trust people sometimes, right?" Nobody trusted Javon—that's how he got popped in the first place. Nobody trusted me when I told them Nic was missing and didn't just run off. I didn't trust Bowie enough to let him in my business. But Riley trusted me. Look at how that turned out.

"I should've trusted you," I continue. "I should've believed you no matter how much Hunter got in my ear. But I treated you like how everyone treated you. How everyone treats people who look like us and live where we live. And for that, I'm sorry." I'm not just gaming Javon. I actually mean it. After leaving my family at the hospital, I tried to remember the last time I saw Javon's people, and I couldn't. Don't even remember Nic mentioning them. It hits me even more sitting next to him: the only reason I didn't become Javon is because I had a MiMi. A Nic. A Man Boo. A Riley. Hell, a village. I glance over at Javon. He's so still, so steady, that I can't tell if he fell asleep with his eyes open.

Finally, he nods toward Lil Chuck and them. "Remember what it was like to be that age?" he asks. "All carefree and laughing all the time. Not worried about what others thought about you. Back then, everyone's your friend until they don't share their snack cake with you or some shit. And you can be anything you want to be, you know?"

I give a slight nod. I grew up a little too fast after what happened to my parents, but MiMi tried her best to keep me and Nic young.

"I miss that feeling, yo." Javon looks over at me. "I'm going back to community college. Turning my business over to Slim and Quan."

The breeze from under the trees just about knocks me over. "You trust those clowns?" I ask.

Javon snickers. "They've been doing it long enough to know the game. But it won't be my problem anymore. I have enough bread saved up. I'm gonna tell them to find a new spot. Get up out of the Ducts. Those kids deserve better." He nods over at Lil Chuck then sighs. "How's Nic?"

"She's good. She's getting out of the hospital today, actually." I pause. "You coming by to see her?"

Javon tilts his head, like he's really considering his options. "Nah. That's not a good look anymore, you feel me?" He glances at me again like he wants to make sure I do. "What you said to me . . . in my car the other night? I get it. It's not

Nic's job to make me feel like a king. I need to handle my own shit." His eyes squeeze closed for a few seconds, like the thought of letting Nic go causes him physical pain.

I get it, too. I feel the same way about Riley. That's why I'm going to try to be a better person. Take care of my own things so she doesn't feel like she has to do it for me, but she wants to because she loves me. Javon and I continue to watch the kids play football. They laugh as one of the kids fumbles the ball and Javon joins in. I can get used to this lighter Javon. Even though he won't be around Nic much anymore, maybe I can check in on him sometimes to make sure he's still floating in a good way. The kids keep laughing and it's contagious. Their laughter so sweet it should be the theme song to the Ducts.

THIRTY-ONE

NIC AND I WALK THROUGH THE HALLS OF YOUNGS MILL HIGH. Of course, heads swivel in our direction. A few polite waves are thrown at Nic, followed by curious whispers.

"I wonder how long this is going to go on," I mutter.

Nic waves at a classmate and smiles. "I mean, it's not every day that someone rises from the dead. I'd be nosy too." We reach her locker and she looks at me. "Don't you have your own class to get ready for?"

"I'm making sure you're straight."

"You don't have to babysit me, Jay. I'm fine. Much rather be back in school than cooped up in my bedroom or a hospital." She pauses as she grabs a book. "Wow, it's been a long time since I said the words 'rather be in school' together."

I laugh. "I'm sure that'll grow old soon."

Nic frowns. Not a frown like she's pissed or anything—more like she's had a moment to think about something. "You know, I don't think it will. I mean, yeah. I'm sure I'll complain about getting up early or writing an essay that I'll forget about a week later. But there were times over the last few weeks that I thought I'd never see you, or MiMi, or even Principal Gilbert." She laughs at that. "Every night in that basement, I kept praying to God that if He got me out of there, I would do everything better. I'd take advantage of every moment I had. He did His part, so I got to do mine."

I smile at her, impressed. "You getting all biblical on me?"

"Bruh, I'm going to start spitting verses at you on the regular now."

We both laugh as Sterling timidly walks over to us. She gives Nic a tiny wave as Nic's laughter dies.

"Hey, girl," Sterling says, tucking her hair behind her ear. "I wanted to come visit you in the hospital, but . . ." Her voice dies out. Nic and I stare at her, waiting for her to continue. Not letting her off the hook. "So anyways, you look great."

Nic nods at Sterling. "Same to you."

Sterling raises her eyebrows, her face all filled with confidence. "You want to leave campus during lunch? Maybe hit up Tropical Smoothie like old times?"

"I'm eating lunch with my school counselor," Nic says.

"Oh." Sterling blinks. "Well, maybe we can catch up over

the weekend. You could stay the night. We could call that lady from the mobile spa over and get our toes done."

Nic sighs. "I have a lot of schoolwork to catch up on. My nights and weekends are going to be booked. Probably for a long, *long* time. Maybe even for the remainder of the school year."

I stifle a laugh. Sterling looks over at me and I start clearing my throat. Even hit my chest to get up more imaginary phlegm.

"I'll just catch you whenever then." Sterling gives another wave to Nic, then scurries down the hall, her head hanging low.

I look over at Nic and raise my eyebrows at her.

"'Remember not the former things, nor consider the things of old.' Isaiah . . ." Nicole pauses. I wave my hand at her, try to get her to conjure up the chapter. "Look, I just recently turned a new leaf, okay? It'll come to me later." She closes her locker and playfully pushes my shoulder. "No stalking me today. I'll see you this afternoon."

I give her a salute to show I'll follow her orders. But I still watch as she walks down the hall, make sure she remembers the way to her first class. Our conversation hangs in the air over me. About doing better. About taking advantage of every opportunity. Youngs Mill may not be the best school, but at least there were people here that wanted to see me do my best. Like Mrs. Chung. Or Mr. Booker. Hell, Mr. Branch even gave me his home email address in case I needed to bump gums about more than matrices.

I head toward the main office and the person I'm looking for stands at her hall duty post near the entrance, reminding students to take off their hats and pull up their pants.

"Mrs. Pratt?"

Mrs. Pratt looks up from scolding a girl about wearing a camisole as a shirt. "How's it going, Jay?"

"You said you had intel about SAT registration, right?" I ask.

Mrs. Pratt's face lights up like it's Christmas morning. "You have a minute to come to my office now?"

I shrug. "I have more than a minute." I follow Mrs. Pratt into her office, this time remembering every step.

✹ ✹ ✹

MiMi sets a platter of freshly baked cornbread that's been cut up into equal squares right in front of Bowie. Bowie's eyes look like they're about to roll right onto the kitchen table.

"Is all this for me?" he asks.

Nic and I crack up laughing. MiMi smiles as she takes a seat across from him.

"What?" Bowie blinks. "I'm not scared. I'll knock this whole plate back in five minutes flat."

"You take one and pass it, fool," I say to him. "Just like you do with everything else."

"You sure? I just figured you were bribing me with all this fickin' food to make up for lost time." He raises an eyebrow at me and gives me a smile. I give him a lazy roll of the eyes, then smile back.

When I texted MiMi from school about Bowie coming over for dinner tonight, she warned me that she might have to scrape something together. Of course, she still managed to go all out. Fried catfish, dirty rice, cabbage stir-fried with real bacon and not that rubbery turkey stuff she's been buying lately. She even baked a yellow cake with chocolate frosting for later.

I was surprised Bowie even said yes to the invite, what with me being a certified ass to him for the past few weeks. But he did. Didn't ask why there was a need for security. Didn't comment on the stray cats that roamed the parking lots. Didn't even flinch when he walked through our cramped living room. All he did was hold up two bottles of soda and ask: "You have ice for this?"

"Bowie, baby, we take hats off at the table," MiMi says.

I shake my head at her. "Don't even bother, MiMi."

Bowie scoffs. "What? You think I'm some kind of caveman? I have manners." He peels his Steelers cap off his head and fluffs out his hair. The purple dye has faded some. Just hanging on at the tips.

"You look like the Joker," Nic says to him.

"The Joker's hair is green," I say to her. "Besides, leave my boy alone. You're one to talk, walking around here like you just got electrocuted."

Nic gasps as she fingers one of her crinkly strands. She had taken her braids out a few days ago. Another step toward her moving forward. "It's called going natural, punk," she says. "Just like you naturally have a big head. You wish your hair could grow out to cover up that real estate you got."

MiMi chuckles and turns to Bowie. "Looks like you're the only one with table manners."

Bowie smiles and leans back in his chair, like he's taking in the whole scene. "No, this is great. We don't do this at my house."

"Do what, baby?"

"This." He waves a finger around the whole table. "None of this. We bring our plates to our respective rooms to eat dinner. I'd much prefer to get ragged on about my hair than watch another episode of *Jersey Shore* by myself."

MiMi smiles at him as we all join hands to say grace before dinner. As everyone bows their heads, I can't help but peek up. I want this image seared into my brain. My grandma and sister back together. My friend at my side, smiling like he's always been part of the family. We may not have a lot, but I'll take what we have over what we didn't for the past couple of weeks. I close my eyes again and exhale.

EPILOGUE

I STARE OUT THE CAR WINDOW AS THE INTERSTATE DRIFTS into rows upon rows of trees. We've definitely left the city. Cows graze the sides of the road, and every now and then we pass fields of cotton. It's like I'm taking in the scenery for the first time. And it is my first time. At least my first time in a while. I had just entered middle school the last time MiMi took me on this route. Not that she hasn't asked if I wanted to come back. It's just that the rides back home were always a sick reminder that someone was missing. That we were leaving someone behind.

My phone buzzes.

Riley: You get there yet?

Me: Not yet . . . almost . . .

Riley: Come see me when you get home. We'll talk as much or as little as you want.

I send three heart emojis to Riley. Again, because I'm that guy now. Then I rest the back of my head against my seat. Nic peers at me through the sideview mirror of the passenger seat.

"You good?" she asks.

I give her a thumbs-up sign, even though my hand feels weak. She smiles at me through the mirror. She's tough. Way tougher than me. I lost count of how many times she had to tell what happened to her. What happened to Kenny. Any time a detective or one of those frat mofos' lawyers tried to find holes in her story, Nic would patch them right up. She remembered every moment, every detail, without so much as a sneeze out of place that there was no plea deal that the frat guys could offer to the prosecution.

"Looks like there's going to be a trial," Officer Hunter had told us yesterday. He's been making daily treks to our apartment. Claimed the Ducts was just added to his patrol, but we all knew there was more to it than that. Hunter needed to see we were all okay. "The State really wants to throw the book at them. Nic's story stayed the same no matter what anyone threw at her. Plus, there's enough physical evidence to corroborate her comments. You did good, kid." Hunter glanced over at Nic like he wanted to pat her on the back, but that's not his style. Instead, he went with a wink.

"Will she have to testify on the stand?" MiMi asked as she handed Hunter a jar of sweet tea. She always had a batch waiting for him for his daily visits. "They have enough of her comments on record. The judge could just use those, right?"

"It all depends on what the State thinks will best win the case," Hunter explained. "Usually, actually hearing from a firsthand witness is just the icing the jury needs to do the right thing." He raised an eyebrow at Nic. "Think you can handle telling your story again? More than likely, they'll want you to share . . . everything."

The way Hunter said *everything* sent my nerves on edge. Like at any moment one of them might blow. "Wait . . . what do you mean?" I asked.

Nic looked at MiMi. MiMi looked at Hunter. But nobody wanted to look at me.

"Hello?" I tried again.

Nic finally took a breath. "One night, Liam got too grabby."

My hand clutched around my jar of sweet tea. Clutched around Liam's neck. I waited for the jar to crack under the pressure and spill a river of Lipton.

"It didn't go as far as it could have," Nic quickly added, then looked down at her lap. "Tyler was home, at least. But it was bad enough."

I propelled from my seat, stormed to my bedroom and punched a hole in my wall. Nic grabbed some ice, held it against my knuckles while she sat on my bed next to me. "This will only be my fuel, not my combustion," she said. She told me her postsecondary plans. Do two years at community college. Transfer to Hampton University and go prelaw. She wanted to fight against the system that for so long fought against people who look like her. Yeah . . . my sister's tough as titanium. And I'd have to steel myself to help her through these next few months.

"What are you going to say?" Nic asks me from the front of MiMi's car.

I shrug at her through her sideview mirror and Nic smirks at me.

"Come on, like you really didn't practice what you were going to say in the mirror?"

"Ugh, naw. What kind of clown do you think I am?" I ask. Truth is, though, I practiced with Riley. Everything down to the length of the first hug. If they were even going to allow us to hug.

"How about you just play it by ear?" Riley asked me, my arms still wrapped around her lower back. "If the hug feels right, keep going. If not, pull away and try to smile."

"What if I can't smile?" I rested my chin on top of Riley's head. Her ponytail tickled the tip of my nose. "What if my cheeks freeze up on me and she can tell?"

"I think she'll just be happy to see you." Riley rubbed my back, reassured me. "You guys have a lot to catch up on.

You're editor of the lit mag, you did well on your SATs. You have an amazing girlfriend who roleplays with you for hours and hours on end." She pulled away from me and smiled.

"Speaking of which . . ." I laced my fingers through hers. "Let's practice that hug again." We held each other until it was time for Riley to get home. I made sure she got there five minutes before her curfew. I definitely did not want to get on the Reverend's bad side. He was *this close* to inviting me to their home for Christmas Eve dinner. Maybe I'd get MiMi to show me how to make her banana pudding for bonus points.

"Well . . . we're here." MiMi parks her car in the parking lot of Spotsylvania State Prison. My mom's home for the past few years. Her home for the next few years to come.

I reach to unbuckle my seat belt but my hands won't stop shaking. What did she even look like now? Would I see that the prison has eaten away at her? Would her eyes look different—hardened from years of being cooped in a six-by-eight-foot cell? What if she forgot what it felt like to even be a mom? That's probably my biggest fear. Going in to see her, and she stares back at me like I'm a stranger.

I feel Nic's hand cover my trembling one.

"Hey." She leans back to me. "Me and you against the world, right?"

I squeeze her hand back and nod along to my heartbeat: *Thump, thump, thump.*

ACKNOWLEDGMENTS

Wow, I've always wanted to get a chance to write my own acknowledgments page as a published author. I hope I get this right!

First, I have to thank Sarah LaPolla—who always managed to believe in me and keep me motivated during this roller-coaster ride called publishing. Thanks for seeing my potential in the slush pile—I wouldn't be here without you.

To the incredible Natalie Lakosil—thanks for taking me on as a client and helping me navigate the world as a debut author. You've asked questions about my writing that truly helps me get to the soul of my story.

To the amazing team at Alloy: Viana Siniscalchi, Josh Bank, and Sara Shandler, thanks for making this girl's dreams come true. You have given me a voice throughout this process and allowed me to put so much of, well, *me* into this story. I'll never forget my trip to New York to start this journey with you—and I still covet that whiteboard wall.

To Andrew Eliopulos, my wonderful editor, it's taken us a few years but I'm so grateful that I finally get to work with you. You knew exactly the type of story I wanted to tell and stretched me so much as a writer that I'm still recovering. But seriously, it has been an honor receiving your insight for this novel.

To all those lovely hands that contributed to the final creation and promotion of this book: Rosemary Brosnan, Bria Ragin, David DeWitt, Shona McCarthy, Lana Barnes, Valerie Wong, and Aubrey Churchward—thank you times infinity. This book wouldn't be what it is without your talents. If I left anyone out, please blame it on my head and not my heart.

To my wonderful cover artist, Shane Ramos, thanks for translating my ideas into a powerful image. You brought Jay and Nic alive for me.

Now, on a personal note, thank you to my parents— Tammy and Shelton. I was a strange kid (probably still am), but that never bothered you. Thanks for reading to me, buying me Lisa Frank notebooks, and pocket thesauruses to expand my vocabulary. I won the lottery with parents like you.

To my son, Easton—I started this book with you in my belly and am now ending it with your little sister in my belly! Thanks for being so patient with Mama when she had to sneak away to finish up revisions. Everything I do is for you.

To my cousin/sister/roommate/best friend and godmother to my children, Marquita Hockaday—you are a superhero. Thanks for picking up the slack when I've been too busy, too sick, or too much in general. I honestly wouldn't know how to change a light bulb if it wasn't for you. Thanks for always having my back. I can't wait for the rest of the world to read your beautiful words.

To my cousin, Patricia Hockaday—you were my first role model. I'll always remember those nights when you, Quita, and I would stay up late writing stories in our notebooks and reading them aloud to each other. You helped to ignite my love for reading and writing.

To my aunt, Pamela Hockaday, AKA PaPam, you've always been one of my biggest cheerleaders. You're the best second mom a girl could ask for.

To my grandmother, Margaret "Peggy" Hunt (formerly Murphy). You were a huge inspiration behind MiMi. Thanks for watching over me. Rest in Power.

To my sister from another mister, Racquel Henry. I admire your creativity, your diligence, and your resilience. Thanks for being an incredible writing partner—and an even better friend.

Finally, to all the kids from Bad News. I got you. I see you. I am you.